Lord of Sherwood

by

Laura Strickland

The Guardians of Sherwood Trilogy
Book Three

Lord of Sherwood

Cover Art by *Diana Carlile*

The Wild Rose Press, Inc.
PO Box 708
Adams Basin, NY 14410-0708
Visit us at www.thewildrosepress.com

Publishing History
First English Tea Rose Edition, 2014
Print ISBN 978-1-62830-348-3
Digital ISBN 978-1-62830-349-0

The Guardians of Sherwood Trilogy, Book Three

He bowed his head over his mother's hands, closed his eyes, and called upon the things he loved best—the trees that arched above him, the water that carried promise and memory, the deep loam, and the eternal light. His heart opened like a new shoot in spring.

"Mother?"

No response. Her flame burned very low but steady. He saw what she saw: Flames on a winter hearth throwing warmth, safety, and comfort. The flash of silver in his father's eyes and the smile Gareth Champion kept for her alone. Himself as a child, lying in her arms, the future in his eyes.

She was not alone where her spirit lay. Others gathered round her, some he knew and some he did not. A few he had met, in spirit form, on his own journeys through Sherwood. He felt rather than heard their message: *You cannot linger here. You are needed. Your time approaches.*

Send her back with me, he appealed to them. We cannot go on without her. He cannot.

Go and play your part, Lord of Sherwood. Uphold the circle.

I cannot. We cannot. We are missing the third of our number.

She comes.
She comes.
She comes!

Praise for Laura Strickland and...

DAUGHTER OF SHERWOOD:

"The imagery is beautiful, the world building is phenomenal, and the descriptions of the spiritual qualities of Sherwood are extraordinary. You will undoubtedly wish you could walk barefoot through her rejuvenating soil for just a moment and feel the connection to the beautiful repertoire of souls she harbors within her midst."

~Daysie W. at My Book Addiction and More

"Laura Strickland creates a world that not only draws you in, but she incorporates it so seamlessly that Sherwood is every bit as much a character in this story as Wren and Sparrow. Throw in a love triangle that has you flipping the pages, and you have the kind of book that keeps you awake well into the wee hours, and sighing with satisfaction when you've finished the very last page."

~Nicole McCaffrey, author

CHAMPION OF SHERWOOD:

"As I read I became so involved with the story, I found it difficult to put down the book. How they fight to protect the village, and how they resolve the situation, if only temporarily, is done so well, you have no doubts as to the magic surrounding them. I really loved this story and would highly recommend it. I plan on finding book one in the trilogy and then the next ones as they are written. Definitely a series and an author to watch."

~Dandelion at Long & Short Reviews, (5 Stars)

Dedication

For my sisters, Joanne and Dorothy—
with me, another circle of three.

Chapter One

Sherwood Forest, Autumn 1260

"Hie, my good man! Can you tell me how far it may be to Nottingham?"

Curlew Champion cursed to himself when he heard the call, and did his best to look as if he had not just run half way across Sherwood pursuing one of the King's deer. His prey, a well-grown hart, had taken his arrow some leagues back, and he had been loath to let the beast go to ground somewhere only to die a slow death from the wound. The hart had fallen at last in the middle of the old road that cut southeast through the forest, and Curlew had ended its misery but an instant before his ear caught the jingle of harness and the creak of wheels that told him someone approached.

The worst of luck, he thought wryly even as he hastily heaved the deer, along with his quiver and bow, into the tangled brush that lined the road. He had time only to wipe his bloodied hands in the grass and turn with a grimace to face whoever approached.

His chest still rose and fell rapidly from his effort as he stood and gazed with narrowed eyes down the road. Naught like getting caught red-handed. Such evidence of guilt might well lose a man his hand or his life. For no Saxon—serf or freeman—was allowed to hunt deer in Sherwood. The Sheriff held the King's authority over all Nottinghamshire, and had no patience for any excuses Curlew might give. The next few moments could cost him dear.

Yet the voice sounded friendly enough, and he saw at once the party looked like a family on the move. In the lead came a man of middle years, only lightly armed, with four outriders and another fellow driving the small wagon with a young woman at his side. All were dressed well. He cursed under his breath again—Normans. Who else would go mounted in Sherwood?

He drew a deep breath and spoke with marked courtesy. "Good day to you, my lord." Respectfully, he touched his brow. He well knew how to play the part of the dutiful underling, even though his heart held the conviction that he owned this place—every tree, stone, and deer of it. "You are not far at all from Nottingham. Be there by midday, my lord, if you keep on steady."

The rider reined his horse and eyed Curlew curiously. Deeply tanned, as if he spent the majority of his days outdoors, with plentiful lines carved into his face and a balding dome, the man went clad less like a noble than a retired knight, all in leathers. He wore a serviceable sword and had a bow strapped across his back as well, the shorter type the Normans favored.

After measuring Curlew for a moment the traveler asked, "And what do you here, my good fellow? Not out hunting, I hope. This is King Henry's hunting ground."

What is it to you? Curlew asked inwardly, while striving mightily to conceal his rising ire. No one ever stopped a Norman going about his business with a demand for him to explain himself. "Aye, my lord. And I know that right well—everyone hereabouts knows it. I am only out on an errand for my old mother, taking herbs to a friend of hers in Haversage." But half a lie, that. Curlew's mother, Linnet, did use herbs aplenty in her healing. But she was far from old, and easily the most beautiful woman of Curlew's acquaintance.

The Norman looked at Curlew's hands. "And, have you hurt yourself? Surely that is blood I see."

Curlew glanced at his fingers ruefully while his thoughts flew. "Ah, just a slip of my knife, my lord, while cutting the yarrow." By the Green Man's horns, how could he have let himself be caught out this way? It would go hard for him, indeed, if this man decided to act upon his obvious suspicions.

Best perhaps to bluster it out now that he was more than half snared. He tossed his head. "Might I offer my services, my lord, in seeing you the rest of your way to Nottingham? 'Tis not as if I am unfamiliar with the forest, though it can be a dangerous enough place for strangers passing through."

As he spoke, his eyes wandered to the face of the young woman on the bench of the cart, and widened. She gazed at him frankly, as surely no well-bred Norman maiden should, out of a face alive with amusement. A curious countenance it was, arresting rather than beautiful, wide of brow, narrow of chin, and well-freckled. Curlew drew a breath, almost convinced she knew he lied, and that she might well point to the saplings that bordered the road and cry, "He is guilty! Look there!"

"Aye," said the balding man, "and we have heard about the dangers of Sherwood—who has not? Infested with churls and outlaws, 'tis said to be. And, my fellow, are you sure you do not number one of those?"

That made Curlew's eyes snap back to the man's face, reluctant as he might be to look away from *hers.*

"Far from it, my lord," some inner impulse urged Curlew to say, "for am I not one of my lord Sheriff's own foresters?"

"Are you, by God?" The Norman looked well interested. "And is it not a remarkable thing, that I should meet you here on the road? For I journey even now to Nottingham to take up my new post there as head forester to my old friend the Sheriff, Simon de Asselacton."

Dismay hit Curlew like a hard blow to the gut. Aye, and what were the chances? Usually he had the very best of luck, scraping through ill-judged exploits by the skin of his teeth. Not this time.

And so this man with the steady eyes and the likeable manner was friend to de Asselacton—or old Asslicker, as the peasantry invariably called him. Ill met, indeed.

The balding man smiled with quiet amusement. "Allow me to introduce myself." He gave a stiff bow from the saddle. "Mason Montfort, late of Shrewsbury. And whom might I be addressing?"

Curlew straightened and gave an excellent bow in return. He knew how to play this game. His father had once lived the life of a Norman knight, though he had surrendered it along with his hated Norman surname long ago.

"The name is Champion," he said.

"Is it, then? Champion the forester?" He could not tell whether Montfort believed him or not. "And so, Champion, what is the true state of things in Sherwood? Is it as overrun with miscreants and murderers as my good friend de Asselacton describes?"

For some reason Curlew's gaze drifted back to the face of the young woman. He wished suddenly he could see the color of her hair beneath her head covering. As it was, he stood too far from her to tell even the color of her eyes.

"My lord, Sherwood stands in good stead." *Magical place, holy place, filled with the light of belief and the spirits of those gone.* "The peasants know better than to hunt here, and the outlaws have decreased in number from what they once were."

"Entirely accepting of the King's justice, eh?" Montfort crooked an eyebrow. "Then I wonder of what my old friend complains so bitterly. Ah, we shall soon see. No doubt with the aid of good men such as you, Champion, I shall be able to provide the vigilance required to keep Sherwood well-guarded." Montfort smiled again and the lines of his face creased into a good-tempered mask.

"Aye, my lord," Curlew replied with a bland expression that hid a flurry of inner alarm. This man was sharp as an iron nail, and would require careful watching. "And," he offered once more, boldly, "shall I escort you the rest of the way to Nottingham?"

Montfort's gaze raked him, still with what appeared to be a measure of amusement. "No need. Just give us our direction"—the eyebrow twitched again—"and be about your tasks for your old mother."

"Aye, my lord. Thank you, my lord. You keep to this road, straight on. Once you leave the forest you will almost be able to see the castle in the distance, on a rise. God's speed to you."

"Thank you, my man." Montfort urged his mount

forward, using his knees. The party started up again, and the cart jerked into motion with a creak. "Oh, and Champion—be sure and report to me on the morrow, eh? At Nottingham."

Curlew bowed again. When the man reached Nottingham and inquired after an under-forester called Champion, he would know this meeting for a farce. But Curlew would be well away by then.

A small, wicked smile tugged at one corner of his mouth. He straightened from his bow just as the young woman's cart reached him. Any well-behaved Saxon underling, as Curlew well knew, would avert his eyes respectfully as she passed. Instead, he lifted them to hers.

And, shockingly, she returned his stare, bold and unswerving as any lad. Nay, not like a lad, though—for she was all woman, this one, her face brimming with character, interest, and mischief. A smile twitched her lips as their eyes met and held—it said many things: that she knew he had just spun a fabrication, that she applauded him for it, and that she found him just as fascinating to look upon as he found her.

His blood leaped at that look, and he condemned himself silently. This, a well-bred Norman miss, was surely no proper object for his admiration. Only, she did not appear particularly well-bred nor well-disciplined. Who was she?

And would he ever see her again?

Curlew stood there with the blood drying on his hands as the small train lumbered past, grateful for his escape, and utterly scorched by her gaze.

Not until they were well past did he draw a deep breath and strive to shake off the spell that held him. A new head forester was not good news for Sherwood or the villages close by. Would Montfort prove a difficult man? And why had de Asselacton decided to bring him here now? The last man to hold the position, Sylvan de Troupe, was not as young as he used to be, and rumor said he had been ill. And true, autumn was when a good forester looked to manage the herds. But Curlew considered Sherwood his own domain, and the last thing he needed was some sharp-nosed git deciding to do an assiduous job of enforcing the King's blighted laws.

Aye, and he would need to take word of this to Oakham and the other villages, let folk know they must set themselves for still another fight. His uncle, Falcon Scarlet, who stood as headman of Oakham and leader of the Saxon resistance, both, would want to know.

But as Curlew retrieved the bow, quiver, and hart from cover and shouldered the last with a grunt, he thought not of the fight against tyranny or even his narrow escape. It was to the trees and the essence of the forest he spoke when he said the words, "Green. Her eyes are green like the holy light of Sherwood. By Robin's heart, I will need to see her again."

Chapter Two

"I do not know when I have been caught so fairly," Curlew said ruefully to his cousin and friend, Heron Scarlet. "To be nabbed red-handed by Asslicker's new man—I should be struck down for the sheer stupidity of it."

"Aye," Heron replied. "You were fortunate to get clean away. But then you always do have the Green Man's own luck in the forest."

"Luck, and a crooked tongue." Curlew eyed the hart he had just laid down near the center of the village. A holy sacrifice it was, like everything he took from Sherwood. Part of him, deep inside, hated to kill, even though he knew he must. Gratitude balanced the scales for him; between the bow and the hoof there existed a constant dance of life and sacrifice.

Heron swept him with a glance, as if he sensed and measured Curlew's stirred emotions. Almost of an age, and with mothers born twin sisters, the bond between them went deep.

Curlew relied upon Heron for the benefit of his intelligence, wisdom, and sound instincts. Heron possessed an almost other-worldly ability to see beyond the apparent. A born shaman, most folk said he was, and sometimes gifted with the Sight.

Now Curlew searched Heron's face for signs of distress. He feared the encounter in the forest, just past, held some particular significance. Should Heron sense that as well... But Heron demonstrated only his customary mild alarm at his cousin's behavior. Curlew knew Heron had long ago given up denouncing him for incaution.

"You will get yourself killed for Sherwood," he had said many a time.

And Curlew invariably replied, "Not until my work is done, and not before we find the third of our number." He had always felt he was meant to accomplish some unnamed task left half done. His birth, as everyone assured him, had been destined. His mother Linnet, her sister Lark, and Lark's husband Falcon Scarlet—those last two Heron's parents—were guardians of Sherwood, members of the triad that held and defended the forest's ancient magic. Four generations, now, had members of their families held those places. The legendary Robin Hood had been great-grandfather to both Curlew and Heron, and they knew themselves destined for a future of guardianship.

Yet the third member of their triad proved elusive. Their families teemed with offspring—Curlew had two younger siblings and Heron had four. Yet none had proved to carry the threads of magic needed to weave the last third of the spell.

It made no great difficulty now. The triad in place stood strong, yet despite appearances Curlew's mother and Heron's parents aged. Life in Sherwood often proved hard and dangerous, and disaster lay only a battle or an illness away.

It would take but one member of the present triad to fall in order for the magic to waver and eventually fail. Curlew had lived all his life in the knowledge of that. But wishing for the third of their number to appear had not made it so.

He looked now into his cousin's face, which he knew better than his own. Heron had inherited his mother's golden eyes—those of a hawk—and the yellow mane of his father, Falcon. He carried almost visibly his knowledge of the other world, a potent combination that made the lasses of Oakham and many other Saxon villages follow him like helpless thralls.

The truly maddening thing was Heron neither invited nor welcomed such attention. It merely trailed him like radiance.

Curlew knew himself to be dull and ordinary compared with Heron's brilliance. Aye, he had caught glimpses of his own reflection in pools and in the village pond—he had even seen himself, quite startlingly, in the fire once whilst Heron sat in a trance. A blend of both his parents, he had his father's height and gray eyes and his mother's deep brown hair. Folk said he had her grace as well, but what was that worth? He cared far more that he had inherited both his Grandfather Sparrow's and his great-grandfather Robin's skill with the bow. Aye, that was a talent to have, and he rarely missed a target.

But something in the Norman maid's bold gaze as she passed had dubbed him attractive enough. Ah, he had to stop thinking of her. It made a futile occupation, and a distraction he did not need.

Curlew knew very well how the triad worked: three held the magic; two bonded together as man and wife. Wherever the missing woman was, she would need to wed with either Curlew or Heron.

On the chance it would be he, Heron turned a

shoulder to the bevy of winsome lasses who pursued him, and kept himself always for the unnamed woman. But by the age of four-and-twenty, Curlew felt the strain, as Heron must also. Not that Curlew had saved himself completely—far from it. But Heron had, and he quested like a walking arrow for their missing third.

"Do you think this new man, Montfort, will be a problem?" Curlew asked Heron now.

Heron narrowed his eyes. Curlew knew that expression: it meant Heron looked beyond the apparent, a thing he could do almost effortlessly.

His brow wrinkled. "I cannot tell, Lew. There is something—a quickening."

"Change," Curlew supplied. He had felt it too, from the party in the forest. "Maybe for good, maybe not."

"Not, I fear," Heron decided. "'Tis always so when something new is thrown into our lives, even a new forester."

"The last thing we need is someone nosing his way into what occurs in Sherwood." Since their parents' time there had existed what amounted to a running war between the outlaws and peasantry of Sherwood and their Norman overlords. Thanks in part to the skill of the present triad who balanced duty and magic, things had lately been peaceful. But Curlew would be a fool, indeed, if he believed such a state would last.

Heron nodded. "True." He gestured to the hart stretched at their feet. "If the good de Asselacton finds out just what we are taking from Sherwood, there will be a heavy price to pay."

Curlew's head came up like that of a pony scenting water. "Sherwood is ours," he declared. "It sticks in my

craw that anyone else should tell us how to manage it."
He gave a crooked smile. "I told Montfort I was one of
his lord's foresters."

"Eh? What daft thing is this?"

Curlew's grin widened and mischief flooded his
eyes. "When he stumbled upon me, it just came out—
that I was one of the men who would be working under
him and thus had a perfect right to be in Sherwood." He
sobered suddenly. "As I have. Who better at liberty
here, Heron, than you and I, whose blood is the same as
flows through this earth?"

"Aye, but it is a dangerous game, that."

"'Tis a dangerous way of life," Curlew agreed.

"What did you think of the man? You are usually
good at measuring people."

"Aye." Curlew could not deny he had a talent for
it, as for shooting an arrow. "A clever man and not
unkind, so I think. But he says he is a personal friend of
Asslicker's. So I do not doubt he will seek to do his
duty completely and well."

"We had better learn all we can of him. Will you
go to Nottingham? Ask Diera to go with you—'twill
look less suspicious that way. And tomorrow is market
day. Search out Ronast or Abery and discover what you
might." They had more than a few contacts in
Nottingham proper. And Diera, Curlew's friend, would
be willing to go. In truth, she had been more than friend
to him on several occasions, but she knew all too well
the situation and the ties that held Curlew fast.

He protested, "And what if Montfort should see
me? 'Twill be all too obvious I am no underling of his."

"You will spin some lie—you always do."

Curlew grunted, half an acknowledgement. "Why

do you not go instead, and give the wenches of Nottingham a treat?"

Heron gave Curlew a cool stare. "Because I am preparing for a pilgrimage into Sherwood."

"Oh, aye?"

"I think it time." Heron's expression turned serious. "I mean to sue the Lady's favor, and ask her for the answer to the puzzle that beleaguers our days—just where we are to find our third, our missing guardian."

Chapter Three

"Daughter, I trust you will keep out of trouble whilst I am off seeing to my duties this day."

Anwyn turned from the window and the bustling activities below to regard her father. She loved the man dearly—he had been everything to her since the passing of her beloved Winifred, the companion hired after her mother's death. But he vexed her at times, if only because she knew how sorely her waywardness vexed him.

And now what had she done but exchange one prison for another? When they left Shrewsbury, she had dared hope—heaven knew why—things would be better in Nottingham. But she found herself in yet another set of rooms with little to occupy her besides needlework. And the saints knew she would as soon plunge the needle into her own eye as sit and ply it.

She saw real concern now in her father's gaze. Her willful and headstrong disobedience truly distressed him; he had been more than glad to leave behind the whispers and disgrace she brought him in Shrewsbury.

But how could she assure him that the restlessness which pulled at her unceasingly these last months would not cause her to break free of these rooms and all his careful restrictions?

His lips twisted at what he saw in her eyes. "Anwyn, dear…" He spoke again before she could. "I know how hard it has been for you, losing your mother and then Winifred, who was so dear to you. I thought it best to wait until we reached our new post to find a replacement for Winifred, but I promise I will do so as soon as possible. Likely my lord Simon will be able to suggest someone, possibly a younger woman. You would like that, eh?"

"Aye, Father." The words might be obedient, but there was little compliance in Anwyn's voice or in her demeanor. Her fingers clenched on the stone window embrasure. Could she hope to tell this man, who loved her, how she felt driven to the wild acts that so dismayed him?

"Anwyn, please." His voice dropped. "Do not spoil this chance for me—for us. 'Tis too fine an opportunity for us to squander."

"Is it?" Anwyn Montfort tipped her head, and her mane of shining, wheaten hair slid over her shoulder. She knew her hair for her one glory; she had been told so by many a man, the words usually whispered into her ear at a heated moment. She had also been told she had fine breasts. The rest of her warranted little remark—a freckled face and green eyes spiked by dark brown lashes. But men cared little for a woman's face whilst thinking to take their pleasure in the dark.

Her father's expression tightened. "It is high time you were wed, Anwyn. I mean to find you a suitable husband here, perhaps someone high ranking among my staff, or a member of the Sheriff's guard."

"One of your foresters?" Anwyn thought to the man they had met on the sun-dappled road and her pulse leaped, wild and hard. All the night past, and even last evening while they busied themselves settling into their new quarters, she had been unable to chase him from her mind. She did not know why. Was he not just another man among the scores that thronged the world?

Perhaps not. She thought again of the look they had exchanged as her cart lumbered past him yesterday. She recalled his eyes—pure silver they were, like the chain her father had given her last Christmas, like the band Da wore on his thumb. Tall and graceful as a young tree, and supple like one also, he had a mane of hair the deep brown color of chestnuts. He looked more a spirit of the forest than a real man.

But that had been real blood on his hands—quick, long-fingered hands they were, too. She would almost have thought him a poacher, an outlaw. Surely not part of Da's new crew.

What had he said his name was? Champion.

"I am trying to do right by you, Anwyn," her father spoke again. "But you must meet me half way."

"I am willing always to do that." She smiled. "Trust me, Da."

"That is just it. Each time I do, I live to regret it. Promise you will stay here in our quarters today."

She hated giving promises she knew she would not keep, especially to him, and especially with all that tantalizing activity down below. "Aye, Da, of course."

"Occupy yourself with finishing our unpacking. Lord Simon has asked us to sup with him this evening. 'Twill be our first chance to make an impression on the company, so make yourself lovely."

"Aye," Anwyn agreed. And how many dreary hours stretched between her and that dubious honor?

Her father gave a nod and went out; she could not tell whether he believed her, or no.

Anwyn turned back to the window. The sounds and colors below immediately caught her attention. Market day and the castle grounds were crowded with folk come from far and wide, eager to buy and sell.

Surely she would not be noticed among so many.

She bit her lip and tried to decide where her father would have gone. To meet with Lord Simon de Asselacton? To review members of his new staff, or to inspect the King's forestland? Surely he would be far from all that clamor below.

She strove to determine when and why she had turned so disobedient. Her Da blamed it on Winifred's death, but she knew it had started before that, when she had refused young Arkwright's hand in marriage. Handsome he had been, aye, and a good enough match, but not the man for her—that she knew to her bones. Da would have liked to see her settled, but he did not worry about it until she took to slipping away on her own and staying out late. He warned her she would ruin her reputation, and his. He told her Shrewsbury, so near the Welsh marches with all their unrest, was the last place she should be on her own.

"Do you wish to be snatched, Daughter, and held for ransom—or worse?"

Did she? Of course not, but she discovered she did like courting that bright edge of danger. She did not know what she was looking for, but it proved to be none of the young men who subsequently vied for her hand.

Another bright vision of the man on the forest road sprang alive in her mind. It made her mutter to herself irritably before she donned a head covering and fled the rooms intended as her new home.

Ah, and out in the castle grounds she encountered movement, sound, color, and life. Anwyn craved it all, and she slipped seamlessly into the crush of folk milling in the courtyard and beyond. Peasants laughed and talked and argued, watched by soldiers who looked, for the most part, bored. The scents of cheeses, ale, and currant buns mingled with those of manure and folk who had given their summer bath a miss. Anwyn felt her heart rise.

A man carrying a tall wooden rack of ribbons caught her eye. She stole one, just to see if she could get away with it, and then pitched a coin at his feet. Startled, he swiftly snatched his payment from the dust.

She ate a sticky bun and watched a couple behind the next stall as they indulged in a kiss and cuddle. The restlessness she felt increased.

What would happen if she tried to purchase a mug of ale? She had to exercise some caution—her father had threatened more than once lately to send her away to the good sisters at the nearest nunnery. And she would rather end her own life than be confined in such a place.

She watched a rough man, a farmer from one of the villages, perhaps, buy a flagon of ale for himself. Before he could drink it, she edged up and spoke from the corner of her mouth.

"I will give you twice what you just spent, in exchange for that."

Startled, he turned his head and their eyes met. He wore a squat woolen hat over hair like brown straw. His eyes were brown also, almost the exact same shade as the ale. They moved over her face slowly and then down to her bosom, where they lingered.

"Well, now." He grinned, revealing a big gap between his front teeth, hesitated, and added, "My lady."

Anwyn dug into her pocket pouch and brought forth a coin. "Here, trade me."

"You want my ale, do you?" His gaze shifted to her mouth. "Tell you what, let's share it. We shall go someplace quiet—"

"The coin," Anwyn insisted.

He shook his head and stepped closer, his eyes issuing a dare. "Not for no coin, but I will give you this flagon for a kiss, my lady."

"Just one?" Anwyn had bargained far more, for far less. Before she could let herself hesitate, she leaned forward and pressed her mouth to his, which was half open in surprise. He tasted of the pork pie he must have just eaten, and like blatant, healthy male.

"Not bad," she told him, and extracted the flagon from his suddenly limp fingers. She raised it to her lips and drank deep, letting the ale wash her senses. A goodly measure of it spilled down her chin and the front of her dress, making those standing nearby laugh in appreciation.

"See here." Her benefactor eyed her now-damp breasts. "I could help you wi' that."

She wagged a finger at him. "I will just bet you could." She drank again, and the circle about her increased in number. None of those here had ever seen such a spectacle—a young woman, likely of some quality, judging by her clothing, at large and unescorted, chugging ale like a soldier.

She grinned at the fellow with the gap between his teeth and thought about taking him up on what he offered. Likely she could string him along quite a while before turning him away.

"My lady?" The courteous and serious voice spun her around. Speaking of soldiers, the scene had snagged the attention of one of those on duty, who now scowled at her. Ah, and she had barely begun to have fun.

She treated him to a glare. "Are you not supposed to be guarding the battlements, my good man?" The ale, strong stuff, already threatened to trip up her tongue. Another swig or two and she would go away somewhere quiet with the young farmer.

The onlookers chuckled, but the guard drew himself up and seized her arm. "Just you come along with me."

"Why? Do you want a tumble?" Anwyn laughed into his face, then kneed him with an ease born of experience and sprinted off, the flagon of ale still clutched in her hand.

The guard—or someone in the crowd—called another and, just like that, Anwyn found herself pursued. She ducked and wove through the gathered throng, her skirts bunched high in one hand, the flagon in the other. She collided with a cart and bounced off a large man with a bale of wool on his shoulder. Hearing a cry from behind, she headed for the main gates, which stood wide open, thinking to lose herself in the freedom beyond.

A hound darted out in front of her. She leaped over it but landed unevenly and stumbled into a number of people on their way in. The ale upended itself all over the chest of the man directly in front of her. Someone guffawed, and a pair of hands came out and caught Anwyn by the arms.

Her breath hiccoughing in her lungs, she looked up into a face that appeared to hover between annoyance and amusement, and a pair of clear, intelligent, gray eyes fringed with lashes so dark brown they looked almost black.

Every bit of her desire to escape fled her body and was replaced by delight as bright and sudden as pain.

"'Tis you!" she exclaimed. "The forester with the red hands."

Chapter Four

"Hush, will you?" The man from the forest road spoke in a low tone, tempting as warm honey. The sound of his voice seemed to go through Anwyn the way a hot knife might, too swift to hurt. "Else they may haul me away and relieve me of one of these hands. Is that what you want?"

Anwyn pressed her lips together and shook her head. His hands most assuredly belonged where they were—not only attached to his wrists but touching her, searing her flesh right through the fabric of her sleeves. Her eyes clung to his the way a woman hanging from a cliff might grasp her handhold, and she could not seem to catch her breath.

Surely she had heard this man's voice before, curling through her as he held her in the dark, as his beautiful hands touched her where she had never been touched, as she gave herself to him, body and spirit.

"What are you doing here?" He shook her gently. "Where is your father?"

The devil that dwelt inside her made her ask, "Why, have you come to report to him?"

An answering spark of mischief caught in his eyes. "Never mind me. I doubt he would want to find you running amok through the rabble with a measure of—is this ale dripping all down my tunic?"

"It is," said a second voice, beside him.

This one belonged to a woman, and Anwyn turned to survey her through narrowed eyes. Prepared already to dislike her—just because she stood at this man's side—Anwyn scarcely needed to take in the loveliness of her face, her smooth black hair, or her merry eyes.

"You will smell, Lew, like you have had your head in a barrel all night."

Lew? But that was not what he should be called. Anwyn's mind stumbled over it.

"You are Champion," she said aloud.

The raven-haired woman gave him an incredulous look. "You know each other?"

"We have met." He still had hold of Anwyn; she prayed he would not let go. "This, Diera, is the daughter of the Sheriff's new head forester."

"You jest." Laughter spilled from the woman, making her even more beautiful. Did she belong to Champion? Might she be, even, his wife? A hot feeling burgeoned in Anwyn's chest.

She glared into the woman's eyes. "And are you Mistress Champion?"

Diera shot another disbelieving look at her companion. "Me? Not likely." But she added, "Leave go of her, Lew. You are attracting attention."

Champion released Anwyn's forearms. Swiftly, she twisted her hands and captured his fingers. Her skin tingled when it encountered his. "Wait." She simply could not allow him to walk away from her.

He quirked a brow. She could now clearly see the amusement, mingled with caution, in his eyes. He thought her naught but an errant lass, a naughty child escaped from her nursemaid. And why should it matter so, what this stranger thought of her?

"So you have not come to see my father?"

He shook his head. "To learn of him."

She lowered her voice. "You are an outlaw."

His companion seized his arm. "Come along out of it, Lew."

"No. I can help you. Who better than I to tell you whatever you wish to know of Mason Montfort?"

"Come away. She is clearly mad."

But Champion's gaze still held Anwyn's. He shook himself slightly. "Why should you seek to betray your father, lass? He seems a good man."

"He is a very good man," Anwyn agreed, heartfelt. "And why should it be a betrayal? You merely seek to know of your..." she suggested, "opponent."

"Ha." The sound contained little humor. "I do not know what game you play at, mistress, but I assure you it is most dangerous. You concern yourself in matters you do not understand."

"Come, we must go in search of"—Diera caught herself up—"those we have come to see."

"Aye." Firmly, Champion released himself from Anwyn's hold. "Good day to you, mistress." He bent his head toward hers, almost as if he meant to kiss her on the cheek, and spoke into her ear. "And if you would do aught to assist me, forget you saw me here today."

Then he was simply gone, melted into the crush of people around them, with the tall woman at his side.

Only her words trailed after him. "I will." But could she?

Back in her quarters, she paced like the madwoman Diera had accused her of being. She trembled, raved inwardly, and spoke to herself.

"What is this? How can he make me feel this

way?" Like a river rising inside her, set to flood; like she harbored a desperate need that knew nothing of reason. She could not even be sure of his name. "Lew," his companion had called him. But Anwyn knew to her heart that was all wrong. He should be called for some bird, one that came with the spring.

She stopped pacing near the window and looked out at the waning crowds below, where people began to wend their ways homeward. With the autumn full on, daylight faded early. Last night, when he greeted them at their arrival, she had heard Simon de Asselacton tell her father the roads—especially those within and bordering Sherwood—were scarcely safe for travelers.

"That is one of my priorities," Lord Simon had said, "to wipe out the outlaws who still infest the shire and, in particular, the forest. You can help me accomplish that, Mason. I am determined the King's laws will hold in Sherwood."

The man with the compelling gray eyes and the magical touch was an outlaw; Anwyn knew it. He represented the very thing her Da had been brought here to eradicate.

Anwyn clenched her fists, threw back her head, and emitted a groan of frustration. Despite all the travail she had caused her father these years past, she loved him and had no wish to hurt him. She had no desire to spoil this place for him. But she knew to her soul she had to see Master Champion again.

How? When? The second question might be more readily answered: naught could be soon enough. As for the first, she would go to Sherwood, if need be, and hunt him out. Yet, were he in truth an outlaw, he must be adept at hiding from pursuers—far more adept in the forest than she.

Despair pronged through her like the point of a spear. Aye, but she could be clever if need be, and devious. She might learn what her Da learned—she could even offer to ride out with him on his patrols as she used to do when she was small, back on the borders.

She laid the palms of both hands on the wide stone windowsill and lifted her gaze northward to the place on the horizon where the distant forest lay gathered like a dark threat, or a promise. And she spoke aloud to the aging day. "I will get myself to Sherwood, whatever it may take."

Chapter Five

"And what did you learn in Nottingham?" Heron asked Curlew and Diera when they returned to the village just before nightfall. "Anything about the new man?"

"Aye," Curlew responded, testing his friend's expression and emotions almost unconsciously, as he was wont to do. Through the bond that connected each of them to the guardianship—as well as the bonds of blood and friendship—he could usually tell how Heron felt about most things.

At this moment Heron appeared serene, yet Curlew could feel a tension in him, running like a current beneath deep waters. He felt, too, a spike of emotion from the woman at his side.

Not too surprising. He had known Diera from birth, grown up with her, played and argued. As young adults, the play had moved to something more, and it was in the safety of each other's friendship, and arms, they had discovered what it was men and women got up to together. But the last time he had held her so—way back last winter that was—she had confessed her love for Heron.

"Tell him," Curlew had bidden her then, and more than once since.

"I cannot," she had replied. "I know the importance of the guardianship and for what he saves himself.

When the woman destined to become your third appears—and I know she will—he thinks he must be free to bond with and possibly wed with her."

Since then, Curlew had possessed an amplified awareness whenever the three of them were together. At least, he sensed feelings on Diera's part. Heron, for once, seemed oblivious.

Heron wrinkled his nose now. "You must have spent the afternoon in an alehouse."

Diera laughed. "Nay, and that was due to another encounter altogether. A fair maid threw herself at him, and drowned him in ale, as well."

Heron lifted both brows. "Perhaps I should have gone to Nottingham after all. Trust Lew to find all the fun."

"Aye," Diera went on, a glint in her eye, "and who did she prove to be but the daughter of the new head forester?"

"You do not say! Come, have some supper and tell me all about it."

Diera hesitated. Curlew could feel her longing and saw the way her gaze lingered on Heron's face, but she shook her head. "I will be needed at home. Thank you for the edifying day out, Lew." She leaned in and kissed Curlew's cheek. He turned his head so his lips brushed hers lightly and tasted only sweetness. All her desire flowed toward the man who stood beside them.

"Good night, love," Heron told her. "Thank you for keeping our Lew in line."

"No one can keep him in line," she returned.

Heron laughed. "Do I not know it! Thank you, then, for trying."

She touched his arm and moved off into the dark.

Heron gazed after her, and Curlew ached to speak. But the secret was not his, and he said instead, "Are your parents about? They should hear what I have to say."

Heron's father, Falcon Scarlet, might be headman of Oakham, but everyone knew he led jointly with his wife, Lark. Curlew's Aunt Lark was a true fury, a warrior to her heart and a force in her own right. There could be no question Falcon deferred to her in matters of decision making and even battle planning. As two threads of the current triad, they made a formidable couple, and Curlew would not dream of bypassing their authority.

But Heron answered, "Mother beat me in going off to Sherwood. One of her spiritual pilgrimages, I expect. She said she went to speak to the Old Ones."

By "Old Ones" Curlew knew Heron meant the spirits that dwelt in Sherwood, who inhabited its deep magic and survived beyond death. A woman with Lark's deep faith and commitment could commune with them. Curlew himself had experienced a few magical encounters over the years. Yet Aunt Lark tended to seek such guidance mostly in time of trouble. Curlew fixed Heron with an inquiring eye. "Do you know what prompted her journey?"

"I do not, for certain. She and Pa were talking in whispers. I think she senses the same things you and I do—approaching changes. And you know Ma; she will not rest until she learns all."

Curlew caught and held Heron's gaze. "You do not think 'tis something dire?"

Heron made a helpless gesture with his hands. "Either way, she will want to know. But I will fetch Pa, and you can tell us what you have heard about our new opponent."

That made Curlew think of the bright-faced lass again. What was it she had said? "You merely seek to know of your opponent." How had she been able to sense so much about him? And what was it he had sensed in her when she laid hold of him—like a storm rising, unstoppable and reaching for him. He had never before encountered its like.

Ah, but she was a bonny, wild thing, like a fox set loose in the courtyard. Alluring though, with her head covering askew, that wheaten hair spilling all down her back, and those eyes filled with green light.

"Only let me change out of this tunic," he told Heron, "else surely I will put you off your supper."

****

"The man is from the Welsh borders," Curlew said around a mouthful of venison, "and you know what unrest lies there now."

His uncle Falcon—Heron's father—nodded. Fair-headed, steady-eyed, and with a deep fund of gentleness, he sat with the two younger men beside their fire outside Heron's hut just at the edge of Oakham, with the open sky and a hundred-thousand stars spread above. Curlew loved this time of night, when the new dark came down and the remembered light of the day still tinged the edges of his sight. On such evenings he felt as if he could see eternity.

This particular night looked to prove cold. No matter that; he loved every season in Sherwood. All freedom lay here for him, and all being.

And there was such comfort to be taken in the company of these two, especially Heron. It felt as if he found a missing part of himself when they came together. But they were both still well aware there remained a third part missing.

"Aye, Henry pushes the Welsh hard," Falcon mused. "There will be much more bloodshed and much grief before that business is done."

"At least it takes the King's eye from us," Heron offered wryly. "Or it had done, up until now. Why do you suppose he has decided to step up his efforts against us?"

Falcon shrugged. "Quite possibly it is the Sheriff moving on his own, seeking Henry's approval or just looking to give a place to a friend. You did say, Lew, this Montfort is an old acquaintance of de Asselacton's?"

"Aye," Curlew affirmed, "though I can only wonder at the connection. I would say they had trained together, yet Montfort has not the feel, quite, of a noble."

"They may have fought together at some point," Falcon suggested. "Such things bond men."

"Most of what Abery was able to tell me was rumor and talk. With the man newly arrived, few have had dealings with him yet. But there can be no doubt de Asselacton has brought him in to clear the vermin from Sherwood, as he puts it."

Falcon raised his gaze from the fire and narrowed his eyes speculatively. "I remember the last time a man determined to do that—Robert de Vavasour and his captain, Monteith, launched a reign of terror that saw most of the villages 'round Sherwood burnt to cinders."

"Aye." That had been before Curlew and Heron were born, but they had heard the stories. No matter that the man of whom Falcon spoke—Robert de

Vavasour, then Sheriff of Nottingham—was in truth Curlew's own great-uncle. When Curlew's father, Gareth, had thrown in his lot with the outlaws of Sherwood, he had renounced that name and taken the one Sherwood itself granted him: Champion.

It was one of many ironies that Curlew, destined to serve as guardian, carried a measure of Norman blood.

Aye, but he lived like no Norman, nor thought like one, either. His heart and his life were all for Sherwood. And this man beside him, whom he called uncle, had never held his Norman blood against him. Falcon Scarlet was wise and kind, and fair to a fault.

Falcon said now, "Abery and Ronast will keep us informed, no doubt. The rest of us shall just have to sit tight until we see how this new wind blows. Though I doubt it bodes well for us." He wrinkled his brow in a frown, and his gaze took on a faraway look. Curlew wondered if he were speaking to his wife, Lark, in his mind, an ability both they and Curlew's own parents possessed, gifted by the magic of Sherwood.

He felt a pang of sudden longing. Would he ever experience that form of spiritual communion with any woman? Probably not. Given Heron's total devotion, it seemed likely that when the third member of their triad appeared, Heron would wed with her and claim that precious right.

Falcon got to his feet. "I am away to my bed. Heron, pray your mother comes back soon with good news." He touched each of their heads lightly, and Curlew felt the love flowing through him. "Blessings, lads."

"Aye"—Heron spoke softly once his father had gone—"and I fear we shall need them. Something begins, Lew." He raised his gaze, suddenly serious, to Curlew's face. "I can no longer put off my own journey into Sherwood. We need answers."

"Your mother will bring them," Curlew assured him, trying to deny his own disquiet.

"I do not mean that. It is time we knew the identity of our third guardian, and when she will come to us."

That sent a spear of emotion through Curlew. "Aye, but we have asked before." They had, both together and separately.

Heron's eyes, deep gold in the firelight, took on a curious expression. "This time I mean to go to the source. I intend to lie with the Lady herself."

Curlew's brows soared. The patterns governing Sherwood's magic were complex and vastly interwoven. They were also what Curlew's grandfather, Sparrow Little, had often called ineffable—sensed rather than known. But that magic fell under the governance of the Lord and Lady—male and female deities who caused all life to flow, brought the spring after winter's freeze, and quickened both faith and flesh. Tradition dictated that among those who held the triad, two wed together and the third bonded with and in essence wed Sherwood itself, and even lay with the Lord or Lady.

Over the years and generations, those details had altered but never failed. Falcon and Lark had bonded together, while Curlew's mother, Linnet—a healer— had gone to live deep in Sherwood and bond with not only the forest but its chosen champion, Curlew's father.

Did Heron now volunteer to take the sometimes lonely path of the hermit, leaving their third member to

Curlew, should she appear? Or did he speak in a purely speculative fashion of a spiritual body?

As if he sensed Curlew's question, Heron gave him a wry smile. "It is time, and past time. I intend to offer myself to her, lie with her if she will have me, and ask what is to come."

Curlew blinked. Had it been any other man, Curlew would have considered him raving mad. Yet he knew Heron to the heart and could doubt neither his honesty nor his devotion.

"Then you have my blessing also," he said.

Chapter Six

"Daughter, we need to speak together."

Anwyn turned her head as her father entered the chamber. A patient man, as she well knew, and often far more generous with her than she deserved, he now wore a serious expression, and his words were weighted.

She sighed. A mere four days had they been in Nottingham. During that time he had ridden out every day, with or without Lord Simon, becoming acquainted with his new duties and the country all round. And Anwyn had been left to her own devices—a dangerous proposition.

Now, as evening came on, he had returned from his day out, with the mud of Sherwood on his boots and his bow on his shoulder. He looked weary and troubled, and her heart smote her that she should be the cause, for that much she knew.

"Father," she said. "How went your day?"

"Well enough, though there is work here for a thousand foresters and I have been given but eight. 'Tis not that which troubles me now. What should reach my ears upon my return this evening but tales of you?" He added deliberately, "Yet again."

Anwyn's breath caught in her throat and formed a lump of pain. She did not want to vex her father, nor to hurt him—God knew he had been hurt enough by her mother's death.

He set aside his bow and quiver and came to the hearth where Anwyn sat. For a long moment he stood studying her, and she braced herself for what must come—an onslaught of disapproval and, worse, disappointment.

As he sat down at her side she could not keep from asking, "What have you heard? Who has been speaking out of turn?"

He did not answer but instead said, "You promised you would not do this, Anwyn. You vowed we would make a new beginning here at Nottingham."

Her shame on his behalf made her defensive. "What have I done? What, that is so terrible?"

"Four days we have been here," he said heavily, "and already they speak of you, the folk of the castle. The Wild Lass—that is what they call you. You lied to me, Anwyn."

The accusation struck deep, but she managed to raise her eyes to his, which were full of sorrow.

Before he could continue, she lifted her hands and spoke, still defensively. "You cannot expect me to stay trapped here like an animal. I will go mad."

"You could not give me four days? We are barely settled in; there is much to occupy you."

"What? What is to occupy me? Folding away our clothing? Arranging the trinkets we brought from Shrewsbury? Nesting? I am, Father, not meant for nesting."

"Quite plainly, and yet, Daughter, you will need to learn. Care you nothing for your reputation, or mine?"

Anwyn shook her head.

Her father's expression hardened, yet his voice

remained gentle as he said, "Then I must care enough for both of us. I love you, Daughter. You are all that is left to me of your dear mother."

Anwyn felt her heart break. Tears filled the back of her throat. "I know."

"But I cannot have you behaving with such abandon, running about unescorted and with your hair loose, stealing from the market stalls—oh, aye, you were seen. Speaking to strange men in a provocative manner. Are we truly to have all that ugliness again?"

Anwyn met his gaze with a combination of shame and defiance. "I have done naught I should not."

"By the grace of God! Do you not know what would have happened at the hands of that soldier back on the borders, and likely all his companions, had you not been discovered? You promised me, Anwyn, it would not happen again."

"It has not."

"It begins! You play a dangerous game, as I have told you. Not every man will allow himself to be put off at your whim."

"I know that." Anwyn got to her feet, no longer able to sit still. "How can you expect me to remain here endlessly? Let me ride out into the forest with you, Da, as we used to do. Let me be of some service."

"I cannot."

She ignored him and hurried on, "You know you have taught me to shoot almost as well as you do, and I have a good eye."

"Nay, Daughter—it would merely cause more scandal. What served on the uncivilized Welsh borders will not do here."

"Is Sherwood not uncivilized?"

He raked her with a troubled look. "You are a child no longer, but a woman full grown. That is what makes your disobedience all the more dangerous. It is time you made your mind up to live the life available to you."

"And what is that?"

"Marriage." He raised a hand. "Now, Daughter, before you fly at me, only listen. There is a man among my foresters—"

"The one we met in Sherwood?" Fierce hope rose in Anwyn's heart. Was it possible he might be part of her father's company after all?

"Nay." Her father's eyes took on a rueful look. "That blackguard must rather have been one of the very miscreants we are set to hunt down—he lied to me also, it seems. There is none such among my band. But there is a man who has impressed me right well."

Anwyn began to tremble. "In four short days?"

"Aye, indeed, for he is foremost among my men, one Roderick Havers, by name, a widower with two children half grown. I believe he would suit very well."

Anwyn stared in horror and repeated, "Two children?"

"A son of about ten years and a daughter eight."

"I can scarcely imagine anything that would suit me less."

"Yet he needs someone to take them in hand and thus may be willing to overlook your...past transgressions. Anwyn, lass, you have left me little choice. I need to be able to devote myself to my work here. And you have said yourself you need an occupation."

"Not two no doubt troublesome waifs."

"You think too often of yourself, Daughter, your

wants and needs." His mouth tightened. "Since your mother's death I have indulged you too much. But it ends now."

Anwyn stared at him, mutinous.

"I want you to meet Roderick tomorrow evening. I have invited him and his children, so you will prepare a meal here in our quarters and you will make yourself pleasant and accommodating. Do you understand?"

"Father." Anwyn laid her hand on his arm. "This is misguided. It will never suit."

"You do not know that until you meet him. He is strong and steady—"

"Hard, you mean."

"It becomes apparent you need someone far more firm than I. In the days to come, Anwyn, I will be much away from Nottingham. We begin a campaign to reclaim Sherwood and search out every man thieving the King's deer. I cannot be worrying about what you will do in my absence."

"You would rather fob me off onto a stranger?"

"Have you left me any choice?"

"There is always a choice," Anwyn answered defiantly, though she knew choices were few enough for women. Contracted, traded, even sold—it was a miracle she had remained unwed so long, and she acknowledged her father had indulged her much. Now it seemed she might have pushed him too far.

"Only meet the man," her father urged. "'Tis a simple enough thing and, for now, all I ask."

Chapter Seven

"This new man tries us sorely," said Falcon Scarlet with bitterness. "He certainly makes his presence known in Sherwood."

"Aye." Curlew could not help but agree. Night had fallen; the dark came ever earlier now they were well into autumn. He and his uncle sat together in Oakham, sharing a meal and a fire. It should have been a peaceful time, yet for the last four days stories had filtered in about a party of foresters moving hither and yon through the villages that bordered the great forest, searching out evidence of what the Sheriff liked to call the King's property.

So far, only warnings had been issued—no one had been hauled away for sentencing or punishment. Yet they all felt the new hand descending heavily upon them. No one could doubt it was merely a matter of time before arrests were made.

"I do wish your aunt would return from Sherwood—or Heron," Scarlet said.

Curlew nodded. Falcon seldom found any ease when Lark was away from him. Yet she still had not returned from her pilgrimage.

Heron's absence troubled Curlew more. When last Curlew spoke with him, he had said he meant to seek the Lady and a measure of enlightenment. But that had been fully two days ago.

"This is the time when the deer run," Falcon added. "If this man, Montfort, begins looking in earnest, he will find venison in plenty. And so a new reign of terror begins."

"I think—" Curlew had just begun to speak when he caught movement from the corner of his eye. A shadow materialized from the darkness, took form, and joined them at their fire. He felt his uncle's emotions rise in instant gladness.

Aunt Lark. Aye, and there was much of the spirit about her. She often moved soundlessly, and her emotions changed as quickly as the weather. Now she stood for a moment with her hands on her husband's shoulders—a small woman, but fierce with it—before she bent to kiss his cheek.

But Falcon turned his face so his lips met hers instead in a moment of blinding sweetness. Curlew blinked. As two parts of the guardianship, these souls were linked on a score of levels, not least the physical.

"Love," Falcon said in joy and claiming.

"Love," she returned, and added with amusement, "you wished for me; I came."

"I always wish for you," Falcon admitted ruefully.

Curlew wondered if they said even more to one another between their minds, words not meant for his ears. Aye, Sherwood gave much. He wondered again if he would ever know this kind of close bond for himself. Having witnessed it all his life, could he hope to be satisfied with less?

"What news do you bring?" Falcon asked his wife even as she seated herself at his side.

"Naught good." Lark's bright, golden gaze touched Curlew. "This concerns you, lad, as well as the rest of us. Where is Heron?"

"Not here, but gone into Sherwood on a pilgrimage of his own. Why, Aunt? What is amiss?"

She did not answer at once but instead took the cup from Falcon's hand and drank deep. Curlew felt the stir of her emotions—he could often glean the edges of feelings from those close to him. Yet he was ill prepared when she settled her gaze on his face and said, "'Tis your mother, lad. I bring grave news."

****

"I knew something was amiss." Lark spoke low and steadily so only the two of them might hear. "'Tis what took me to Sherwood, withal. But I did not expect what I found."

She stopped abruptly and Falcon seized her hand. He had gone pale and sober like a man who had received a blow to the heart.

"What has befallen my mother?" Curlew demanded.

"That I cannot say."

"She lives?"

Lark nodded. "Oh, aye, she lives, lad. But she has been...stricken. Three days ago, your father said it was. She arose as usual, spoke her prayers, and then went down like a young tree riven by lightning. She lives, she breathes, she shows no sign of pain, but he has been unable to rouse her." Lark's lips tightened. "Nor could I."

Falcon stared in horror. "Gareth did not send us word?"

"He wanted to, but he refused to leave her. You know what he is."

Aye, Curlew thought, shock and pain curling

through him, they all knew of his father's attachment to his mother. Gareth Champion lived for his Linnet, unsparing. Curlew could scarcely imagine his devastation now.

Sherwood gave, but when it took, it took much.

"What does it mean?" Falcon appealed to his wife.

"I confess, Fal, I do not know. She is there, yet not there. Gareth has tried calling her through his mind, as did I. Both of us can sense her thoughts—they move yet. But she does not respond."

"Poor Pa," Curlew murmured, and Lark looked at him.

"He does not do well, Lew. It is as if both his arms have been struck off—he founders in a dark, angry sea. Fal, I came to fetch you. I thought the two of us together might call upon the powers of our bond and so draw her from this dire sleep."

Such, Curlew knew, had been done before. Members of former triads had been called back even from death. Aye, surely that was the solution.

Falcon asked softly, "What does this mean for the guardianship, for Sherwood?"

Lark made a helpless gesture with her hands. A forceful woman, Curlew saw her so seldom at a loss it shocked him now. "Linnet yet lives, and thus the triad still holds." Her eyes returned to Curlew's face. "But I think we must be prepared for anything."

A shudder moved through Curlew. Anyone raised on the magic of Sherwood—and by its three guardians—learned early of life and death. He knew to his soul that death was an illusion, a mere altering of form, and that all that lived came again. Had he not met with and conversed with the spirits who dwelt in

Sherwood? Yet these three, who held the power of the current guardianship, had always seemed unchangeable to him. And his mother—

Memories of her rushed upon him—the warmth of her smile, the otherworldly wisdom in her dark eyes. The gentle touch of her hands that seemed to shed mercy and healing wherever they reached. The constancy of her love for his father, for the members of the family they had created together, for the greater family that included the folk of Sherwood and beyond. She had given so much to others. How might she best be repaid now?

"This will wound us all," he said. His two sisters, Dove and Petrel, both born after him, were already wed and moved away to neighboring villages.

"You will need to carry the word to your sisters," Lark told him.

He nodded. Dove lived in Ravenshead, where her husband was smith, and Petrel, who would soon give birth to her first child, in nearby Little Wold. He could not duck the duty of informing them of this tragedy. But what he wanted was to go to the forest and see his mother.

Lark rose and her fingers twitched on Falcon's. "I go now to my prayers. Come with me?"

He nodded, still looking as if someone had punched him hard in the gut, which was very much how Curlew felt.

"But tomorrow," Falcon said, "we go to the forest." He looked at Curlew and vowed, "We will bring her out of this, lad, if anyone can."

Chapter Eight

"Cousin, I have just heard the news. How do you fare?"

A hand dropped onto Curlew's shoulder while he sat with his head lowered into his hands, locked in a fog of despair. He had spent the day tramping to the nearby villages and meeting with his sisters, advising them of what had come to pass. Neither of them had taken it well. Petrel had clung to him, and Dove had wept in his arms.

All the while, his heart had journeyed with Falcon and Lark, into Sherwood. He longed to see his mother so badly he ached. But when he looked up now into Heron's face, he found himself somewhat comforted.

"By the Green Man's horns, I am glad you are back," he said. "Who told you the news?"

Heron made a wry face and seated himself at Curlew's side. "Who did not tell, would be a better question. I was swarmed as soon as I stepped into the village." He lowered his pack and bow from his shoulder. "Not but I knew something was amiss—there is an imbalance. It haunted me the whole time I was gone."

"You had no glimpse of your parents in the forest?"

"Nay, but I went nowhere near the hermitage. My business was nothing I wished to have observed."

"They have gone to try and bring Ma out of this sleep, or whatever it is that holds her."

"Peace then, Curlew. If anyone can, they can."

"I know that." Curlew believed it to his very soul. "But what if she cannot be brought?"

Heron smiled quietly. "If they cannot call her with the power of Sherwood, surely your father's love can. It is at least as strong."

True enough. Curlew had never seen a love to rival his parents', not even that of Lark and Falcon, who were bonded on an inestimable level. His parents quite plainly lived for one another.

"What will happen if she never comes out of it?" he asked of Heron, and the night. "What, to him?"

Heron looked thoughtful. He poured a draught of ale from the flagon that stood at Curlew's knee and placed it in his hand. "Drink that."

"I do not want it."

"Drink, Cousin. Your father is a strong man—none stronger."

True also, and yet… "He is strong because of her."

Heron's golden gaze grew serious. "We are all strong because of each other, especially here in Sherwood. The magic will save her, lad. And if it does not—"

"Aye?"

"Your father will either go on without her or lie down and follow her wherever she has gone."

"I cannot bear it."

Heron let those words hang in the dark air for several moments before he said, "But you will have to bear it, lad. 'Tis what we were meant for—born for—is it not? To take their places when the time comes."

"But it is too soon. We are not ready. We have not even found the third guardian."

"Then have faith in Sherwood, Lew. Your mother will not surrender her place just yet."

Aye, comforting words—or they would be, did Curlew not know the history of past guardians so well. Many had held the power of Sherwood over the years, and for all, change had come too soon.

The first triad had been made up of his great-grandfather, Robin Hood, who had held the power shared with his wife, Marian, and the living sentience of Sherwood itself. That circle, though, had been uneven, and when Robin fell, cut down by the Normans, both Marian and the circle had broken. Unwilling to surrender Sherwood's magic to their overlords, another three had stepped up—the healer Lil, the village headman Geofrey, and the mystic Alric. Upon their deaths, the circle had wavered perilously again, only to be taken up by Robin and Marian's daughter, Wren, along with the sons of those who had worked so hard to keep Robin's legend alive—Sparrow Little, son of Little John, and Martin Scarlet, son of Will Scarlet the renegade soldier.

And when Martin died, when Wren and Sparrow, together, disappeared into the mystical depths of Sherwood, Curlew's mother and Heron's parents had stepped in.

And held strong until now.

"We can do nothing without the third of our number." Curlew spoke the words aloud and yearned with them. He turned his gaze on his cousin. "Tell me your pilgrimage to Sherwood was successful."

Heron met his gaze with one that glowed. "It was

successful."

Curlew's heart rose. "You know who she is? Where she is?" A woman in one of the nearby villages, perhaps, who had somehow escaped their attention all this while.

Heron leaned forward and his tawny hair slid over his shoulders. "Not that, Lew. You forget I knew not the urgency of the need, when I left. Yet," he drew a breath and finished, his words full of wonder, "I lay with the Lady, Lew. She came to me on my third night out, while I lay sleepless and aching. She gave herself to me even as a flesh-and-blood woman might, as a lover might."

Curlew stared. Always had he known the thread of mystical belief ran deep through Heron's being. But this made a powerful magic indeed, the sort that might have been experienced by Robin Hood himself. A rush of wonder, like an echo of Heron's own but touched with envy, arose in his heart. He could sense Heron's jubilance, catch its reverberations. If anyone deserved such an honor, aye, it was this man. But why could such an experience never find him, Curlew? Aye, he was the ordinary one, the one who must walk the path of hard work and struggle. Sherwood, it seemed, had chosen Heron for great things.

"I am glad for you," he said softly, and he was. Heron deserved this honor. He walked half the time clothed in magic. Why should this come as a surprise? He asked, because he felt he could ask his cousin anything, "What was it like?"

A smile came to Heron's face, unlike any other Curlew had seen. Half bliss and half devotion, it seemed to elevate Heron's very spirit. "Far more than I had anticipated, though I believe I waited for it all my life long. She formed out of the very air, Lew; I felt her arise from the elements of Sherwood itself. She came into my arms and loved me. It was—ah, but words fail." Heron lifted his hands in a speaking gesture.

Curlew's mouth went dry. "How did she look?" As lads, they had speculated over it—how beautiful might be the spirit of all womanhood?

But now Heron smiled and shook his head. "I do not know; I could not see her. She came to me in darkness. There was naught but sensation. I could feel everything about her—her skin, and the softness of her hair that wrapped around us as we—" He stopped abruptly and an incredible look invaded his eyes. "Forgive me, Lew. I cannot speak of that even to you."

Curlew struggled with his feelings, which seemed predominately jealousy and longing. "What said she to you?"

"All manner of things. She whispered to me—and through me—all the while, Lew, of how blessed we are to carry Sherwood's magic, how favored we are with both her and her Lord. She told me I took his place on this night—that I was him, whilst I lay with her."

"Said she aught of the missing guardian?" Curlew's voice sounded hoarse, and Heron gave him a sympathetic look, as if he could feel Curlew's desire.

"Aye. She comes, and soon. She comes to Sherwood."

Curlew's heart leaped and began to beat madly in his chest. "Who is she?"

Sorrowfully, Heron shook his head. "You must understand, the Lady communicates not so much in actual words as in knowing. And I was somewhat otherwise occupied at the time. Her favor is strong."

"Did she let you know to which of us she comes?" Heron had experienced this wonder—should Curlew not, then, possess the real woman?

"Nay, only that she comes here to Sherwood. That was emphasized. Also"—Heron frowned—"that her coming is in some manner a returning. I did not completely comprehend that part of it."

"Ah. Someone who lived here before, perhaps, was born here and then moved away, and was raised elsewhere. 'Twould explain why we have been unable to find her. For it seems these last years we have gleaned for every possible candidate and found only disappointment."

"So we have. I know not, Lew. Only that she will come in the fullness of time."

"The time is now." Curlew thought again of his mother lying senseless. Should she slip away from them, how long could the magic of Sherwood endure without a new threesome of guardians?

Yet he could sense something new about Heron, brought from his encounter in the forest, a quickening, a certainty.

"You are changed," he said, soft as the night.

Heron gave him a smile. "Who could lie with her and not be changed? She has left part of herself inside me."

"So. You are to be our priest—the one of us who bonds with Sherwood itself." Curlew should, indeed, be glad. How could he be jealous of his closest friend, dearer to him than a brother? But Heron, it seemed, had been given so much: intelligence, a kind of male beauty that invariably turned female heads, and ease with

Sherwood's magic that far surpassed Curlew's own. He could even shoot an arrow—not, perhaps, so well as Curlew, but then, few could.

"Do not despair, Lew," Heron said, as if he could hear Curlew's thoughts, which, in part, perhaps he could. "She told me that we move toward a prize of inestimable worth. And she sent me a message especially for you."

"For me?"

Again, Heron smiled. "Aye, she bade me tell you to go to the heart of Sherwood even as I have done, and there she will come also with you, the holy Lord's Lady."

Curlew's brows flew up. "Lie with me, you mean? With both of us? But 'tis unheard of, that."

Heron shook his head. "What is the value of wondering? Sherwood makes the rules and then loves to break them. I do not believe there is a precedent for this. For our case is unique, is it not? There has never before been a triad like ours—two parts without the third. All I know is she bade you come." A hint of mischief invaded Heron's eyes. "And then, *come*. Prepare yourself—she is a wild ride."

Heat seemed to rush through Curlew's blood until he sat enflamed.

But he raised his gaze to Heron's face. "You do not mind if I have her also?"

Heron's smile deepened. "How can I mind? This is not, Lew, like lying with a mortal woman. The sensations are all physical, aye, but she is spirit. As such, there is enough of her for both of us. As I have learned, there is no lack in the spiritual world. She—like her Lord—is everywhere and within everyone, in the stag that runs, the child who cries, and the smallest flower that lifts its head from the soil. She is life. She is the fundamental magic of Sherwood."

He paused, and the night moved around them; the trees stirred overhead. In the far distance an owl called, plaintive and echoing.

For several long moments Heron waited, and then he fixed Curlew with a golden stare. "And so, will you go?"

Curlew's heart still beat high and hard in his chest. He might tell himself he went for his mother's sake, or that of the guardianship, or even the future of Sherwood itself. He knew all three would be a lie.

He drew a hard breath and answered, "I will."

Chapter Nine

"Daughter, come and greet our guests."

Anwyn turned to the door with dread in her heart. She had done her best this day to comply with her father's expectations. For love of him she had put their quarters in order and made herself presentable, even going so far as to don her best gown and tame her thick hair into a knot beneath her head covering. She had planned a meal and struggled to prepare it at the small hearth, her uneasiness increasing all the day long.

And they came late, her father and his guests, when the dark had nearly fallen and the meat was spoiled and her heart felt like a trapped bird suffering in her chest. She whirled about, telling herself she was prepared for anything, and froze.

There stood her father, indeed, with a man and two children at his side. Her poor heart struggled even more wildly at the sight.

The children—ah, and they were just ordinary children, the boy thin as a bundle of sticks and the lass dressed in a drab gown like the fur of a mouse. All Anwyn's attention settled on the man. Only, surely he was no man—her father had brought home a troll instead.

Nearly a head shorter than her father, who was not particularly tall, the fellow appeared almost as wide, clad in a leather vest and leggings. Arms beefy as an ordinary man's legs and a thick, muscular torso contrasted almost grotesquely with a pair of bandy legs.

His hair lay thin on his domed head, patchy and brown, and he had a face like a weathered stump, eyes as small as those of a boar. He resembled a boar withal—squat, bristling, and all strength.

Anwyn smoothed her suddenly damp hands down the front of her dress. Ah, but her father could not be in earnest! He made some cruel joke, a mere attempt to shock her into obedience.

"Daughter, I would have you meet Roderick Havers, the foremost among my foresters, and his children, Agnes and Dennis. Roderick, my daughter, Anwyn."

The troll grunted. Anwyn could not possibly interpret the sound he emitted any other way. But his eyes were all over her, avid and grasping. Anwyn had seen that look before and knew what it meant.

"Welcome," she managed to say. "Please make yourselves comfortable. I fear the meal I prepared is a bit overcooked—"

"I am sorry for that, Daughter. We were delayed. Chased a miscreant well into the forest, did we not, Roderick?"

"Tricky devil," Havers rumbled. His voice sounded like thunder approaching from the distance. Anwyn suddenly imagined hearing it in the dark as he ordered her to his bidding, his hands mauling her as his gaze did even now.

No, no, and no.

"Will you not sit?" she invited, and indicated the table she had laid. The rooms Simon de Asselacton afforded his new head forester were not large but provided a measure of comfort. From the way the two children glanced about, Anwyn could see they were impressed.

And to what quarters were these three entitled? Where would her father expect her to live, if she accepted Havers?

Which she would not. She would sooner decapitate herself.

"I am learning well the abilities of those who dwell in Sherwood," Anwyn's father said ruefully, "and around it. The villagers in league with the outlaws will look you straight in the eye and lie barefacedly. 'Tis nearly impossible to tell what is truth."

"Very little of it," Havers said, lowering his bulk onto a bench. "We have long been in need of a man such as your father, mistress, to lead this war we wage on behalf of our King."

"But we need more men," Montfort put in. "I cannot hope to make inroads with but a group of eight. Anwyn, Roderick here is the best of my men—a fierce fighter and virtually unstoppable when on a charge."

Like most boars, Anwyn thought, as she brought the food to the table and struggled to look polite.

"If I had another two like this man, I would be well served," Montfort said.

Havers eyed the food Anwyn had prepared and did not appear impressed. From the look of him, he must be a serious trencherman. Again, Anwyn's heart struggled in her breast. Perhaps he would refuse to consider her for the sake of his stomach—and her obvious lack of domestic skills.

Yet if he were like most men he was far more interested in her other features. Even as he began eating the food Anwyn served—subjecting each bite to dubious scrutiny—he continued to shoot her glances that stripped her bare: her neck, her shoulders, and on downward, lingering at her breasts as if he sought to measure them.

The two men discussed the situation in Sherwood, Havers roundly denouncing those who dwelt there, while Anwyn fought to remain silent. Women, she knew, were expected to be quiet and respectful, and she could almost feel her father willing her to hold her tongue.

But her father had brought her a troll. Should she care for his wishes?

The ruined meal served, she took her own place at the table and looked at the children. Both were silent, but neither was still. The lad squirmed and emitted an air of spitefulness. He had little resemblance to his father, being thin and sharp featured. The girl, Agnes, the younger of the two, did have the look of her father—poor lass.

"Anwyn is an unusual name, mistress," Havers said abruptly, apparently having exhausted the sins of the peasantry while Anwyn's attention strayed.

She looked at her father uncertainly, and he answered, "It is a Welsh name. Her mother came from Gwynedd."

"Lot of trouble with the Welsh just now." Havers shoveled a chunk of bread into his mouth and spoke around it. "Treacherous lot, they are. I doubt Henry will ever succeed in putting them down."

"They have their own laws," said Anwyn's father, who always strove to be fair, "and believe in their own sovereignty."

Havers grunted again. "Aye, but their King is their King. They need to be knocked down a few pegs, just like that lot in Sherwood. Allowed to run wild too long, that is what." His tiny eyes, the color of dried mud, moved to Anwyn's face. "Time to apply some discipline. 'Tis the only way. Is that not right, children? Tell Mistress Anwyn how often you two have felt the strap."

Agnes's face took on a painful flush, but Dennis slid his eyes to his father's in a sly look. Anwyn felt for the girl but guessed the lad would be a right handful, the sort who pulled the wings off honeybees, no doubt.

Havers went on almost proudly, speaking to his host but with his gaze still on Anwyn's face. "I have lost count of the times I have whipped these two since their mother died. But 'tis the surest solution for disobedience."

"Aye, well…" Anwyn's father began.

"You cannot be soft, man. It only leads to trouble. And a child—or a wife—will only make mischief when she thinks she can get away with it."

Anwyn stared at him in horror and then looked at the children again. The lass appeared close to tears. Young Dennis, though, looked like he might cut his father's throat some night, while the man slept.

Anwyn found herself firmly on Dennis's side. If ever Havers tried to take the strap to her—or if he attempted to maul her with those rough hands—she would cheerfully stab him in the neck.

"So, ah"—Anwyn's father cleared his throat— "you have said, my good man, that you are looking to remarry."

Anwyn glared at her father. He could not be in

earnest! Would he still contemplate handing her over to such a brute after hearing his opinions? Her heart smote her. Had she troubled him to such a great measure, with her disobedience, he would be rid of her any way he could?

Sudden tears blurred her vision. In that moment she saw herself as she was—naught but a problem to this man she loved right well, and a source of shame. Surely he meant this encounter as a kind of warning? Surely he merely intended the threat of marriage to this beast-man to frighten her into proper behavior?

Somehow, she endured the rest of that meal and the distressing, limping conversation. She said little and the children less. Havers bragged of himself in a backhanded way, and spouted opinions on everything from the treatment of the peasantry to the actions of his King. With every word he spoke, Anwyn's opinion of him worsened. By the time he and his two children rose to leave, she could not have been more relieved.

Having spoken her goodnights, she busied herself clearing away the remains of the meal. That did not mean she failed to hear the two men's whispered conversation at the door.

"Well, Roderick, will she suit?"

"Truly, Master Montfort, there is a deal of rebelliousness there. I can see it clear in her eyes. The unfortunate legacy of her Welsh blood, no doubt."

Aye, and that would do it, Anwyn thought triumphantly. Her father would never stand to hear a word that impinged her mother, the woman he had adored.

Yet he hissed, "You say you are still willing to take her on?"

"Even Welsh blood can be tamed by the proper hand. And she looks as if she would provide strong sons."

"She is barely twenty, and in good health." Her father sounded as if he strove to sell a wayward hound.

Havers lowered his voice further. "You swear to me she is not ruined? I will not take another man's leavings."

Anwyn twitched and waited for her father's reply; he hesitated an instant too long. Did he truly doubt her virtue?

"She vows to me she has kept herself pure."

Pure, and what was that? Anwyn raged inwardly. Should she save herself only to be violated at the hands of a brute such as this? Pawing at her in the dark, lowering his great bulk upon her—she would never endure it.

Predictably, Havers grunted again. "Aye, well, I will speak to the priest. Pray, Master, keep her close until then."

"Aye. Good man."

Pain seared Anwyn's heart as her father closed the door behind his guests. She turned to face him.

What had she done to make him so eager to be shed of her? Had she killed the great love in his heart?

"Well, Daughter. I know Roderick Havers may not be the sort of husband that ever you thought to accept."

"He is not."

"Yet we must consider the present situation. Things are much different here at Nottingham. I will not be able to devote to you the time I did at Shrewsbury. And it becomes evident you are not happy here on your own. I cannot allow a scandal to ruin my chances with Lord Simon. This is a fine place he has given me, one in which I could well rise if I do my job well."

"So," said Anwyn, her heart breaking, "you would give me to *him?* Father, what have I done to make you hate me so?"

Her father's face crumpled in a troubled frown. "Anwyn, I do not hate you. Quite the contrary. Can you not see how I fear for you? Left to your own devices, you can only come to great harm."

"And," Anwyn's voice trembled, "will I not come to grief beneath the strap that brute means to use on me? Da, would you truly condemn me to that?"

Her father caught her hands in his. "Anwyn, lass, he will only use you ill if you push him to it. He is a good, steady man."

"I do not want this!"

"Aye, but Anwyn, you leave me no choice." His fingers clasped hers painfully. "Can you promise me you will no longer run wild about Nottingham?" His eyes caught hers. "Can you vow it to me once more, and not lie?"

Tears choked Anwyn so she could not speak. She did not want to lie to him. She shook her head. How could she hope to explain the great restlessness that possessed her, that pushed and pulled until she felt half mad with desire for something she could not name?

Her father's expression cooled. "Then, Daughter, I must think of myself for once, and of keeping this fortunate place that has fallen to me." He drew a breath. "Accept it, Anwyn; Roderick will speak to the priest, and you will be wed."

Chapter Ten

"Six days she has lain like this. So still. No sign that she feels any pain."

Curlew's father spoke the words quietly and revealed little emotion, yet Curlew felt the storm inside him, so intense he could virtually taste it.

Since his arrival at their hermitage early this morning, Gareth had looked at him but once—all his attention remained fastened on the woman who lay like an effigy on a coffin.

Now he whispered, "Is she not beautiful?"

She was. Curlew firmly believed his mother, Linnet Champion, to be the most beautiful woman he had ever seen. Now she lay stretched on the pallet his parents had once shared, her eyes closed, her face serene, and her hair flowing about her like a brown veil. Her hands, which Curlew had all his life seen moving, ever moving in compassionate deeds—healing the sick, uplifting her children, or giving a loving caress in passing to the man who stood beside him—were at last still, folded on her breast. Curlew thought that hit him hardest of all, made this impossibility seem real.

He looked from her to his father. What must he be feeling? These two had always been connected so deeply they often did not even need to speak words aloud. Ma had always said with a radiant smile that their hearts spoke together instead.

How long could his father last without that, without her? Already he looked honed, his tall, slender body whittled down somehow, and his handsome face drawn. Aye, and his hair still made a smooth, shining cap on his head—more silver than gold now, true. But the look in his gray eyes, so like Curlew's own, made Curlew ache.

'Twas not fair. This man had given his life in service to the people of Sherwood, to his family, to the magic of the forest itself. He did not deserve this blow.

Curlew said, hushed, "You cannot reach her, Pa?"

"I cannot. Lark and Falcon could not, though they formed a circle and drew down enough power to fell these trees, so I thought." Gareth glanced at the great beeches, oaks, and ash trees that surrounded them like sentinels before his gaze quickly returned to his wife. "They said she is there but distant—held from us."

"Held by whom?"

Gareth gave a grim smile. "Sherwood. Safe, but kept."

Sherwood gives. Sherwood takes much. How many times had Curlew heard those words in his youth? He sometimes thought he had been weaned on them.

Gareth tipped his shining head as if listening to something. Curlew was not sure he believed in angels—were they not a construct of the Church, like hellfire and eternal punishment? But if they did exist, he thought they must look like his father at that moment—otherworldly, righteous, and strong.

Gareth said almost lightly, "You know, I have seen Falcon weep more than once over the years—when your aunt Lark gave birth to that stillborn babe, when we lost so many to the cold that harsh winter, even when a beloved tree came down. Falcon has a loving heart. Do you know, lad, how many times I have seen your aunt Lark weep? Yet they sat together and wept like terrified children when they could not pull her back for you, for me."

Emotion clutched at Curlew's heart, so tight it ached. If the other two thirds of the circle could not rescue her, what could? Only the love of this man beside him.

But he would have already tried, and tried again.

"Pa," he whispered around the pain that possessed him, "what does this mean? What, for the guardianship of Sherwood?"

Gareth shook his head. "I do not know. Lark and Falcon do not seem to know. Both have prayed on it. A day and a night they stayed here, praying. As I say, they raised a fearsome magic. It was not enough."

"She still lives." Curlew asserted it like a demand. But for how long?

"Aye, there is that. So long as she lives—even thus—the circle and the protection stand. I keep thinking she might just awaken in her beauty, as she has done every morning, in my arms."

The pain that held Curlew's heart increased. All his life had he wished for a great love like that his parents shared, in total devotion to one another. This, then, was a glimpse of the other side of it, devastation beyond imagining.

He said, though he did not want to, because he must, "Six days, you say—she will need food, water. What of that?"

"No food has passed her lips. I have dribbled water between them. I cannot tell if she swallows it. But you know what the water of Sherwood is."

Curlew did. It had healing properties, magical ones. Yet could a few drops sustain a woman and keep her alive?

And if she died...

Curlew swiftly shut that thought away. He would not entertain it, would not contemplate it. For her death would mean that of this man beside him, and of the triad, as well. All personal grief aside, he and Heron were not ready to take their places.

His father's voice interrupted the dire thoughts. "I wondered if you would try."

"Eh?"

Gareth reached out and grasped Curlew's hand. "Son, you were conceived here in the magic of this place. Even before your birth we were told you would be the most important person ever born in Sherwood. Perhaps you are the one who can catch hold of her and call her back."

Tears blurred Curlew's vision. Aye, such tales had been told of him before his birth. But what had come of them? He had grown well and strong, yet with nothing extraordinary about him save the ability to hit a target with great precision, an uncanny sense of the forest, and a penchant for mischief that often caused more trouble than otherwise. It was Heron who possessed all the important gifts, the talents, the otherworldly grandeur.

Curlew came to this armed with only love. And much as he might adore his mother, if love alone could call her back she would have answered that of this man beside him. Yet he would try, of course he would try. He nodded.

He lowered himself to the ground beside his

mother, reached out, and took her hands in his. Aye, he loved his mother's hands, quick and gentle, that never so much as once struck one of her children in anger. How fortunate they had been to have such a woman for mother! He would gladly lay his life down now for her and his father.

He bowed his head over his mother's hands, closed his eyes and began to pray. He called upon the things he loved best—the trees that arched above him like a living roof, the water that carried always promise and memory, the deep loam, and the light, the eternal light. He felt something come alive in him, take hold, and flare bright. His heart opened like a new shoot in spring.

"Mother?"

Never had he called her that she had not answered. Her soft voice and reassuring touch when evil dreams found him in the night, as they sometimes did, leaving him convinced he lay wounded and bleeding in the forest, struck to the heart. And the time when the boar caught him and he could not get up the tree fast enough, when everyone thought he would lose his leg. When he lay parched with fever his tenth winter—always, always she came.

Could she fail to answer him now?

What ties lay deep, twined and tangled, between a mother and her son? He hauled deliberately on them now and located her essence—a mere spark of radiance.

Gladness uplifted him. Aye, she was here, not gone from them yet. But so far, so very far away.

Come back to us. I need you, all of us do. Father needs you.

No response. Her flame burned very low but

steady, not affected by a breath of wind. Curlew focused himself and reached for her still more intentionally.

He saw what she saw: green leaves dancing overhead, dawning, birds darting through the light in bright shards of color. Flames on a winter hearth, throwing warmth, safety, and comfort. The flash of silver in his father's eyes and the smile Gareth Champion kept for her alone. Himself as a child, lying in her arms, the future in his eyes.

Blessed child.

She was not alone where her spirit lay. Others gathered round her, some he knew and some he did not. A few he had met, in spirit form, on his own journeys through Sherwood—the great man wearing the sheepskin who, he knew, was his grandfather Sparrow, now deceased, and the woman as ever at his side—she who had Aunt Lark's golden eyes—his grandmother, Wren. And a man with a thick, tawny mane, one with a bristling, brown beard, another with a lion's head of hair.

They all looked to him. He felt rather than heard their message: *You cannot linger here. You are needed. Your time approaches.*

Send her back with me, he appealed to them. *We cannot go on without her.* He *cannot.*

Remind him he is never truly apart from her, not here in Sherwood.

Please.

Go and play your part, Lord of Sherwood. Uphold the circle.

I cannot. We cannot. We are missing the third of our number.

She comes.
She comes.
She comes!

They thrust him away from them, out of that deep and silent place back into the light of the autumn morning. It rushed in upon him with its scents of damp earth and dying leaves, the much-loved essence of Sherwood itself. His mother's hands were still clutched in his, and she still lay like a carved effigy of herself.

He turned his head and met the gaze of the man who crouched beside him. "I could not bring her, Pa. She is not alone. A host of other spirits hold her. They said to remind you she is here with you always."

His father bent his head and wept like a man heartbroken.

"Aye," Curlew whispered, "it is little enough comfort now."

Chapter Eleven

"You there! I saw you take that. Put it back, lass. Hie—After her! Thief!"

Fleet of foot, Anwyn whirled like a dancer and sped off, the hard words and more than one set of feet following. Market day again, one hung in gray cloud and chill, with a damp wind. She had been unable to force herself to stay inside, even with the best of intentions. For this very morning her father had informed her Roderick Havers had arranged with the priest for a marriage on Sunday next.

She had demanded that her father refuse it now, before it was too late. She had wept and threatened and stamped her feet. Her father, for once in his life, had remained unmoved.

"You have left me no choice, Daughter," he told her once again.

Nay—he had left *her* no choice. Face screwed up in concentration, hair flying loose behind her, she dashed through aisles and alleys between carts and stands, twisted and turned away from pursuit. She would not wed with the vile Havers. But the only way she could see out of it was to make certain he refused to accept her.

And the only way she could see to assure that was to ruin her reputation most thoroughly. Had she not heard Havers ask her father if she remained "pure"?

Aye, well, she meant to convince him she did not.

Her knee caught the edge of a barrow in passing and knocked it over, spilling an array of vegetables. A rutabaga flew into the air and arced gracefully before striking the nearest stallholder square in the head. Cries arose all around, not the least those of the people still pursuing Anwyn. She gasped, spun again, and leaped over two casks, her skirts flaring high.

Where to turn? Surely the men after her would tire long before she did, and give up. She had taken but one small ribbon, and that only because the imp inside had bidden her to it.

"Catch her!" The cry rang out like the bright blare of a clarion. Several people responded and moved toward Anwyn. She ducked again and changed direction.

And ran straight into a wall of solid muscle.

She rebounded slightly with the force of her impact. Hands came out and captured her, hard enough to leave bruises.

"You, lass!"

Anwyn, the air heaving through her lungs, looked into the last face she conceivably wanted to see. How came Roderick Havers here? Given, she had just been thinking of him, but must that cause him to appear like a devil? Her knees wobbled beneath her and she gasped, "Leave go of me."

"I do not think so." He smelled of unwashed male and something else—dead animal, perhaps. He clutched her close enough that she could also smell his breath, a hot miasma striking her face. "What are you doing here? Does your good father know where you are?"

"You know this lass? Does she belong to you?"

The persistent stallholder, much disheveled, had caught up, and addressed Havers with a modicum of respect. Foresters, favored by the King, were men few wished to cross.

Havers raked Anwyn with his small, porcine eyes and clutched her still more cruelly tight. "Why? What has she done?"

"Stolen from me, as well as left a trail of ruin through the market." Several other panting stallholders, including the owner of the vegetable cart, had now reached them and stood looking on angrily.

Havers returned hard eyes to Anwyn. "What did you take?"

"Nothing."

He raised one of her hands, his fingers wrapped around her wrist. She tried to resist but might as well attempt to fight a bull. Her fist concealed the ribbon. He forced her fingers open, also against her will; it felt as if he would snap the bones of her hand like twigs.

He glared at the ribbon revealed. "You took that?"

"I saw her," the first stallholder put in, "bold as you please."

"Why?" Havers asked Anwyn.

"It was green."

"But why steal it? Your father would afford you a score of ribbons."

She shook her head. How could she hope to explain to this behemoth? But maybe a kind fate had brought him to intercept her. Surely if he saw that of which she was capable he would abandon all intention of taking her to wife.

"Give it back."

Anwyn shook her head again.

Havers let go of her with one hand, drew it back, and slapped her face so hard she saw stars.

Several people cried out. Anwyn made not a sound, but her eyes burned and she tasted blood in her mouth.

"Give it back and apologize," he ordered, and shook her like a rat in the grip of a terrier.

Anwyn extended her trembling hand and the crumpled ribbon to the stallholder. Her parents had never done more than swat her when she was small. Now anger surged inside her, along with a good measure of indignation.

The stallholder snatched the ribbon. Scurvy thing—Anwyn did not want it any longer. Havers shook her with the meaty fist that still held her trapped. "Say how sorry you are."

But Anwyn was not sorry. At that moment she hated everyone, including the stallholder, her father, and especially the man who pinioned her.

Havers raised his hand again.

Almost, Anwyn let him strike her. But her head still rang from the first blow, and the inside of her mouth still bled.

"Sorry," she choked out.

The stallholder snorted. He and the others drifted away—a small crowd still stood watching, but they had already begun to lose interest.

"What you need," Havers told Anwyn, "is a good thrashing. And once we are wed, you will have it."

"Take your hands from me."

He leaned still closer so the smell of him assailed her more intensely. For her ears alone he said, "Very soon, lass, I will have more than my hands on you. Do you know of what I speak? No matter, once we are wed, you will. Perchance you will learn some manners on your knees."

Anwyn's eyes widened. How dared he speak to her so? Aye, she knew of that to which he referred; most women knew. But if he ever forced such an act upon her, she would vomit all over his feet.

"You do not wish to wed with me," she told him, holding hard to her defiance. "I am wild and disobedient."

"I have said I can cure that. With some sense beaten into you, you will soon settle down. A wench worked hard enough has no time for mischief."

Anwyn glared into his eyes. "You do not want me. I have been with three men."

His gaze stabbed at her, weighed the look in her eyes and then dropped to her bosom where, Anwyn was dismayed to realize, her top two laces had come undone.

"You lie," he said. "'Tis something you seem to do uncommonly well. Your father has sworn to me you are intact."

"He does not know," Anwyn retorted, now wholly desperate. "I did not tell him that I sneaked out while back in Wales."

"Why, you bitch," he said so softly she almost thought she did not hear him right. "If that is the case, I could have you now myself, and need not wait for the priest."

Anwyn gasped. How could the game she played turn back upon her so? "You would not. My father—"

"Your father, as I say, is a good man. I will do well under him if I can keep his approval. I think the best way to do that is solve his problems for him, and the greatest of them is you." His grip on her arm tightened still more brutally. "Come with me."

"Nay!" Anwyn tried unsuccessfully to dig her toes into the soil of Nottingham. She would go nowhere with this man. "I will scream."

"Go ahead. Folk have already seen me discipline you. What more will they expect?"

He dragged her away, his strength such that she had no opportunity to resist, not back through the stalls the way she had come but in another direction, toward a part of the castle grounds where she had never ventured. Her mind raced, seeking an escape or some hope of one. He would not do as he threatened—surely he would not dare. Yet she realized belatedly that the blow he had delivered, and the very act of laying his hands on her, had inflamed him.

Aye, and she had played the tease many times—too many, she must admit. She knew well enough what usually heated a man's blood, and it was rarely violence. This man, she sensed, harbored a cruelty— well-disciplined, perhaps—linked to his desire, the like of which she had never before come up against.

Always had she been able to put men off, sometimes with difficulty, aye. Always had she met them, though, in public places. This man dragged her away into the quiet, and her heart beat harder as they went.

"Leave go of me. What is this place?"

Gray stones and a cluster of what looked like huts huddled beneath the gray sky.

"Never you mind. I know where we will not be disturbed. You will learn a few lessons this day, lass. And by the time the priest speaks over us, you will know how to behave." He paused outside one of the huts and gave her a mirthless leer. "Maybe you will even carry my babe by then."

"I swear I will tell my father—"

"Tell him what you will. He already knows you lie. And he will be so glad to be rid of you he will not mind."

Anwyn's head jerked up. It could not be true. Her Da adored her. Or was this beast right, had she truly killed the last of the deep affection between them? That possibility struck her to the heart, froze her where she stood, and gave Havers the opportunity to haul open the door of the stone shed.

"In with you."

The interior of the hut was dark and smelled like something had died inside. Anwyn knew if she entered that place she would come out changed. Her spirit reached for freedom—she had been meant for something more than a sordid tumble in a wretched hovel. The knowledge of that made sudden sense of all her restlessness and the unnamed desire behind it.

The belief gave her strength. Even as Havers pushed her through the door she reached out for a weapon, any weapon. Her fingers closed around the first thing they found, a stout length of wood that leaned against the wall just inside the door.

She drew it up into the light. As soon as he saw it, Havers' face changed. He bared his teeth in a grimace, seized her wrist, and forced it back against the wall of the shed.

"No," he growled, "you will not."

Anwyn felt a flash of pain as her wrist made contact with the stones. His fingers, relentless as when she held the ribbon, forced the spar from her hand.

If she had thought him angry before, she knew him enraged now. He pressed his bulk against her and spoke directly into her face.

"You think to strike me? I will give you back two blows for every one. You, lass, play a dangerous game, running about with your hair and skirts flying. You need to learn: if you can hit, so can I. And," he raised his voice, "if you can lie, so can I. Your father is in charge over me. Do you truly suppose I would do aught against him?"

Anwyn's head spun in confusion. Did he not mean to force her, then? Was all this some terrible attempt to frighten her?

He continued, harsh and low, "I no more believe you have slept with three men than with King Henry himself. I will have you first, but not until we stand before the priest together."

"Leave go of me," Anwyn gasped. If she got away from him now, she would run long and far.

To her surprise, he released her. His bulk still had her trapped against the wall, but she was free of his hated touch.

"Aye, go home, lass, and think about the fact that you have met a man a far sight smarter than you. I give you but one warning: do not come to our bridal bed ruined. Do not even attempt to lie about it. I told your father I want none of another man's leavings."

"Let me go."

He stepped aside. Her heart beating like that of a dying hind, dizzy with repugnance, Anwyn ran.

"You will not have me," she vowed half beneath her breath. "Not now, not ever." If he refused to take her ruined, then ruined she would be. "I will give myself rather to the first man I meet." Her spirit lifted unaccountably. She turned her feet not for home but for Sherwood, and freedom.

Chapter Twelve

"She comes!"

Curlew's eyes flew open onto dark so deep it left him blind. Who had spoken? The voice of memory, repeating the same words he had heard when he reached for his mother's spirit?

He heard nothing now but the movement of wind through the trees above him, the eternal breath of Sherwood, as comforting to him as a well-loved whisper. Quite possibly he had fallen into sleep and dreamed the words, but his heart told him not.

Who came? The holy Lady for whom he waited? He had brought himself here as Heron bade, alone under the trees like a sacrifice. He had bathed himself in Sherwood's waters—no treat on an autumn day moving toward evening. He had spoken his prayers, the same he had learned at his mother's knee, and then had tried to quiet himself and wait as Heron said he must.

Only, his thoughts refused to still. Rather, they ranged wide with doubt and wonder. Would the Lady come to him? Why should she? He was clearly no Heron, and she answered not to his bidding. What would it be like to couple with a spirit? He had little talent for these otherworldly things. He did not doubt the existence of magic, but rather than congress with a spirit he would prefer answers to when the missing part of their triad would arrive.

She comes.

This time the words sounded only in his mind. He sat up from the moss bed he had chosen for himself and stretched all his senses.

Sight served him little now. But Heron had said he saw not the Lady when she came to him. He had felt her, oh, aye, and tasted her—bonded with her on some mystical level. Could Curlew expect as much?

A whisper of sound from his left caught his attention and spun his head. Could he hear breathing? Did the Lady breathe? A frisson of awareness chased down his spine and anchored him in the soil of the forest. He ceased moving and waited.

Definitely breathing he heard. The Lady must be real enough to breathe, else how could she be real enough to couple with a man, give him strong favor, as Heron had said?

Madness, he said in his own mind.

Nay, not madness—belief, Sherwood answered. He felt the magic, the power, gather around him. He lived with Sherwood's magic, aye—in part it always accompanied him. But not like this, for now he could actually sense it move and gather in the darkness.

Suddenly the branches overhead tossed in a strong wind. The clatter of dying leaves assailed his ears; they rained down around him and covered any sound of footsteps.

And all at once she was there—a presence in the darkness—standing above him. He could feel every part of her even though they touched not—her skin, her hair, the heat of her mouth. He knew the taste of her already, remembered and desperately needed.

He gasped.

She moved and came very softly down into his arms.

Did he reach for her, or she for him? He never knew. She was just there, held fast, an answer to every unknown desire. And by all that was holy, she felt real, substantial, warm. His heart struggled and paused in his chest. When it started up again, it shook his whole body, and hers as well.

"Lady?" He whispered it hoarsely in a voice that did not sound like his own.

She began to touch him, her fingers on his face, exploring, then down across his jaw to his throat, his chest, which shuddered with the blows of his heart, and on downward.

Curlew had doubted, when Heron told his wondrous tale, he would be able to respond to a spirit woman. But he was up instantly, high and hard, before ever her soft hands descended that far.

"Who are you?" she asked.

Surely she knew who he was, else why had she come? Had she not bidden Heron send him? And had she not answers for him, as well as loving?

But he answered her as he must, "Curlew Champion."

She gasped in turn. He felt her breath gust across his cheek, sweet and warm. He raised hesitant hands to touch her in turn.

Her hair—ah, it made a glorious curtain all around her, like water flowing. Her back, narrow and slender, revealed she wore clothing like a mortal woman. Her shoulders held a delicate strength, as so they should. Her breast—

His fingers fumbled there, and froze. She spoke,

wild and desperate. "It is well. Touch me."

Her fingers brushed past his to unfasten her bodice. Oh, if only he could see! But his hands possessed their own sight as they slid gently over the smooth softness of her skin to cup the delectable weight of her.

The moment his palm found her breast, she leaned forward and pressed her mouth to his.

Light exploded in the darkness, or perhaps only in Curlew's head. It raced through him and brought with it a thousand images so bright they seared his mind: the promise of love in tawny eyes, laughter curving pink lips, a flash of auburn hair with the glint of sunlight on it, the flow of magic from narrow, white hands as they moved over his body, and tears, tears, tears.

He broke the kiss even though he needed it more than breath, terrified at what he held in his arms.

"Lady," he whispered brokenly, "what do you bring to me?" Why would she bring him memories of what he knew not, that both hurt and fostered unbearable gladness?

"Only myself," she returned.

"And why have you come?"

"Only to love you. Will you take me, Curlew Champion?"

Could he do otherwise? With this powerful combination of magic and desire flowing through him, he could not pause to contemplate the fear that accompanied the upsurge of passion. Ah, and he had thought he might not be able to serve the Green Man's Lady.

"You feel so real. You taste so real."

"Then by all that is holy, taste me once more."

Delight joined the other emotions crowding his

mind. Their mouths found one another in the dark; she parted her lips beneath his and he dove into her the way a man might partake of Sherwood's sacred waters. A new sensation hummed in his blood, like nothing he had ever experienced. Strong and unstoppable, it moved with him as, never taking his mouth from hers, he began to remove her clothing and then his own. It tingled through his hands as he ran them over every part of her and drew her closer to lie full atop him beneath the restless trees.

She clove to him. Her flesh molded itself and fused to his before he ever thought to enter her. Almost, that contact was enough. Almost, the slide of her hair across his hands and the scent of her surrounding him. Should one be able to catch the scent of a spirit? Yet she brought to him all things and asked from him all things, each of them to the other a willing sacrifice.

When at last he rolled her beneath him, when she parted her thighs for him in sweet invitation, he managed to lift his lips from her breast and ask, "You are certain of this, Lady? You will have me?"

"I will have you, Curlew Champion." She ran her hands down the muscles of his chest and still lower. Unseen fingers wooed him, and with glorious, breathless abandon he slid into her—home—where he had never, and always, been.

And how could it be that she came to him a virgin, this Lady who had lain ageless with her Lord and with Heron and countless other true believers? Yet so it was, for he felt her pain, as she tensed in his arms, but for an instant before she quickened into passion so powerful it lifted and convulsed them both.

After—but there was no after. Curlew lay with his

cheek against her breast and wanted to rejoice and holler and make impossible demands. He wanted her to stay with him always. He knew a part of her would, just as part of him would be ever and undeniably inside her. He understood then the beauty of this mystical joining. For he had bonded with Sherwood in the most fundamental way.

And she? What did the Green Man's Lady, once the gift was given? She lay quietly, her arms wrapped about him so tightly it felt she would never let go. She breathed shallow breaths and her heart pounded against his cheek. Strange wonder that he could feel even her heart.

"I have questions for you, Lady," he said into the softness of her breast, his breath coaxing her nipple to tighten once again.

"Ask. Ask of me anything."

"How can I save my mother?"

She went very still. Even her breath ceased for an instant.

He continued, as if bidden, "I cannot bear to lose her. My father cannot."

"All loss is unbearable." Memory sounded in her voice, and her arms tightened impossibly about him.

"Aye, so how might I call her back to us?"

"I do not know that you can."

His heart sank like a stone. He had hoped for another answer. But aye, Sherwood gave—and took— much. And when Sherwood decided the wheel must turn and the next three guardians take their places, there could be no argument.

"Then, Lady, where is the other of our number? Where the third guardian?"

Again, she remained silent.

He rushed on. "Heron and I cannot move forward without her. All is lost without her—the very magic that holds you safe lies in peril."

She sighed. "Will you make me a promise?"

"Anything, Lady."

"Promise you will keep me, always. That you will never send me away from you."

Ah, how could he ever send her away? Raw need burned inside him, and even the idea of turning from her caused pain. But Heron had not spoken of this. He had said nothing of demands.

"I will keep you always," he vowed. "Can it be otherwise?"

"Nay, this is forever. I have not the answers you seek, Curlew Champion, but I do know if you hold to your promise, 'twill be as meant."

Aye, it was as he had feared—the wheel turned, inexorable.

"If you have faith in me, then I have faith in you also," he whispered.

"Then, my Lord, make good on your promise: hold me and love me once more."

Chapter Thirteen

"Do not leave me."

The words curled into Curlew's ear even as the morning light teased his eyelids. He had slept long and deeply, and he had dreamed the most miraculous, wondrous dreams of darkness and loving. *The Lady*.

His eyes flew open to discover the sun well up, light filtering through a roof made of leaves, russet brown and gold, that turned the whole world amber.

Had he spoken the words or merely heard them in his mind, an echo of those the Lady had said to him last night? He could not tell, for tendrils of her spirit wrapped around him yet.

Ah, and Heron had not lied about the magnificence of it. How many times had they coupled before he fell asleep in her arms? Almost he could still feel her presence. Indeed, and swore he could.

Startled, he turned his head and looked at the woman who lay beside him. Awareness and disbelief hit him at once, a blow to the gut that stole all his breath. He sat up slowly, eyes wide and thoughts rushing.

She lay naked, curled on her side with her back touching him. Her hair, a glorious and tangled curtain, covered most of her from his gaze, but he had touched every part of her last night, of that he had no doubt. This, and no spirit Lady, was the woman he had loved so long and vigorously. By all that was holy, what had he done?

Aye, but the sight of her stole his wits and his sense, even now. Her hair, ashen in color, picked up the amber radiance of the forest. Her skin, milk white, bore a scattering of pale freckles. Curlew's gaze traced the sweet curve of her buttocks, the even sweeter swell of one breast that peeked from the bend of her arm. She slept yet.

And who might she be? How had she come to the depths of Sherwood even as he lay waiting for Heron's Lady to appear?

As if she felt his attention even in her sleep, she sighed and turned toward him. Curlew gasped again, for he saw none other than the lass who had run into him at Nottingham market, the one who had ridden past him on the forest road when he chased down the hart—Montfort's daughter.

Oh, by the holy Green Man himself, he had deflowered the daughter of Asslicker's head forester—for he remembered that part of it perfectly well. By his blood, he remembered every part of it.

She opened her eyes and he lost all his regret. His spirit rose and surged, and his flesh with it, so he became caught and helpless all over again.

She smiled.

Mischief lay in that smile and, somehow, innocence, and a woman's knowing. Everything Sherwood had to give lay there, and everything it could take.

Curlew's heart trembled and bounded, and ached in his chest.

"Lady," he whispered.

"My Lord." And hers was the voice from the dark that had curled through him as he plunged into her in rampant delight.

Her smile deepened into a lovely thing. She had dimples, and eyes the exact color of new leaves in the spring, speckled with flecks of gold and fringed with long, brown lashes. They captured Curlew and held him while she examined his very soul.

And what was he to say to her now? I thought you were someone else? Not a thing any woman wanted to hear following the intimacies they had shared. Indeed, her lips were still swollen from his kisses, and the tips of her lovely breasts, as well.

Ah, he would send her back to her father unharmed, yet he could never undo what he had done.

Before he could speak, she reached out with one hand and touched his face hesitantly, almost reverently. Her fingers slid across a cheek now rough with new beard, and her gentle touch slammed through him, setting every part of him alight.

He realized then that she could not have seen him either, last night. Why, then, had she come into his arms? He had been waiting for the Lady, but what could have brought her from Nottingham to the forest and led her to give herself to a stranger?

And why did her touch affect him so profoundly? Why, even now, did he ache to close his eyes and lean into her hand, lose himself to her presence?

By the Green Man's horns, he needed to keep his wits about him. He needed to send her safe home.

He reached up and caught her hand. Her wrist felt fragile, and she let her fingers rest quietly in his. "How do you come here?" he asked. "What are you doing in

Sherwood?"

Emotions chased their way across her face like light on water. He knew she considered many answers before she said, "I came to find you."

"Why? What do you know of me?"

She shook her head. A tendril of wheaten hair slid across one breast and made him ache to touch. Her fingers twitched in his. "You are Curlew Champion."

"Aye, so?" True, she had asked his name last night—he had supposed, then, that the Lady asked. That explained nothing.

Her gaze rested on his face, studied him intently, and moved slowly down his naked body, lingering on his chest before coming to rest upon the undeniable evidence of his arousal. Aye, well, nothing he could do about that—after last night she must know how her presence affected him.

He jostled her hand gently and her eyes returned to his. "How came you so far into the forest alone and in the dark? And why would you give yourself, so, to a stranger, met by chance?"

"Not to a stranger. To you."

"Lass, you make no sense." And he found it difficult to think clearly when he wanted so badly to take her again, to run his palms over those luscious breasts and those smooth buttocks, to taste every part of her. "Does your father know where you are?"

Her eyes clouded. They reflected her emotions the way a forest pool mirrored the sky. "Nay."

"He will be fretful and searching for you, will he not? With you gone all the night—"

"You do not understand. I could not stay in Nottingham."

"He has never used you ill," Curlew declared. "He seems a decent man."

"He is a very good man, and I have tried him much." White teeth caught at her lush, lower lip. "Indeed, I think I have run him out of patience with me."

"A father's patience is right near limitless." At least, that had been Curlew's experience. His own father had rarely, if ever, lost his temper with his family.

"Aye," she agreed, "yet I have exhausted even that." Again, her eyes caught at Curlew's. "I am not so good a daughter as he deserves."

Curlew's heart wanted to protest it, but had he not seen her running unfettered in Nottingham? And was she not here, so, with him now?

Awkwardly, he said, "I am sorry, lass, for what passed between us last night."

"Are you!"

"Had I known who you are—"

"You never asked."

"I know that, and I regret—"

"Why did you take me, then?"

"How could I refuse?" he returned helplessly. Surely she saw his condition now, just from being near her. How to tell the lass he had come looking for magic and found her instead? How to explain the way she affected him when even he did not understand?

She said defiantly, "I regret nothing. You ask how I came here last night—I tell you, I was led. Oh, aye, it began in flight. I ran away, not toward. But once within the forest, once the dark came down, I followed—but I do not even know what it was. A flicker of light, like memory, or like a wisp of song. I know that makes no sense, but 'twas as if a presence went before me and beckoned me on. It led me straight to you."

The breath caught in Curlew's chest. Deep magic, indeed. But why? It could not have been meant merely for his pleasure, for only look at the tangle in which it had landed him. Was he to send Montfort's daughter back to him plucked?

"From what did you run?" he asked gently.

"My father plans to marry me to one of his foresters, a brute called Roderick Havers. He thinks that will put an end to my disobedience. Havers will discipline me, right enough. He means to use a strap."

Curlew felt the impact of those words all through his body. That anyone should harm one precious hair of her, or one freckle—nay, and it would not be, not while he drew breath.

Defiance and triumph mixed together in her face. "Havers said he would not have me if I came to our marriage bed ruined."

"Ah, and so you chose me for the job."

"The darkness chose you, and blessed good fortune. I would not change a thing."

Aye, Curlew thought ruefully, and she could not be ruined more completely than at his hands last night. And if he sent her home with his child in her belly, what then? He realized, with a shock, he did not even know her given name.

A bit brusquely he said, "Gather up your clothing, lass. Cover yourself. You must go home."

"Nay."

"Do not be daft. Of course you must. Your father will be beside himself."

"You promised."

"Eh?"

Stubborn light flashed in her eyes. "You gave a vow last night that you would never send me away from you."

Had he? Dismay crashed down upon Curlew like a hurled stone. But he had thought she was the Lady, asking from him a vow of devotion. He did not know he spoke words to a mortal woman.

He got to his feet, heedless of his nakedness, and began collecting her shed garments and thrusting them at her.

"To be sure, you will go home."

"Nottingham is not my home." She tipped back her head to look at him. "I belong nowhere, except maybe here with you."

Curlew shook his head violently. He turned from her and took up his own clothing, pulled his sark over his head even as she watched, donned his leather tunic, then slid into his leather leggings.

"Master Curlew?"

He turned back to her swiftly. She sat with her chemise clutched to those tantalizing breasts, her eyes wide with inquiry.

"Listen to me, Mistress Montfort. You are not for me, nor I for you."

"But last night—"

"Despite last night." In spite of the wonder and magic of it, the undeniable sense of rightness. "For I have a destiny before me, one I cannot escape, and would not if I could. I regret, but you have chosen the wrong man."

She got to her feet, her clothing still caught against

her. The autumn sun, filtering through the leaves, warmed her hair to amber-gold. "I do not believe that."

"You must. Now dress yourself. I will see you safe to the edge of the forest."

She did not move. Like a goddess she stood and looked at him with defiance.

Curlew felt an unexpected twinge of sympathy for Montfort. Who could fail to love this lass, or be driven beyond endurance by her?

"Please," he said.

The corners of her mouth twitched. "I regret, my lord, I would do most anything to please you. Anything but that."

Chapter Fourteen

"You are angered with me." Anwyn directed a searching look at the man who strode beside her. Each time she so much as glanced at him, she saw him again standing naked in the forest, strong and proud with the leaves dancing behind him and the light in his eyes. She could not identify the source of that light, did not understand it, but it drew her irresistibly.

She still tingled all over from his touch—and ached in a few places, if she were honest. She had never imagined lying with a man could be like that. Aye, and she had come close before, but she did not deceive herself that lying with anyone else could affect her so, could claim and consume her. Only this man. She did not comprehend it, but she knew it to her very soul.

And now she had annoyed him, even as she always annoyed her Da. Aye, and she regretted that but could find it in her to rue nothing else that had taken place between them. A miracle had brought her through the dark to his arms, the one place she needed to be.

She would do it all again. Indeed, she longed to.

A small smile curved her lips. He turned his head sharply and looked at her.

"Why do you smile? Do you not see the trouble you are in?"

"I see it," she told him comfortably. Trouble could blow right past her, now she was at his side. "Where do you take me?"

"To Oakham." He scowled as he said it. A village, she presumed, though the name meant nothing to her.

"Is that where you live?"

"I live here." He lifted his hands in an encompassing gesture.

"Aye, well, since you told my father you are a forester, it seems I am not the only one who utters lies."

His eyes flashed silver fire. Beautiful eyes they were, full of bright intelligence and, she thought, more than a hint of magic. Aye, but he was beautiful withal, from that mane of chestnut brown hair to those wide shoulders, those narrow hips, and the glorious endowment with which she had become so well acquainted last night. She might never look enough.

"I am a steward of Sherwood," he told her, "a guardian—that was truth."

She nodded. Had he told her he was a hobgoblin, she would have accepted it. "A lord of Sherwood."

His step faltered. They both stopped walking and faced one another.

As if he could not help himself, he reached out and brushed the hair from her shoulder. His fingers lingered, and everything in her leaped toward his touch. "You must return to Nottingham, you know," he told her almost regretfully. "You cannot stay here."

"I will not marry that hulking, stinking brute."

His lips twitched. "You said he would not take you ruined. Lady, you are most surely ruined."

"I am." She fought the desire to lean up and press her lips to his. She craved the taste of him, burned into her last night.

"Then what need you fear?"

Being away from you, her heart cried, though she did not say it. *Not being able to watch the light dance in your eyes. Not being at liberty to reach for your hand.* She could not live so.

"Surely," she proposed, "folk flee to Sherwood every day and seek refuge. My Da says that is whence half the outlaws come."

"True."

"Then why not me?"

"Because you have someone fretting over you, and he is not a man I would have for an enemy."

"He is already your enemy, so it seems. You stand on opposite sides of the King's law."

"But I would not give him the cause of his daughter's virtue over which to contest me."

"Too late," she reminded him blithely. "You should have thought of that last night."

"I did not know who you were, last night." But a spark of mischief appeared in his eyes, and the corners of his mouth twitched again.

"We can go round and round it, or you can take me to Oakham and give me breakfast. I am perished."

"Aye?" He quirked a brow. "And will you partake of the King's deer?"

"Gladly."

"Then come along."

Had he given in? Not so easily, Anwyn thought. She guessed he just bided his time. They turned and resumed walking, she smiling all the more to herself.

"Tell me of this brute your father would have you marry."

"Ah, well—he is squat and rancid, wide as he is tall."

"Rancid?" She could hear the smile in his voice.

"He stinks like a boar, has little eyes like a boar also, and is every bit as mean. He believes in keeping his wife well-beaten and heavy with child. He has two vile children—"

"This paragon has been married before?"

"Aye, and killed his first wife with cruelty, no doubt. The daughter is a sad, morose creature with the look of her father, the son far worse—sharp and sly. Havers wishes a new wife to raise these two cubs."

"A fate worse than death."

"Far worse." She directed her most beguiling look at him. "You would not send me back to that?"

He smiled, and this time it reached his eyes. By God, but they stole the breath from her, so full of quick wit and that indefinable light. "Surely 'twould be a shame to do so."

She slanted another glance at him. "Keep me with you and we can do what we did last night again—and again."

"Nay." All the humor fled from him. "I told you, I am not at liberty, child, to be with you that way."

"I am no child. If what we shared together failed to convince you of that—"

"Aye so, but I am not free to be with anyone."

Anwyn's heart sank in her breast. For an instant she felt as if she could not breathe. She fought the terrible feeling. "Are you promised to another, Curlew Champion?"

"Nay."

"Then—"

"But I am promised to duty."

"Does this duty preclude you ever taking a woman

to wife?"

He paused and stared at her in bemusement. "It does not. But she must be the right woman, one to fill a particular place."

Anwyn resolved at that moment to be that perfect woman, no matter what it required. She would trade whatever she must.

"'Tis a difficult thing to explain," he went on. "I and another, my cousin, hold a kind of trust."

"This cousin—male or female?"

"Heron is male."

"Heron? It is an odd name. Can he not choose whomever he wishes to wed, either?"

Curlew shot her another measuring glance. "The trust is to be held by three. The third of our number will be a woman, and she has yet to make herself known. She will bond with both of us and wed with one of us— how can we say which, yet?"

"And you will keep yourself free, unclaimed, for this?" Ah, but she had claimed him for hers last night, in her heart, each time he entered her. "It sounds daft."

"Aye, so it must. Yet 'tis for this I was born." His tone told her there could be no argument. Yet her whole being wanted to argue it. She wanted to claw and thrash, to fight for him.

"How come you to be an outlaw?" she ventured to ask.

"Not an outlaw. A free man, rather, living on what Sherwood provides."

Anwyn looked away from him. "There were many such 'free' men in the Welsh borders where I grew. They, too, thought themselves masters of their own lives. King Henry teaches them differently now, though."

"The Welsh will not fold. They are brave, strong fighters, as well as good bowmen."

"My Da says they fly to the hills when the King's forces come—melt away like the snow in springtime. But he is not willing to wager who will win in the end. He did not wish to be caught in the midst of the fight, so when his old friend Simon de Asselacton offered this place, he decided we should come."

"And your mother, lass?"

"She died some years ago of the fever." The pain of that still caused Anwyn's eyes to fill with tears. "He has not been the same since."

"I am sorry." A faraway look settled over Curlew's features, as if he thought of something grave and troubling. "A hard loss to bear."

"She was a kind woman, warm and beautiful."

He nodded. "Is that not all the more reason for you to go home? If your father has lost her, will you make him bear the loss of his daughter, as well?"

"In due time I will send him word that I am alive and well and mean to stay in Sherwood." She hesitated. "Do I need your permission to stay?"

"Nay, lass, not mine. You might ask permission of the headman of Oakham. He is my uncle, one Falcon Scarlet." He stopped suddenly, as if struck. "By the light, I do not even know your given name, Mistress Montfort."

"It is Anwyn." She bade him, "Pray you call me by it."

Chapter Fifteen

"Hie, Curlew! How went your pilgrimage?"

The cry met Anwyn and Curlew as they entered the village, and stopped them in their tracks. Anwyn turned her head sharply to locate the speaker, and her eyes widened.

The most beautiful man ever she had beheld strode toward them. Beautiful, aye—it was not a description she ordinarily applied to males she encountered, but this man deserved no other. Golden he was, from his head to his feet, tall and slender, and lithe in his movements. Tawny yellow hair flowed over his shoulders, and his face might easily grace one of God's angels. He wore leggings and a tunic of golden deer hide, and the laces on his high boots only served to show the length and grace of his limbs.

"Heron," Curlew said.

Ah, so this was Heron, the cousin somehow linked with Curlew in this mysterious duty of which he spoke. Anwyn could only stand and stare as he approached.

Curlew slanted a rueful look at her. "Aye—Heron affects most maids so, at first sight."

The beautiful man even had golden eyes, set like jewels between deeply-fringed lashes. They regarded Anwyn and warmed when he smiled. "Well, cousin, I knew you went to meet a lady in Sherwood but, faith, I did not expect you to bring her back with you."

Anwyn's heart sank once again. Curlew had gone to the forest to meet someone? Was that why he had seemed so unsurprised when she fell into his arms? Was it why he had loved her so eagerly, because he thought she was someone else? Dismay tasted bitter in her mouth.

Curlew did not answer directly. "This is Mistress Montfort, who is fleeing Nottingham for the refuge of the forest."

"Montfort?" Heron tipped his head. Light shimmered around him like fractured radiance. "Is that not the name of de Asselacton's new head forester?"

"He is my father." Anwyn spoke with only a slight tremor in her voice and held out her hand. "I am Anwyn, and most pleased to make your acquaintance."

Heron fairly shone with delight. He made an obeisance worthy of King Henry's court, and his lips brushed her fingers. Anwyn felt that touch reach inside her, like the toll of a bell.

"Most pleased to meet you, Mistress Anwyn. I am Heron Scarlet. Welcome to Oakham."

Curlew cleared his throat. "She cannot stay but for breakfast. She will have to be sent back to Nottingham."

You promised you would never send me away from you, Anwyn protested silently, and Curlew twitched, almost as if he heard.

"Well, we will speak of that anon," Heron said soothingly. "Meanwhile, you will break your fast on bread baked by these hands."

"You know how to bake?" Anwyn could not help but ask.

Curlew snorted. "He cooks astonishingly well—

manages most things well, does my cousin."

Anwyn sensed sincere affection between the two men. Close as brothers they must be, possibly closer. Oh, she thought wistfully, to be part of something like that.

Heron led them to a hut, one among the others. It had the figure of a stag carved above the door—nay, it was a man with antlers on his head.

"Any word?" Curlew asked his cousin as they went.

"Your sisters have both been and gone. They brought word of no change."

"And your parents?"

"Remain with her. We will need to go, the two of us, and make our attempt." Heron's eyes slid to Anwyn. "Just as soon as matters here are attended."

She felt instantly in the way, as if she did not belong. But Curlew only nodded, and Heron pushed wide the wooden door of the hut and invited her in.

The interior of the place felt cool and smelled wonderfully of things Anwyn could not begin to identify—herbs, possibly. The hearth took up most of the space in the small room. To the right Anwyn saw stools and a bench, to the left a narrow bed. Only one window opened onto the autumn light, but Heron left the door standing wide.

Anwyn had been in similar dwellings in the Welsh borders, had played with and been invited home by children who lived there. She had seen desperate poverty but did not sense that here. The room, though spare, gave off an air of comfort.

"Please, Mistress Anwyn, sit. Will you take some ale?"

"Aye, thank you." Whatever this beautiful man offered her, she would gratefully accept.

He poured three mugs of frothy ale and placed one at her hand. When he bent over her, she caught a hint of his scent, very similar to that of the house, and beguiling.

He brought a basket of bread and a pot of honey, then sat down between Anwyn and Curlew.

"So, Mistress Anwyn, tell us why you have fled Nottingham."

She froze with her mug halfway to her lips. Parched, and hungry as well, she nevertheless hesitated. "Do I need your permission to stay here?"

He lifted arched brows. "Nay, but I promise you I can put in a very good word with our headman. He is my father."

"Then, please." She slid forward and touched his hand. "I pray you will convince him to let me stay."

****

Yet another woman fallen victim to Heron's redoubtable charms, Curlew thought sourly as he watched the smiles his cousin and the lass, Anwyn, traded to one another. He wondered why the idea made him ache inside. He barely knew her. Well, aye, he knew her in the carnal sense, right enough. His flesh still leaped for hers every time he looked at her, and to save his life he could not keep from looking. Even now, as she leaned toward Heron and touched his hand, he saw how her breasts pushed against the fabric of her bodice. He knew those breasts as well—the size and taste of them. He knew her sweetness and her heat.

But he should be used to coming second to Heron. Had he not done so all his life? Truly, never before had he resented it. The only thing at which he excelled was the longbow—there, at least, he knew himself unmatched.

He could not deny the two of them made a bright picture together, all ashen and golden like the autumn day outside. 'Twas as if they brought its beauty inside with them, to light this ordinary place.

"Only tell me your circumstances," Heron bade with an interested look, "and I will gladly speak to my parents on your behalf."

"My father has made a marriage agreement very little to my liking." She bit into her crust of bread with her white teeth; Curlew could not but remember them also, sliding over his flesh.

"Who is the man?"

"The foremost of my father's foresters, so Da says, though I can scarcely warrant it. I have told your cousin all my objections to him." She glanced at Curlew, and away.

"Why would your father settle on such a man for your husband?"

"To tell true, I have not made things easy for my Da since my mother's death. This is a fine place my lord de Asselacton has granted him, and he wants to keep it."

Heron's eyes flashed. "A fine place hunting down my good neighbors, who seek only to keep themselves and their families fed?"

"I know little of such matters, only that if I prove disobedient I shame him, and if I shame him it does not sit well."

"And are you so disobedient?" Heron asked, looking suddenly amused.

"Aye." Again, Anwyn glanced at Curlew. Did she think he would bring forth what had happened last night? Did she suppose him such a man? Aye, but she knew little more of him than of the trials of life in Oakham.

Heron looked at him also. "What say you, Lew? Shall we offer her sanctuary?"

Curlew took a deep draught of ale and shook his head. "A dangerous proposition. Her father will no doubt come looking for her. What father would not? And when he does come, he may well find other things." He tried to ignore the stricken look in the eyes Anwyn turned on him. Aye, but she feared returning to her monstrous forester rather than parting from him, Curlew. Just because they had shared one mistaken night of passion did not mean she harbored genuine feelings for him.

She asked him softly, "Would you truly send me back to a man who has promised to beat me?"

Implacably, he said, "Tell your father what you have told me and Heron. You say he is a good man. I do not doubt he will take your part."

An accusing look came to her eyes. Curlew could almost hear her thinking, "But you promised never to send me from you."

Aye, he had promised in the heat and beauty of the moment. But he had to think of his people, and of his mother lying near death. Could he allow this woman's presence to bring more risk upon them?

He spoke in a voice that did not sound like his own. "I do not see how we can allow you to stay."

She looked like he had slapped her. All the light fled her eyes, and she clenched her hands together.

"Aye, well," Heron said comfortably, "'tis just as well for you, Mistress Anwyn, the decision does not lie with Lew. You will need to ask my father, and he is away just now." He gave a curious smile. "It seems you will have to stay long enough to await his return."

Chapter Sixteen

"A word with you, Heron," Curlew requested irritably.

His cousin turned to him, his face calm in the golden afternoon light. Almost a full day had the lass, Anwyn, been in Oakham. Curlew could not help but think of her as a trap waiting to spring upon them all.

The urgency inside him increased, making him edgy and impatient. His inner desires and his practical sense warred with one another. He did not like being at odds with Heron, but he felt very much so now.

"Come and sit," Heron bade. He waved Curlew to the fallen log from which they often watched target practice. The life of Oakham bustled all around them: children laughed and cried, women gossiped together, men hauled in the last of the harvest. The rhythm of it should have comforted Curlew, but it did not.

Heron, on the other hand, looked very much at ease. He met Curlew's gaze and lifted both brows in query. "Something troubles you, cousin?"

"What have you done with the lass?"

"I? Nothing."

"Then where is she?" Annoyance stirred in Curlew's heart.

"With Diera, who has agreed to give her a bed for the night."

Aye, and Diera would agree to whatever Heron

asked.

"I think 'tis a bad idea for her to remain here."

"That, Lew, is more than plain."

"Then why would you go behind my back and arrange for her to stay?"

"I have not. I meant what I said—the decision to let her stay or send her to Nottingham lies with my father, or, more precisely, with my parents, for you can be sure Ma will have a say."

"And where are they but struggling with the possible collapse of their triad? Surely they have enough to juggle now. We all have. Why trouble them at such a dire time with the fate of one errant maid?"

Heron drew a breath and gave Curlew a thoughtful look. "You feel very strongly about it."

"I do." Curlew's emotions were tangled impossibly between the desire that still kicked him hard every time he so much as glanced at the woman and his conviction that her presence promised to change everything.

Heron settled himself more comfortably. "Why not tell me how you came to meet her in the forest? I thought you went to await the ministrations of the Lady."

Curlew frowned. Could he explain to Heron what had happened? Could he even explain it to himself? "You will scarce believe it."

"Only try me."

"I did, indeed, go into Sherwood as you bade, deep into its heart. I bathed myself, invoked the Lady's presence, and waited."

"Aye?"

"Dark it was, dark as if I lay blind. And then," a thread of wonderment crept into Curlew's voice, "she

came. And I took her into my arms and loved her well."
That made a vast understatement. Curlew had never
dreamed of coupling with anyone as they had.

Heron's eyebrow twitched. "And so?"

"At the height of things, she extracted a promise
from me that I would never send her away. I thought
her the Lady, Heron—I supposed it some kind of
mystical binding to do with the guardianship. I agreed."

"Aye, so? I would have done the same."

"Only, she who extracted this promise was not the
Lady. It proved, in the end, to be this lass, Anwyn, in
my arms—a mortal woman, and I could not tell. I know
not how she came there, to the heart of Sherwood in the
dark."

"Do you not?"

"Nay. She has some mad tale of being led by a
glimmer of light."

"Does she!"

"But it can only be a vile trick, Heron. I was misled
into giving that promise, and now she seeks to hold me
to it."

"Ah." Heron's golden eyes turned thoughtful.
"Quite the tale, that."

"Aye, if someone else brought it to me, I would not
believe it."

"That is plain." A hint of irony colored Heron's
voice. "For you do not believe it now, even though it
has happened to you."

"Eh?" Curlew scowled.

"Do you, lad, remember none of the old stories?
Have you forgotten their meaning?"

"Of which stories do you speak?"

"Many they are. Take the one your father tells of

how he found himself led through the depths of Sherwood by the glint of a bird's wing, a spark of light."

"Our parents tell many tales. You know I am not one for living in the past. 'Tis the present that concerns me, and the future of the guardianship."

"And it is just that I believe confronts us now. Why did you go to Sherwood last night?"

"Because you sent me," Curlew said, not without resentment.

"Nay, because you sought an answer, among other things, about our missing companion. I think you have received it."

For the space of several heartbeats, Curlew failed to take his cousin's meaning. The look in Heron's eyes directed him to it.

"Nay," he breathed then. "You are mad."

Both Heron's eyebrows rose. "No doubt of that. Yet I am surprised you did not tumble to this conclusion."

"What conclusion?"

"You went to the heart of Sherwood seeking. Sherwood gave."

"Not this. Not her."

"You lay with someone you believed to be the Lady, did you not?"

He had, indeed. Every moment of the encounter remained burned into his flesh and spirit. "Aye."

"Why is it difficult to believe Sherwood placed into your arms the woman we seek?"

"Because," Curlew sputtered, "because she is all wrong."

"What is right, then? You tell me how she must

appear, this woman we seek."

"Not like that. Not like her!" Curlew insisted again. "She is naught like I imagined."

"Must we always receive what we imagine? Or sometimes more—what we need?"

"How can this wayward lass be what we need to complete our circle?" Curlew scowled. It irked him that Heron sat there so smug and calm. "She is not even born of Sherwood but comes from the west—part Welsh, and with that unwieldy name."

Heron began to laugh softly. Curlew fought the desire—heretofore unheard of—to slap the smirk from his cousin's face.

"What is there to make you laugh?"

"You denounce her name, and us a flock of birds!"

Curlew managed to damp down his irritation. "Aye, make light as you will. You are wrong about her. You have no real cause to say she is the one we have awaited so long. As she pointed out to me herself, many folk flee into Sherwood."

"And she just happened to flee into your arms."

"Heron, listen to me. This is no time for fancy or uncertainty."

"It is all uncertainty."

"Do you think her father will fail to come looking for her? She will have him and his foresters down upon us like a pack of hounds. Send her back."

"That is not up to me, Lew. I say again, it is a decision for the members of the current triad."

"Which is broken."

"Not yet. You and I need to go together and attempt to rouse your mother from her sleep. I am thinking we can bring my parents back with us and let them make the decision about Anwyn. Meanwhile, she will do well enough in Diera's hands."

"And if Asslicker's men come looking for her while we are away?"

Heron shrugged. "They are bound to come. Something has been set in motion by the arrival of this lass and her father in Nottingham. The wheel begins to turn again. I believe, Lew, we face our challenges even as did those who came before us."

"The risk is high."

"And has always been so. We would not be worthy guardians were we not able to face the dangers and stand strong."

Aye, bold words for Heron to say, Curlew thought bitterly. It was not *his* mother lying still as death and holding the welfare of all they loved in her slender hands. He did not have to face the heartbreak in his father's eyes.

Yet he could not allow Heron to become his opponent. And anger would benefit them not at all.

He drew a deep breath, looked Heron in the eyes, and nodded. Heron reached out wordlessly and they clasped arms as they had done a thousand times.

"Aye," Curlew said then, "together we shall go and make our bid for my mother's life."

Chapter Seventeen

"I did manage to reach her when last I came," Curlew said hoarsely. "I felt her where she lies, held by many spirits. Her flame burns low and steady. But I could not bring her forth."

Heron nodded, his face tensed in concentration. They sat one on either side of Linnet's still form, with their hands linked.

Not far from them Heron's father, Falcon Scarlet, paced. He looked tired, aged in a matter of days, his eyes wild and his hair mussed as if he had pulled at it.

Curlew could almost taste his pain. The first thing he had said upon their arrival was, "We cannot bring her; she still will not come back with us."

"We have tried everything we may," Lark added. She did not look quite as distressed as her husband, but pain shone in her golden eyes. Twin to Curlew's mother and doubly bonded with Linnet through the ties of the guardianship, she must feel this loss full well. But Lark Scarlet had fierce hold of her emotions.

And Curlew's father? He sat, even now, not four feet away from his wife, his head bent and his hair, golden-silver, spilling over his knees. Curlew could not tell but thought he might be praying.

"Come"—Heron's eyes caught at Curlew's—"let us do our best."

Curlew's heart struggled and then rose. Heron

possessed a deep affinity for magic and had the strongest ties to Sherwood of anyone he knew, including his Aunt Lark. If anyone could return Ma to their arms, surely 'twould be Heron, with Curlew's own assistance.

Heron bowed his head and Curlew closed his eyes. Heron whispered a prayer, the ancient words flowing from him, invoking the powers that ruled life and all things it contained: air that moved the spirit of man, fire that burned in his heart, water that washed through him in eternal renewal, and earth that anchored him and gave him strength. Curlew felt the power come in response to Heron's call, felt it twine and swirl and begin to rise.

Ah, and by all that was holy, it came strong. Curlew rejoiced as it possessed him and danced against his closed eyelids—the amber gold that seemed always to stream from Heron and, a bit more slowly, the deep hunter green that seemed to reflect his own light. They met and fountained up into a blinding glow of bright green.

Curlew fell—or, nay, he flew, weightless—his only anchor the hard grip of Heron's hands. Together they rose, and he strove to make sense of what he saw. Sherwood lay spread beneath him, not green, no, but a pattern of autumn brown and gold. A tunnel of light closed round him and he saw a succession of things, so quick they flickered: his grandfather Sparrow and his grandmother Wren, who touched his hand with hers. A man covered in a welter of blood, swinging from a wooden frame in what looked like the forecourt of Nottingham Castle. His father looking young and strong, facing a youthful Falcon Scarlet in a green field, both with bright swords in their hands. A hart with steaming flanks—but nay, it was a man with a tumble of brown hair and blue eyes so bright they burned. The man's lips moved—he spoke—but Curlew could not hear what he said.

And then everything abruptly stopped and centered upon one scene. Curlew blinked rapidly, trying to make sense of what he saw.

He lay on his back very much the way his mother did now, with the eternal, beloved green of Sherwood arching above him. He burned with pain that reached down into his soul—he knew he had taken mortal wounds, many of them. He was dying. Yet Sherwood held out her arms to him and he would rest there, as enduring as the forest itself.

But someone wept. As if her heart broke she sobbed, and he knew it was for him. Against the weight of eternity, he opened his eyes, for she had the ability to call him from anywhere—even hold him a few precious moments from death.

She bent above him, her auburn hair loosed and hanging down. Her face, beloved to him, had showed him many moods during their time together: love, merriment, mischief, desire, devotion—even the light of worship. He had never seen an expression such as he now beheld: sheer, desperate need and terror so stark it left her white as bone.

"Do not leave me. Robin, you cannot."

He tried to speak, but the flowing blood had stolen the ability. His blood covered her hands that clutched at him in demand and supplication. He knew his blood would flow back into the soil of Sherwood where it belonged.

"Please." Hot tears struck his face. "You must stay with me. You must stay and see your child."

Aye, and she was great with the love they shared—she carried the future. His heart struggled to beat for her, for both of them.

So beautiful, you are so beautiful, he tried to tell her, and knew she heard in her mind. And she was, despite her visible agony—all amber like the light he loved. *From the first moment I saw you. Stay strong. Stay strong for me, Marian.*

She gasped like a drowning woman. *I cannot. My love, my love, my love, you are my strength! You are all my world. I need you to keep my heart beating.*

I do not go far. Watch for me, listen for me. I do not leave you. Inevitable as the setting sun, his eyes closed.

She wailed. He felt her pain rise up in a wall of agony and protest. He knew it kept her from understanding what he said: that they could not truly be parted, that his love would surround her every day of her life, and that one day they would be together again.

I need you, Robin! I need your touch, your warmth, your presence. I need your strength. Oh, please, my love, do not go from me.

He sank and flowed away from her with his blood, into the earth of Sherwood and thence into its waters below and then burning, burning up through the trees themselves and, like radiance, into the holy air.

But she did not see. In her vast pain, she could not see him.

All the radiance behind Curlew's eyelids died to a small, steady flame—his mother's essence still burning. And he heard her voice in his blood and bones.

I cannot come with you. But do not doubt all love lasts forever. Go to her, son—she needs you now even as she did then.

At once he flew backwards through darkness. His mother's flame grew more distant. He felt only the grip of Heron's tensed hands.

Grief accompanied him from the vision, both that felt by she whom he had seen weeping and his own, caused by the knowledge he would not be able to fulfill his father's greatest wish. He came to himself with a sob in his throat and tears blurring his eyes. Heron's face swam before him, as did that of his mother, so still.

Heron released Curlew's hands. Curlew did not know if Heron had seen the same terrible vision as he. Blinking rapidly, he observed that his cousin's expression looked grave and grim. Gracefully, Heron arose, turned to Curlew's father, and placed both hands on his head.

"Uncle, I am sorry."

****

"I did reach her you know, Pa," Curlew said awkwardly. He and his father sat together beside the fire, not far from his mother's quiet form. Gareth fretted about keeping her warm enough, with the chill night coming on. How to explain that his mother would not return to the man she loved and who loved her so well? "She gave a message."

His father raised his ravaged face. A handsome man, save for the old, thin scar that snaked down his left cheek, he now showed his age for the first time.

"What message?"

"She said to never doubt that love lasts forever."

Gareth gave a hard laugh. "I knew that already. It

does not keep my heart from breaking each time I look at her."

Still more awkwardly, Curlew said, "You are strong, Pa. None stronger. You can endure this."

Slowly, Gareth shook his head. He spread his hands. "I cannot."

"Do not despair, for she lives yet."

"Aye, son, so she does."

"Let us carry her back to Oakham. You stay there with us. I do not like to think of you here on your own."

Gareth's gray eyes met Curlew's. "That is what your aunt suggested. She and Falcon must go back to deal with this new threat from Nottingham. But if I come..." Gareth corrected softly, "If *we* come, then my choices will not be my own."

"Choices? Of what do you speak?"

His father did not answer.

"Pa?"

"I must be free to choose, Lew, to not go on without her."

Horror twisted through Curlew's heart. He thought of the woman in his vision—Marian, his own great-grandmother and wife to Robin Hood—and her despair as her husband lay dying. She had not grasped how Robin's essence had become part of the air itself, so that as long as she kept breathing he remained with her.

He bade his father, "Do not make the mistake others have made in the past." Surely he had received that vision just so he could bring this warning. "What of the rest of us, should both of you perish? Please come back to Oakham with me."

"You are a good son." Gareth's hand, scarred from many battles, came out and cupped the side of Curlew's face. "But I am where I need to be."

"Can you not speak to her?" Curlew knew his parents communicated by thought far more frequently than in words.

Gareth shook his head. "I speak. I do not know if she hears."

"She hears you, Pa, always."

"Sherwood gives," Gareth said heavily, "and it takes much. Go home, son, and leave me to my vigil."

Chapter Eighteen

"Where is your headman? I would speak with him."

Anwyn recognized the voice even through the wattle wall of the hut in which she sat sorting berries for Diera, the young woman she had met with Curlew Champion at Nottingham market. As well she should, for that was her father calling out firm and steady in the golden afternoon.

"He is not here," someone spoke in reply. "Called away, my lord."

"When will he return?"

"We do not know, my lord."

Anwyn, alone in the hut—for Diera had gone out a short while ago and her grandmother, with whom she lived, was at a neighbor's—crept to the window opening and sneaked a look out. She did not want her father to see her, yet her curiosity refused to be denied.

And what she saw chased the breath from her lungs. Her father, aye, dressed all in his hunting leathers with his bow on his shoulder and a small troop of foresters at his back. They made an impressive show wearing the Sheriff of Nottingham's insignia, but that was not what made her duck back down and crouch on the dirt floor. The man on her father's right was Roderick Havers, ugly as sin and twice as large.

What if he should spy her with those little, piggy

eyes that seemed to see so much? He would draw her father's attention to her, and they would come crashing in here to haul her away. Her heart smote her over the worry she must be causing her Da, gone last night and, now, most of this day. It showed his mettle that he carried on regardless, and performed his duty in spite of it.

She heard him raise his voice again. "Hear me, good people of Oakham. In the absence of your headman, I will speak to you all. Already this day we have visited four other villages and found stolen game in each—the King's deer, taken out of hand. I am here to tell you the King's writ regarding poaching will be upheld. Four men have been sent to Nottingham to stand trial for their crimes against their King."

Could this truly be her Da speaking? He knew what it meant to live in want, had been friendly with folk in the borders who did whatever they must to survive. She believed he sympathized with men and women struggling to feed their children. How could he be so harsh now?

"Know that my men mean to search this village. Have you anything to hide? If so, speak up now. It will go easier with you."

No one spoke. A child began to wail but not loudly enough to keep Anwyn from hearing her father tell his men in a low voice, "Spread out and search."

"What goes on here?" A new voice, one Anwyn did not recognize. She slid back to the window opening and peered out cautiously.

A group of three people had entered the village from the north. Her heart leaped momentarily, but none of them was Curlew. The first two, a man and woman

of middle years, she knew not, but the third she did—
Heron.

Diera had told her earlier in the day, when she asked, that Heron and Curlew had gone off into the forest to see Curlew's mother, who lay gravely ill. Even when Anwyn pressed the girl, she would say no more.

Could these be Heron's parents, who headed this village? The man had a look of Heron, and a mane of wild, fair hair. The woman, small and dark, wore a bow on her shoulder like a man.

Anwyn's father turned toward them, and the man said, "I am Falcon Scarlet, headman here. What is your business in Oakham?"

"We come by the authority of Sheriff Simon de Asselacton to enforce the King's writ. I am Mason Montfort, my lord de Asselacton's head forester. We search for stolen venison and will take into custody anyone responsible for its theft."

Falcon Scarlet tossed his head. He wore his dignity like a cloak and stood straight and tall. "Search as you will. You shall find nothing here."

Anwyn's fingers grew white on the window opening. Had Curlew not promised to feed her the King's venison when he brought her here only this morning? True, Heron had given her bread and ale— had Curlew merely been taunting her then? Curlew spoke as if he believed he had full right to take the King's deer. What if venison were found?

Her father's men moved out and scattered. She heard Havers say, "There, master, on that wall— antlers."

"Antlers, not venison." Falcon Scarlet said softly. "Those are old, from my father's time."

Havers growled in reply, "Then, headman, your father must have been a stinking thief."

"Never mind that now." Mason Montfort spoke quickly. "Go help the others search."

Aye, Anwyn thought in sudden panic, and what if Havers or her father came here to look? The door stood open to the bright afternoon. By heaven, was there somewhere she could hide herself?

She gazed about and saw nothing except the cot leaned up against one wall during the day to afford more floor space. Swiftly, she made herself small and hid behind it, immediately losing most of her ability to hear and struggling not to sneeze from the smell of dust and old wool.

She waited what seemed an age, holding her breath, before somebody entered the hut with a heavy tread and began knocking things about. She trembled behind her screen, praying the man would not decide to shift the upturned cot.

A loud cry sounded from outside, and the searcher abandoned the hut. Slowly, but avid to hear what transpired, Anwyn crawled back out.

"—deer hide!" she heard through the open doorway. "And fresh."

Falcon Scarlet's voice was heard once more. "A hide, Master Montfort, is not venison."

"Aye, but it argues misdeed." Her father's voice held a new note, heavy with intent. "Where is the venison, save in your bellies?"

"You have no proof," Scarlet argued.

"A bloodied hide is evidence." Anwyn's father insisted. "Enough, I think, for you to stand trial. That is"—his tone became a suggestion—"unless someone else would confess."

"No." Another voice, that of a woman and flinty as rock. Was that Heron's mother, then?

But someone called from the crowd of villagers, "I confess to the crime."

"Nay, I confess."

"Nay, I!"

Anwyn simply ached to see. She slid forward across the beaten floor until she could peer around the door post.

Two of her father's men held a fresh deer hide. Her Da wore a curious look on his face—mostly consternation. The villagers stood in a ring and continued to call out, claiming ownership of the deed.

And the small woman who stood between Heron and Falcon Scarlet virtually glowed with anger. Indeed, if Anwyn narrowed her eyes she could see a faint haze of reddish light shimmering all around her.

Even as the chorus from the villagers died, the woman stepped forward and looked Mason Montfort in the eye. "'Twas I shot that deer."

"You?" Montfort questioned.

"Do you doubt my skill?" Before anyone could blink, the woman had her bow down off her shoulder and an arrow notched. She drew and released in a blur of speed. Her arrow flew past Montfort's face and Havers' nose and passed through the deer hide.

The men holding it jumped. Anwyn's father directed an astonished look at the woman.

"Ruined, that," she snapped, "and worthless. It has a great hole in it. Surely, Forester, you will not drag someone away to Nottingham over such a pitiful prize?"

Montfort's lips tightened. He signaled his men, who threw the hide to the ground. He gave the woman another hard look.

"Consider yourselves warned. We will return, and we will continue to enforce the King's laws."

He signaled to his men once more, and they all began to move off.

The fierce, small woman called, "You will be careful, Forester, that you do not catch an arrow in the back."

Montfort's head jerked round. Had she not just demonstrated the skill needed to accomplish the deed? Anwyn's heart trembled anew; she certainly did not want her Da to die.

The woman smiled dangerously. "'Tis just that you foresters are so few, and Sherwood is such a perilous place."

Anwyn could feel the woman's anger—and hate—from across the clearing. Her father had to be bombarded with it. But she knew her Da for a clever, canny man. He merely nodded. "And you, my good woman, play at a treacherous game. The murder of a King's forester is punishable by death, and a man's—or indeed a woman's—arrow is an accurate marker."

Anwyn saw Falcon Scarlet reach for the woman's hand; their fingers curled together in an unspoken gesture of unity.

But the woman said, "And dead, Forester, is dead, despite the price paid for the deed."

Mason Montfort gestured yet again. His band of men assembled and, with invisible targets on their backs, moved away.

****

"'Twas Curlew shot that deer, as you know full well." The small woman glared into the faces that surrounded her. "Who was careless enough to leave the hide where it could be found?"

None of the villagers answered. They still stood about, grave faced, but with the immediate danger past, mothers had released their children from their arms and men had eased their stances.

Anwyn ventured from Diera's hut and out into the dying light of the golden day. She could see Diera now, standing beside Heron with her hand on his arm.

"And who is this?" The small woman's gaze found Anwyn the way a hard slap finds a cheek.

Heron spoke wryly, "She, Ma, is daughter to the Sheriff's new head forester, that man you just met. She has come here seeking refuge."

Both the woman's brows rose. "And is her father not likely to hurry back looking for her? She cannot stay."

Should that decision not belong to the headman? Anwyn wondered. But the man with the wild mane did not gainsay the woman and merely stood quiet as she beckoned to Anwyn. "Come here, lass."

Anwyn started forward. Those gathered stayed where they were and stared. A show upon a show, this was, and they were nothing loath.

As Anwyn approached she tried to read Heron's expression and that of the headman, who seemed to hold his opinion in abeyance. She had no trouble discerning the look on the small woman's face, clearly outraged and furious.

"How do you come here? And who let you stay?"

"That would be me, Ma," Heron said. "Since she

sought refuge, I thought she should wait and speak with you and Pa."

Heron's mother waved a hand. "Permission to stay denied."

"Nay." The word burst from Anwyn's lips without her volition. She did not like to defy this woman, but she would not be sent back to Nottingham. "You must let me remain."

"I must?" Heron's mother threw her head back and her face froze.

"Or—or he must," Anwyn quickly amended, gesturing at Falcon Scarlet, "he being headman here."

The woman glared into Anwyn's eyes. "I am his wife, Lark Scarlet. I speak for him and he for me, always."

Anwyn shot a startled look at the man. Rather than offended, he appeared slightly amused. "We speak as one."

"Ah," Anwyn managed. She could almost feel the ties that existed between them, tangible and strong. What would it be like to share such a connection with someone else, say Curlew Champion? Envy stirred in her heart.

"Your presence here is not required," Mistress Scarlet said shortly. "It is a complication, and we have enough of those right now. Heron, pray escort her clear of the forest."

"But I cannot go." Not, at least, until she saw Curlew again. Where was he? Diera said he had gone away with Heron, yet Heron stood here without him. Had he remained with his ailing mother?

"You cannot stay." Lark Scarlet's tone turned vicious.

"Mother." Heron spoke before Anwyn could. "I think you will want to hear my opinion before you send her off."

"Oh, aye?" Lark turned those fierce eyes on him. "You give me one good reason to keep that devil's offspring here amongst us."

"Because, Ma, I think she is the woman we have sought so long."

Chapter Nineteen

"We cannot leave those who were seized to stand trial," Falcon Scarlet said heavily. "We will need to mount a rescue."

Curlew turned his head and looked into his uncle's face. Since his return from his parents' hermitage at midmorning, he seemed able to sense the emotions of those around him far too clearly. Indeed, they came at him like arrows shot fast and hard, broke upon him and heightened his own feelings of distress.

He had hated leaving his father and mother alone in the forest, for he could taste his father's despair and feared what he might do. Curlew could not, he simply could not endure losing both of them.

Yet Gareth had sent him off without reservation. "You have a task to perform, son, new duties to take up. You can help her best by doing them well."

Now he sat with his aunt, his uncle, and Heron, sharing information and a mug of Aunt Lark's vile bark tea. She had taken one look at him and thrust it into his hands.

"Drink, lad. You look shattered."

Aye, and he felt it. He drank the bitter stuff and sat quietly while the others talked over the matter of rescuing the four headmen hauled away from the surrounding villages for poaching. All, if found guilty, would lose their hands or their lives.

And how could they fail to be found guilty? De Asselacton would not have begun this campaign did he not mean to prove ruthless in it.

Lark waved a hand. "They are as good as lost." She turned sharp eyes on Heron. "And what is this nonsense you spout about the forester's daughter? You said to wait and speak with Curlew. Well, he is here."

Heron seared Curlew with a single glance and looked away. "'Twas he who brought her here. 'Tis he who knows."

"Nay." Curlew spoke quickly before he lost the will. "I know nothing."

Because he remained so attuned to others' emotions, he felt Heron's immediate protest. Heron rarely grew angry, but when he did he burned with righteous heat, and surely his anger built now.

But Falcon spoke kindly, before Heron could. "Curlew, lad, Heron has said something remarkable of this lass—that she is the woman you have sought this long while, the missing guardian."

Curlew shook his head and did not look at Heron.

"Then," Lark demanded, "Why has he said so?"

Curlew shifted uncomfortably. He did not wish to discuss this with his aunt and uncle. At this point he did not even want to think about what he and Anwyn had done in Sherwood. Yet the images would not be gone from his mind. And, of all people, these two guardians needed to know. For everyone hung from threads of uncertainty until the third of their number was found.

"The manner of our meeting," he admitted, "was passing strange."

"What was the manner of your meeting?"

Curlew raised his gaze to Falcon's. "I went into

Sherwood to await the arrival of the Lady. This lass came to me instead."

Falcon's lips parted in surprise.

Lark spoke, "So you met with the wench in the forest—sheer chance and much nonsense. How could she be your third, she of foreign blood and not even Sherwood born?"

"You always doubt, wife. You doubted our Gareth when first he came. Does he—does Curlew—not carry Norman blood?"

Lark made a face as if she tasted something unpleasant. "Aye, well, and Gareth eventually proved himself. Besides, he never held a part in the sacred trust of guardianship. Always has that gone to one of us."

"You are wrong, Ma." Heron said it softly, but Curlew could still feel the anger coming off him. "What of Marian?"

"Eh?" Lark looked startled. "That was long ago."

"How long does not matter, for in one way or another we all carry her blood. Was she not a Norman ward when she ran away to Sherwood for the love of Robin?"

Marian. The memory of Curlew's vision slammed through him once more. Tears splashing hot on his face, terror in amber eyes. *My love, my love, my love.*

"Curlew?" He realized Lark had spoken to him; he had not heard.

"I am sorry, Aunt?"

"It is clear Heron, with his mad notions, would have the chit stay. Will you not give us your opinion?"

Truthfully, Curlew said, "My feelings are so tangled right now I am not sure what I think. Change comes quickly." And change, for him, always came hard.

"Well, I do have an opinion," Lark stated roundly. No surprise, there. She usually did. "Citing Marian—my grandmother or not—is no good recommendation. For there was no strength in Marian; she crumbled when Robin died, and abandoned their child. She failed in her role as guardian. The last thing we need is another such miss, and one who is likely to bring Montfort sniffing round is even less welcome."

With deceptive mildness Heron asked, "Would Marian's circle not have failed, regardless, once Robin died?"

"Aye, perhaps." Blindly, Lark's fingers reached for her husband's and clasped them tight. "But what kind of woman is it who does not fight for her child, the child of the man she loves? I would battle to the death for the sake of any of my children."

No question of that.

"She went mad with grief," Falcon said gently. "I am not sure, love, I could go on without you, either."

For an instant pure, blazing adoration shone in Lark's eyes. Wholly mollified, she murmured, "Aye, I know. Poor Marian—and poor Gareth! But that has naught to do with the forester's lass."

Dryly, Heron said, "Should we not give her a chance before denouncing her, even as you have our beloved ancestress?"

All three of them looked at Curlew. "You brought her here, lad," Falcon said at last. "You had best speak to her."

****

A cold wind snaked through the village, promising rain and hinting of winter. Curlew found the forester's lass outside Diera's hut, sorting turnips. She glanced up when he approached and then leaped to her feet, light flaring in her eyes.

And just like that Curlew felt the emotions leap up inside him—desire and something he understood far less well. Aye, and he had known this encounter would not prove easy. A more cowardly man might turn and run.

She looked nothing like the well-tended young woman he had watched ride past him on the forest road. Her clothing mussed and tattered, with dirt on her slender hands, she might have been born in Oakham. Curlew tried to ignore his memories of those hands moving over his naked flesh and found he could not.

She took a step toward him and her eyes reached for his. "Master Champion."

"Mistress Montfort."

A smile curled her lips. "Are we not unaccountably formal, considering—" She did not complete the thought, did not need to.

Hastily he gestured to the vegetables tumbled at her feet. "What is all this?"

She wrinkled her nose. "I am trying to be useful. Diera bade me sort out those that might be stored for winter and those to be used at once, but I confess I cannot tell the difference."

"No doubt you are happier at needlework."

"By heaven, no! That is torture. I always long to plunge the needle into my eye."

"Then for what are you suited, Mistress Montfort?"

Immediately he regretted asking, for the heat leaped into her eyes. He felt it all again—the way she had moved beneath him and fitted her body to his in glorious passion.

He cleared his throat. "I hoped we might speak together."

"So did I."

"Come then. Walk with me."

He led her away down one of the paths that wound away into Sherwood. He felt always steadier in the forest. He would need all his wits about him now.

"I hope you have been comfortable whilst I was away."

"Diera has been most kind, as has her grandmother. How is your mother, Master Curlew? Diera said you had gone to see her because she was sore ill."

"Aye, she lies very ill indeed, stricken. I do not know if she will recover."

"I am that sorry." She reached for his hand. Curlew's fingers moved of their own volition to accept hers; their fingers interlaced without intention. "I know what it is to lose a mother."

"Aye, so you said when—back in the forest. How long did you say she has been gone?"

"Three years. It seemed no more than a winter fever. But it burned her up to nothing and stole her from us."

"I am sorry," he told her in turn.

"My father has not been the same since," Anwyn admitted. "He is changed. I know I try him sorely, yet he has hardened himself somehow. He never would have forced me into an unwelcome marriage before we came here."

"Indeed, and I fear for my father also," Curlew confessed. "'Tis difficult to imagine him going on without her." Difficult to imagine Gareth so much as drawing breath without his Linnet—the memory of his devotion lit all the days of Curlew's childhood.

For a moment Anwyn was silent. Then she spoke with a quaver in her voice. "Is love not a perilous thing? So many go to their marriages without the benefit of it. I have always envied those who do manage to find it, like my parents—and yours, so it seems. Yet it comes at a steep price."

"Aye. Much is given; much is also taken."

She glanced at him in surprise. "Of what did you wish to speak, Master Champion? Surely, 'tis not the pain of love."

He stopped walking and turned to face her. Their hands, still linked, made a bridge between them, and above their heads the brown oak leaves clattered in the wind.

"I wondered if you had changed your mind about going home."

She drew a quick breath. A new emotion flooded her eyes. "You do not want me here."

Curlew had spent the day convincing himself and everyone around him that was true. Now, facing her, he began to doubt. He wanted her near him; that much he could not deny. "I do not think it wise for you to remain here, despite the promise I made when we lay together." He added very gently, "I did not know who you were, then."

"Does it matter so much that I am the daughter of Lord Simon's head forester?"

"Your presence is a danger. He will soon come searching for you."

"But he has no reason to seek me here, of all places."

133

"He will search everywhere, in due course, as any good father must. Mistress Montfort, you see how we are set."

"What said Heron's parents? Did they insist you bid me go?"

Not wishing to lie to her, Curlew said, "That remains in question."

"Did Master Heron speak for me?"

"Aye."

Light kindled again in her eyes: gratitude. "I knew he would."

Corresponding jealousy leaped in Curlew's heart. Had she feelings for Heron? Aye, and would that be so difficult to believe? He spoke quickly, before he could change his mind, "Go home, Mistress Montfort, and set your father's heart to rest."

As soon as the words left him it began to rain, cold drops striking down like knives, slicing through the leaf canopy to beat upon the ground. Anwyn ignored them, her gaze fused with Curlew's, and her fingers tightened on his painfully.

"I pray, Curlew Champion, whatever else, do not ask that of me."

Chapter Twenty

"What must I do to convince you I should stay?" Anwyn spoke before Curlew could voice the refusal she saw in his eyes. "I can prove useful to you and your folk—I know I can. Did I tell you I am well able to use a bow? My father taught me when I was still growing. I often shot in company with the young folk of our town, and you know how good Welsh bowmen are."

A smile curved those lips of his—warm, tantalizing lips that had explored every part of her in the dark. Desire slammed into the pit of Anwyn's stomach. She did not understand the power of her longing, but oh, how she felt it!

"It makes an intriguing picture, that—you with a bow." The hand not fused to hers came up and touched her hair lightly, as if he could not help himself. "But one I think we must neglect."

Anwyn stepped closer. Now only the swiftly falling rain separated them. She knew men and how to manipulate them. Those games she had played at Shrewsbury and, aye, in Nottingham also were all about manipulation. Men wanted but one thing, and a woman could get whatever she wanted if a man thought he might win it in return. Dangerous, aye, and she had nearly been caught once or twice. Yet she had already given this man that prize and, besides, he was like no one she had ever met. She was sure the great

135

restlessness in her had sent her always, always searching for him.

What a cruel irony that this one man appeared to be the only one ready to turn her away! She could not allow it, not on her life.

"I can think of still another reason for you to let me stay," she breathed.

Desire ignited in the silver of his eyes. Even before she pressed her body against his she felt something in him leap to her, a reaching of pure spirit, and she yearned upward to find his mouth even as he sought hers.

And oh, it was as she remembered from the darkness but better, ten thousand times better, for the answer it made to her fierce wanting. Her lips belonged on his, just as her fingers had been made to curl into his. Every separate part of her had been formed, before birth, to fit his flesh. And by heaven, his tongue belonged inside her mouth and the taste of him burning through her. Her spirit needed to be at home with his until she died, and after.

She breathed his name into his open mouth. His hand released hers and she grieved, she grieved until his arms closed around her hard, lifted her from her toes, and gathered her against him.

He knew who he kissed now, right enough. Let him make any excuses he would about what had happened in the dark. He knew who she was and she could feel him strain for her.

She no longer cared who he had thought to meet in the night. She cared not for her sins of the past nor what had brought her to this place. For in this moment she offered him her heart—silently, helplessly—and everything she was, besides.

Love me, she bade him in her mind.

Of course he could not hear, yet his hands moved, slid down her back and cupped her buttocks, coaxing her still closer. The rain fell faster, and Anwyn wiggled her hands inside his tunic, her lips never leaving his. Her fingers encountered smooth skin marked by a tempting trail of hair that led downward, and beneath it supple muscle. Beautiful man, everything she wanted in the world—hers, hers, *hers*.

She trailed her hands still lower and felt his arousal spike. Aye, and try as he might to send her away, he could not deny the attraction, nor the need.

"Soldiers! Soldiers!"

The cry came from the direction of the village, not so very far away. Anwyn distinctly heard the sudden clamor and the disturbance, even through the clatter of the swift-falling rain.

Curlew went rigid in her arms and then drew away, leaving her bereft. He turned back to Oakham, and dread swamped her. She dug her fingers into his arm.

"Nay!"

"I must go see—"

In the village a dog barked, a child began to wail. Anwyn heard a series of sharp demands. She still clutched Curlew's arm tightly, and he pulled her with him back through the trees until they could see what transpired in the village. Between the rain and the intervening huts, Anwyn's view might have been better, yet she could not miss the large troop of Sheriff's men, all on horseback, with swords and shields.

The dread in her heart intensified.

Near the oak tree that stood at the hub of the

village the troop paused and their leader called, "Where is your headman?"

Falcon Scarlet moved forward, his wife predictably at his side.

Curlew murmured, "That is Rassent, captain of the Sheriff's guard. Why has he been sent?"

Anwyn blinked desperately against the rain. Falcon must have said something she could not hear, for the captain on his tall roan horse waved a hand. His reply to Falcon came through the rain in pieces.

"… de Asselacton … good friend … forester … daughter has gone missing. Abducted … thinks."

Anwyn gasped and stiffened. She saw Falcon Scarlet shake his head. Would he and Lark lie for her sake? Would Heron? And why should they, if it looked to cost them? She meant nothing to any of these people; she could not even be sure what she meant to the man at her side. What she had learned since coming here, though, was that loyalties ran deep.

"I do not want to go back," she breathed, and her heart beat painfully in her breast.

Curlew made no response, but his arm curled about her waist and drew her hard to his side.

"I do not say you know where she is," the captain responded to whatever Falcon had said, "but my lord the Sheriff wishes to assure her return … taken for security until she is found."

"No!" The cry came not from Falcon but Lark. A number of villagers started forward, and the sudden threat of violence reverberated through the air.

Anwyn, still blinking through the raindrops, saw Heron move forward to face the captain. "… makes you think she would … forest? … anywhere."

"… give you three days," the captain hollered in reply and mayhem promptly erupted as the villagers charged the mounted men.

Suddenly a bow appeared in Lark Scarlet's hands. As Curlew abandoned Anwyn to rush forward, she saw a man tumble from his horse, an arrow through his throat. A villager fell to a blow from a soldier's sword, even as Anwyn leaped in an effort to catch Curlew.

She failed, for he eluded her and loped away through the trees. With a sob, she followed.

Everything seemed to happen at once: the mounted men attacked the villagers even as arrows flew in a sudden, deadly storm. Screams tore the air. Anwyn, though, thought only of holding Curlew Champion back from danger.

And then, to her horror, she saw Heron's bright head go down. He crumpled, and a host of cries arose all around him.

"Hold!" The demand came from one among the troop of soldiers—the captain, Rassent, Curlew had called him. It froze Curlew even where he stood, for the man held Falcon Scarlet fast, with his sword at Falcon's throat.

"Three days," the captain called into the sudden silence, "and we take this, your headman, for security. Should the girl be returned before then, well and good. Should she not be returned, your headman will stand trial along with the others taken, for violation of the King's law."

"You cannot!" one of the villagers cried. "No venison was found here. You cannot prove—"

A blow from one of the soldiers silenced him and brought blood to his lips.

"The Sheriff has spoken. Take him," Rassent ordered two of his men, and lowered his sword from Falcon's throat.

At once, Falcon began to fight—not, as Anwyn saw, to free himself but to reach Heron who lay on the ground, unmoving. Curlew came to life suddenly and ran forward to throw himself into the fray. But before Anwyn could follow, it was over, for one of the soldiers stood with Lark Scarlet in his grip and a long knife hard against her breast.

Falcon turned his eyes on her and all the fight went out of him. Anwyn sensed that, somehow unheard, they exchanged words before Falcon was dragged onto one of the soldiers' mounts, and with a terrible din the company rode away, leaving devastation behind.

****

"This is your fault." Lark Scarlet's golden eyes, sharp as knives, stabbed at Anwyn, and raw hatred rolled from her. The woman knelt, stricken, on the floor of the hut to which Heron had been carried, her son's head on her knees. Diera crouched beside them, her hands already red with Heron's blood.

Anwyn—always ready with her tongue and seldom at a loss for words—could not speak. Emotion overwhelmed her, both Lark's grief and that of the others present. She could almost feel the pain that possessed Curlew's heart. He stood like a child, stricken.

Lark shot a look at him. "She will need to be sent back at once. You see that." Not a question but the pronouncement of law. "I would be rid of her as I would a contagion."

Curlew glanced at Anwyn and then, ignoring both

her and his aunt's hard words, went to his knees at Heron's side.

"Heron?"

No response; Heron lay like a carving of a god, or an angel, his beautiful face far too still. The blow from the soldier's blade had taken him below the throat and sliced through both clothing and the flesh beneath. The blood welled as from an underground river and none of Diera's efforts so far had made it cease.

Folk crowded the doorway of the hut, peering in. Diera's hands shook, and she lifted an ashen face to Lark. "I have not the skill for this. We could send for Peg from Ravenshead, but I do not know that there is time."

"We need Linnet, with her healing touch," Lark grieved, "but I have lost her. I will be cursed if I will lose Fal and Heron as well. Son, arise!"

Heron refused to stir, and a lump rose to Anwyn's throat. She could not say she liked Lark Scarlet, and she knew how the woman despised her. But her grief was now tangible, alive in the room. And, oh, she did like Heron. It struck her hard to see all his brightness lying still.

And what of Curlew? How must he feel now? His mother ill, his uncle seized, and now his companion in this mysterious, inexplicable guardianship struck down also.

How she wished she could help! She would give anything to be able to mend things for him.

Almost as if he could hear those thoughts, he glanced at her over his shoulder. Then, quite shockingly, he laid both his hands, palms down, in the blood that covered Heron's chest. He bowed his head in an attitude of prayer and began to speak words, too low for Anwyn to catch.

And something came in response to those words. The very air of the hut stirred, the folk at the door murmured, shadows rearranged themselves, and a dim glow appeared around Curlew's hands.

Dark green it was, the hue of fir needles, deep and fathomless. Anwyn blinked as she realized what this must be—power, magic, pure and strong. Awe enfolded her, and she took a half step back even as all her senses responded and came alive.

Curlew—for the first time she saw him as more than just a man. Was this what the guardianship entailed?

Could the power he unleashed call to Heron?

It certainly called to something within her own heart. Every fiber of her being and every speck of her spirit responded and arose, quivering. It was Diera, though, who looked up from Heron's face and noticed her first.

"Look, Curlew—look!"

All three kneeling above Heron turned their faces to Anwyn. Lark's eyes widened, and Anwyn heard Curlew draw a sudden breath.

"By the Green Man's horns!" someone at the door exclaimed.

Anwyn looked down at herself and lifted her hands in amazement. In the dim light of the hut she could just see it—faint radiance outlining her body, a very pale reflection of that which emanated from Curlew. Only it was the wrong color to be a reflection, for it coursed in deep garnet red, nearly the same shade as blood.

"What—?" she began, staring at her own hands.

But Curlew gave her no time to complete the thought. Light flaring in his eyes, he reached one bloodied hand for her.

"My lady, come."

Chapter Twenty-One

"Place your hands just here, beside the wound." Curlew shot a look into Anwyn's face. She appeared too shocked to obey him, yet she hesitated only an instant before pressing her palms into the welter of blood that flooded Heron's throat and chest. By the Green Man's horns, why did Heron not stop bleeding? And how deep did this dire wound penetrate?

He closed his mind to the very idea of Heron dying, and to the faint trails of light he saw coursing about the girl who knelt facing him. At the moment, he had no way to reconcile either.

"Think," he bade her. "Concentrate on Heron's healing. Picture the blood staunching and the wound closing up."

"Aye." Her face had turned bone white and her freckles stood out even in the dim light. But her eyes clung to his, the look in them almost worshipful, and he knew—knew to his heart—she would do anything he asked.

"Reach deep inside," he said hoarsely. "Pull up the power."

"Power?" Her breath rasped in her throat. By contrast, he could not hear, or feel, Heron breathing. Had they lost him? No. He would not allow it.

He wanted to close his eyes, the better to sense his own power, to haul it up by the roots if needed, but his gaze remained snared by Anwyn's. He could no more look away from her than he could abandon Heron.

He began to pray again, the words whispered almost beneath his breath—old words, sacred words.

The power came.

Hard as he had called on it before, when he knelt beside Heron alone, so easily did it now come flowing, surging and burgeoning up through him from the very dirt of the floor, from the roots and waters deeper still, twining and combining with the air of the hut, transforming into internal fire.

His hands, pressed so tightly to Heron's chest, began to glow—not as they had before but with an intensity that nearly blinded him. An instant later, Anwyn's hands flared to light also, deep crimson, like a portentous rising sun.

She gasped but, the Lady love her, did not waver or break her hold. Her eyes, still fast on Curlew's, shone green, and the golden flecks that marked them glimmered.

The power rose, staggering in its intensity. Swiftly, Curlew sought to grapple with and control it. Aye, and he had shared such healings and communions with Heron—most lately in the attempt to rescue his mother. But that had been two, not three.

The realization hit him like a rock between the eyes—'twas what this meant, the ready flow of power, the three of them connected for the first time in flesh. He could almost see the circle forge, form bonds between them, and manifest.

He still did not understand why it should be this lass, of all those born in Sherwood or elsewhere. He simply knew it to be so.

The glow that surrounded Anwyn intensified; she shimmered before his eyes. Light streaked down the length of her hair, whispered over her skin, and ploughed into Heron. Curlew's own power had risen to such a fevered brightness he could hear it, like the music of wind in leaves.

Heron jerked beneath their hands. Lark exclaimed and Diera sobbed. Heron's lips parted and emitted a strangled gurgle, along with a trickle of blood.

Hold him, he told Anwyn in his mind. *Staunch the blood in him. Imagine him well-knitted, inside.*

She nodded. Her face had now taken on the sickly shade of tallow and he hoped she would not swoon. Surely not, while yet this power possessed her. But he extended his own strength around her like a shield and saw her straighten and lift her head.

Heron opened his eyes. They glowed liquid gold, two pools of pure spirit. He gasped for breath, and air filled his chest, one painful gasp after another.

Curlew fought to control the vast magic that linked them and felt it begin to come into line. It took him a moment to realize that was because Heron, awake and aware, now participated. And Heron's affinity with spirit was masterfully strong.

Relief flooded him much as the power had. The unwieldy intensity of the magic steadied and subsided to a rhythmic throb.

Lark, who knelt still, on her knees at Heron's head, swore. Anwyn removed her gaze from Curlew's for the first time and looked at Heron.

He breathed steadily now, the light in his eyes half-veiled by his long, dark-gold lashes. Color had returned to his face and, blinking, Curlew saw that between his hands and Anwyn's, the flow of light had burned most of the blood away. Beneath it the terrible wound had closed into an angry, red line.

Reaction hit Curlew then, a staggering blow, for he saw that had the stroke been a hair higher, it might well have decapitated his cousin.

They had nearly lost him. The triad had, Sherwood had, and he, Curlew, had.

Now the sound of Heron's breathing seemed to fill the hut. Diera began to weep. She reached out and touched Heron with careful hands. Curlew knew how she felt—his own emotions threatened to overwhelm him.

Anwyn, it is enough. Again, unsteadily, he spoke to her in his mind. Again, she seemed to hear. Her eyes flew once more to his, and she jerked her palms away. Curlew followed suit, and the light began to subside gently, small tendrils of it still flowing down their hands and rippling across Heron's skin.

Heron smiled. The folk watching from the doorway began to whisper, and Lark's hands came out to cradle her son's head.

Anwyn sat like one stunned, and stared at her own hands as if they belonged to a stranger.

Easy, Curlew told her. *It is well.*

She nodded and swallowed. Aye, he knew how she felt, punched by such power—both exhilarated and exhausted. And what of the implications? He could barely begin to comprehend them.

Heron's left hand reached up and seized Curlew's. His right captured Anwyn's, and for one blinding moment the circle glowed again, almost visible in the room—forged and nevermore to be broken.

****

"You cannot send her away now. Surely, Ma, you must see that."

Heron spoke hoarsely, his voice roughened and no longer melodic. Well and lovingly bandaged by Diera, he sat in company with Lark and Curlew, weakened but very much alive.

In the corner of the hut, Anwyn slept. She had barely spoken since helping Curlew haul Heron back from the edge of death. Shattered. Curlew knew her to be. Even though she slept, he could still feel the connection between them, could almost sense her emotions and the dreams that flickered through her mind.

Lark wore her stubborn face. She sat rigid, with a mug of ale in her hand, and stark worry in her eyes. Both she and Diera had bid Heron rest, but they might as well try to tie him down. For Curlew could feel his emotions too—a bright mix of wonder and pure gladness.

"And what of your father?" Lark asked predictably. For most of her life, she had loved Falcon Scarlet with a totality that bordered on the worshipful. They were bound not only by marriage but by ties similar to what Curlew had just felt forge into being. He could not imagine losing Anwyn now, no more than Heron.

So this was what it meant to be a guardian of Sherwood, possessed and possessing. This was the terrible wonder that would rule his life.

"We must get him back," Heron soothed her, "and we will. So I do promise you."

"There is but one coin will purchase his freedom," Lark spat. "She must go back."

Curlew's heart protested wildly, but he spoke low, so as not to disturb Anwyn's sleep. "You saw—and felt—what just happened."

Emotion flickered in Lark's eyes. An honest woman, she could not deny the truth; neither would she pretend to like it. "She is not worthy," she declared. "An outsider."

"No longer," Heron spoke in his new rasp. "She could not belong more surely to us."

"She is a bridge," Curlew said. His father always told him how Sherwood had chosen him, Gareth, to be just such a bridge between Saxon and Norman, rendering both *English*. Possibly, Sherwood had made another such choice.

"A lot of blood has flowed into this soil," Heron said. "Perhaps Sherwood no longer minds from whence it originates. 'Tis all about spirit."

And aye, Curlew thought, what a spirit dwelt within the woman now linked with them! He sensed so much about her—restlessness, longing, defiance, burgeoning strength, fragility, and a stark terror that lurked beneath it all. What did she fear so terribly?

And for which of them was she meant, himself or Heron? Him, surely—it had been to him Sherwood led her, and with him she had coupled in the forest. He burned anew, just thinking of it. But this potent circle might change everything. Heron had such a deep link with the forest and, object of any woman's desire, must be the obvious choice.

All he, Curlew, could do was shoot an arrow very well. Why should Anwyn choose him? And, aye, he would now have to let her choose.

She shifted slightly in her sleep as if she felt his

thoughts tease at her. Softly, so as not to spoil her rest, he turned his attention away.

"I wish Linnet were here." The words startled Curlew to the heart. His Aunt Lark rarely displayed vulnerability, but how lost she must feel now, with two thirds of her circle torn away.

Gently, he asked, "Can you still sense my mother in your mind?"

Lark's gaze flicked toward him. She shook her head. "Yet Sherwood holds her—it is my one comfort. I can sense Falcon, and speak with him in my mind—aye, that I can. He bids me be strong. He tells me there is no one who has more courage than I." Sudden tears filled her eyes. "But I am lost entirely, without him."

"You are not without him, Ma, nor will you ever be." Heron clasped her hand. "Sherwood assures that for all of us. We are the fortunate."

"We are the burdened!" Lark cried. "I pity the both of you." She glanced into the corner. "I even pity her. Such gifts Sherwood gives. And such pain, also."

A sudden memory sprang to life once more in Curlew's mind—Marian, her auburn hair streaming down, tears falling from her eyes, unbearable grief and terror filling her.

"Have faith, Ma," Heron bade. "Let your belief be as strong as your courage. All things always come back to us again."

Chapter Twenty-Two

"I must leave at once and go into the forest. We have but three days in which to rescue Falcon."

Anwyn watched little puffs of vapor appear from Curlew Champion's lips. The morning was deadly chill, brisk and alive with color. She tried to understand why it felt as if Curlew's words echoed inside her, and gave it up. She comprehended little enough of what had happened to her since she came to Sherwood.

Only that Lark Scarlet wanted her sent back to Nottingham in exchange for Falcon. That somehow she and Curlew had commanded a staggering, great magic and saved Heron's life. And that she could not bear to be parted from Curlew ever again.

She ached to lie with him—oh, aye—but it was not just that. She ached also for his presence, could sense it when he did or did not remain near. In a curious way she seemed able to feel his moods as well, almost as if they touched upon her awareness.

The two of them stood now just outside Diera's hut. Not far away soared the great tree for which Oakham was named, its dying leaves stained the color of the light on Curlew's hair.

She said the only thing she could: "Let me come with you."

He studied her for an instant and she thought he must agree, but he shook his head. "Better not. I can move more swiftly alone."

"Master Champion—"

"You had better call me 'Curlew' now, given what happened yesterday."

"What did happen yesterday?"

Again he seemed to hesitate. The brightness in his eyes devoured her face, and she wondered what he saw. She had never been beautiful; now perished by the cold and worn by her emotions, she felt fragile beyond belief.

But his expression softened, and his emotions fluttered in her mind before he said, "It seems Sherwood led you to us for a reason, a precious one."

Her heart protested it: Sherwood had not led her to *them*, so much as to him, through the sightless dark. Had he forgotten? She could never forget—each separate memory still had the power to possess her.

"Curlew, please do not leave me. Heron's mother does not want me here."

"She is grateful to you for saving Heron, and she knows you belong."

She belonged with him. But that explained nothing. She reached out and seized his arm. "But just how did I help you save Heron? What was that light?"

Something grave and wonderful looked at her out of his eyes. "You, dear girl, are the one Heron and I have sought so long, the third of our number."

She almost fell down. "I?"

A rueful smile curled his mouth. "Indeed, and I nearly failed to accept it, fought the very idea just like my aunt. But no one can deny what occurred when we called Heron back from death. You must have felt the bonds form and how strongly they now join the three of us."

"I do not know what I felt," Anwyn confessed. Amazement and terror moved within her, and a thousand doubts. From the very beginning Curlew had impressed upon her that an inescapable duty lay before him. She was not a woman suited to duty. Indeed, she had spent most her life fleeing the chains of responsibility. But this duty, these ties, would bind her to Curlew. And she would give her present, her future, her very life to be tied to him.

The uncertainty within her steadied as she gazed into his eyes. "Are you saying we belong together? You, me, and Heron? Forever?"

"Forever." He repeated it like a vow.

She sucked in a breath. Dazzling, momentous miracle! She slid her fingers down his sleeve, which still she gripped, to his hand. She wanted him to feel what she felt, wanted him to know what lay in her heart. For her whole life had led her to this.

"Well, then," she said softly, her fingers curling into the warmth of his, "you can hardly leave me here, can you? Not if we are meant, always, to be together."

****

"Why do you go to see your parents?" Anwyn spoke in a hush inspired by the morning forest. Like something beautiful dying, it was—all the trees sentinel and silent, clad in their brown and yellow robes of mourning. The thought prompted another: perhaps he went to see whether his mother yet lived. Should she have asked?

But he said calmly, "I need to tell my father—and my mother, if she can understand—what has come to pass."

"Explain it to me, first. What has come to pass? What is this triad, exactly?"

He slanted a look at her. They walked side by side when possible through the trackless forest, heading ever deeper into the trees. Anwyn could not guess how he knew where he was going, unless he might be led even as she had been the night she came to him, by inner knowing.

"It is a long and complicated tale."

"This guardianship of which you speak—it is some magical force that protects Sherwood?"

His eyebrows twitched. Had he forgotten she hailed from the Welsh borders? Among her mother's people magic was accepted, an everyday reality. And she could not deny magic existed here, among these trees.

"You have heard of Robin Hood."

She smiled. "Who has not? He is like King Arthur, whom the Welsh claim as their own. A glorious hero who will never die."

"Yet he did die, pierced by nearly half a score of arrows. Those he left behind, who loved him so well, banded together to keep his legend alive. Three of them did so by taking up the circle of magic Robin had once held along with his wife, Marian, and the god of Sherwood, and keeping it balanced among them. So did they become guardians of Sherwood. When they died, the guardianship passed to three others: Robin's daughter and the sons of Will Scarlet and John Little. That daughter, Wren, was my grandmother."

"You are descended from him, then—from Robin Hood."

"Aye. My aunt, uncle, and mother took up the

guardianship in their turn, but with my mother so sorely stricken—well, it becomes our duty and privilege."

"Yours, and Heron's."

He drew a breath and she felt his emotions stir. "And yours," he said softly. "All our lives, Heron and I have known ourselves destined for this. And long did we search for the third of our number. We knew only she would be female."

"How did you know that?"

"Always there are three, all connected—two bound in marriage with each other, the third with Sherwood itself."

Anwyn's mind struggled with it. "But you say your mother is a guardian? Lark and Scarlet are husband and wife, but your mother is also wed."

"My father is not part of the circle, even though Sherwood chose him as mate for my mother, just as Sherwood seems to have chosen you—either for me or Heron."

He spoke the last words carefully, yet Anwyn's heart leaped when she heard them. *Him,* let it be him! She admired Heron, aye, and what woman would not consider him beautiful? She could sense his kindness, his warmth, and great wisdom.

But to think she would ever lie with anyone but this man surpassed imagining. He answered every call she had ever heard, and stilled her fathomless longing.

Again he glanced at her. This time his eyes remained fixed on hers. "That is what my aunt struggles to reconcile. It is a great honor and a great burden. Sherwood bred, she cannot understand why it did not fall to one of our own."

"Are you certain I am the one?"

"There is no doubting what happened yesterday. Surely you felt the power of it?"

Gravely, Anwyn nodded. She could scarcely let herself think about that even yet. The sensations she had experienced defied understanding. "So, that was magic?"

"Deep and wondrous magic, the kind that comes only when three are bound." He added simply, "We would not have been able to wield it, were you not the one."

Anwyn tried to accept that, and a host of emotions rose up inside, too tangled to define. One emerged, dominant over all: gratitude. She was grateful that this meant she had reason to be with him. She would accept far more, dedicate herself to aught she must, if it gave her a right to remain at his side.

"But even you do not know why 'tis I?"

"Sherwood knows, and that must be enough."

Such faith, she thought. The beauty of it sounded deep inside her.

"It will take time," he continued levelly, "to reach an understanding of what this means to you—to us. Heron and I will do our best to show you all you need, so you can make the right choice between us."

Her mind darted, strove to comprehend all the aspects of it. "What about your uncle, though? Your aunt will insist on trading me for him." Anwyn could not but sympathize with the woman. She knew what it would cost her to lose Curlew. The very thought of it terrified her.

She reached once more for his hand. His fingers closed about hers strongly, and a sort of humming started running through her blood, a very faint echo of what she had experienced yesterday when the sparks of light flowed from her hands. Aye, so this was magic, and nearly as powerful as what she felt for this man.

Comprehension touched her. "It is why you told my father, when first we met, that you were a forester," she proposed, "because you are guardian of this place."

He looked at her and his eyes glowed like stars. "Sherwood," he stated, "is and will ever be mine."

Chapter Twenty-Three

"I do not understand," said Curlew, and not for the first time. He stood at the edge of his parents' encampment deep in Sherwood, that which they had always called the hermitage, and wondered if he were losing his senses, or if he might have lost his way in Sherwood for the first time in his life. But nay, this was the place. There lay the ruins of the shelter his parents had shared for so long, all boughs and wattle work, not wrecked but dismantled. And there the great gray stone his mother had used for her altar. There the dead tree his father had used for a target when he practiced with the bow. And there, reaching above it all, clothed in gold, the central ash tree, taller than all those around it. He could not mistake the place.

Yet everything, each living remnant of his parents, was gone.

He stood stricken and stupid, unable to comprehend it. Beside him, the lass, Anwyn, shook her head.

"What is it? What is amiss?"

"They should be here. They are not."

"This is the right place?"

"Aye. There—there she lay the last time I was here with her. There he sat with his head in his hands."

"Could he have moved her somewhere else?"

It made no sense. Why would his father subject her

to a move when she lay so ill? And could he have moved her on his own? Perhaps she had recovered and they had started back for Oakham by another route.

But then why take apart the shelter that had stood so long? Why, unless Gareth believed they would never return?

Had his mother died and his father gone mad with sorrow? Had he buried her somewhere nearby and gone off into the forest to end his own life? But Gareth Champion was not a cruel man, and never to his children.

Aye, and likely Robin's Marian had not been cruel either, yet she had turned her back on Robin's folk and abandoned their child. Grief caused people to do impossible things.

Anwyn laid her fingers on his arm. "Steady on; they may be somewhere nearby. Let us search."

He looked into her eyes and calmed. "You are right. You wait here; I will go up along the stream a short distance. He may well have taken her to the pool that lies there."

He went slowly, calling for his father, and dread gathered on his heart even though he encountered only a sense of peace. Birds fluttered up at his approach, and the trees rustled, whispering overhead.

All at once he caught a swift movement from the corner of his eye. On the far bank of the stream he saw a hart and hind, their coats shining white in the uncertain light beneath the trees. At his approach they turned their heads to look at him—the eyes of the hind were his mother's eyes. He caught his breath even as the deer moved off quickly, together.

And at that moment he knew the truth. Grief and

gladness together filled him. At least his father would not have to live without her. The deep magic of Sherwood had given Gareth fair repayment for all his years of faithful service and love.

When he returned to the clearing, he saw Anwyn waiting beneath the great ash, her hair half braided and hanging down, looking so much a part of the place he could scarcely believe she was not born of it. No matter, though, for she had come to them, and just in time.

She took one look at his face and distress flooded her eyes. She hurried to clasp his hands.

Hers, he had learned, was not a quiet spirit, yet he sensed in her now only support and strength.

"You have not found them."

"I will not. They are free now in Sherwood. It is our turn to take up this burden."

"Oh, lad." She wrapped both arms about him and pulled his head down to her shoulder in an immediate offer of comfort. He accepted it gladly, let the pain he felt rise and flow into her, the ache of it shared. She spoke no words, made no sound, but merely absorbed his hurt. The birds darted and flickered around them, the trees swayed softly as if to an ancient music, and Curlew's heart eased. Whatever he faced, at least he did not have to face it alone.

Anwyn's fingers caressed his cheek and then cradled his head, pressing him closer. He felt the bonds between them flex and strengthen, and when her lips brushed his face he turned so his lips met them.

The kiss held much comfort and very little passion. He drank from her long, and when he paused she said, "There is nothing I would not do for you, Curlew

Champion. I would take your every sorrow. I would accept your every pain. I do not understand this magical burden you have inherited, but I will gladly take it up with you."

He looked into her eyes, green as new leaves on a spring morning, and asked, "Why? You barely know me yet. My troubles are not yours."

"I know you. And they are my troubles just because they are yours."

Something like a sob came from his throat. "Anwyn—"

"Hush. Would you refuse what I offer? Do you not need me?"

"I need you," he said helplessly.

The pricks of gold in her eyes warmed. For an instant he saw glimmers of the light that had consumed her when they saved Heron.

"But," he said carefully, "you must know what you are taking on. There is no going back from this. Guardianship is a grave and heavy duty, and you see how it ends."

"I have never taken on any duty so dear to my heart. Do you doubt? Please, Curlew, do not doubt me."

She kissed him again, and this time the passion came surging. It built inside him, all tangled with his need and her devotion. It flared like the magic of Sherwood and nearly took him to his knees.

He caught her face between his hands. "Stay with me, lie with me here tonight."

"I will stay with you anywhere."

"This is a holy place." And if he loved her here, claimed her here, would she not remain his for all time?

****

"You need not fear for your parents, child."

The words might have been part of a dream, only they roused Curlew from sleep as no dream ever could. He opened his eyes and fought against memory and imagining. He lay in the eternal forest with the woman he loved. Her name—?

Anwyn, of course. She snuggled close against him, one arm curled about his chest, still fast asleep. They had used their clothing for blankets and so lay naked beneath it. The taste of her remained, ripe and sweet, in his mouth.

He tore his gaze from her and blinked, then blinked again. A spirit sat beside him, faintly outlined in radiance, a dim aura of gold. He did not require the moonlight filtering through the autumn leaves to see her.

"Well, then, do you know me?" she asked.

Struck nearly dumb, he did not reply. She had long, brown hair liberally streaked with gray, a strong face, severe and beautiful, and Aunt Lark's eyes.

"Knowing," she said comfortably, "is a curious thing, is it not, lad? There is the knowing you feel down in your gut, the knowing you pick up on your way through life—then there is the knowing that precedes it all. Life is funny, too. It is like a giant wheel that goes round again and again. A circle has no beginning and no end. Your grandfather taught me that."

"You are Robin's daughter, Wren."

She nodded, as if pleased with him. "Robin's daughter and Marian's. It took me a long time to forgive her, you know. But understanding comes more easily when we are not confined to the flesh. We remember so much more about beginnings and endings."

"Grandmother." He had never met her in life. She and her husband, Sparrow, had disappeared into Sherwood before he was born.

"Aye, lad, and is that not why I have come? I would not have you fret and fear for them. They follow a path even I have taken." She raised her hands. "And am I not well?"

Curlew tried to gather his scattered thoughts. He hoped Anwyn did not wake and take fright.

"No worry, Curlew—she sleeps sound."

"You can hear my thoughts?"

"Let me explain to you something of life—and death. Death first of all: it does not exist, save in our minds. All life is in your mind, come to that. Pure illusion. You know that as well as I do, but it is one of those things you have forgotten."

Curlew shook his head.

She leaned toward him. "What if I were to tell you everything that has happened since Robin's death—*everything*—was meant to bring you to this? You, and her." She gestured at Anwyn. "Would you then remember who you are and who she is?"

"Nay, Grandmother, I do not understand."

"Put your head to work on it. Generations of folk have bequeathed you a rare intelligence. Use it now. Use all the power that comes to you." Her gaze softened slightly. "For the past must be healed and the future won."

"What am I to remember? And if 'tis so important, why do I fail to recall it?"

"Ah, lad, 'tis a mercy we forget, for if the memories of so many lifetimes descended upon you,

you would go mad. But I will give you a hint."

She leaned still closer and whispered into his ear, "You are the most important person ever born in Sherwood. Now do you know?"

Chapter Twenty-Four

"I had the strangest dream," Anwyn confessed. "I thought I heard people talking—you, and a woman."

She had awakened in Curlew's arms, the one place she wanted to be. And now, with the sun barely up and the air cold and still all around them, her heart rose wildly. For he seemed to gaze into her, all the way to her heart, as if she were the only thing in his world.

She sat up. "Was it your mother with whom you spoke? Have your parents returned after all?"

"Nay." Gently, he eased her back down to lie against his shoulder. "'Twas my grandmother you heard. It is as I told you, my parents will not be coming back. They have gone to be together in a place that is here, yet not here."

"I do not understand."

He smiled and it lit his face with warmth. "I am not sure I do, either, not completely. Yet with my mother's going, her triad ends, and surely the new one must take its place. Sherwood brought you to us just in time."

Anwyn fought to make sense of it all. "But your uncle, Falcon Scarlet—you need, still, to get him back." She caught her breath. "I think I know a way."

"Aye?"

"It came to me all of a piece while we slept." Born in part of her desire to give anything and everything to him. It terrified her, such desire, made her heart beat high in her breast, made it hard for the breath to come. But she could not fail him. She would not.

"Eh?" His fingers tensed on her shoulder and his gaze became intent.

"Lord Simon acts on my father's behalf in this. They knew each other well as young men, when de Asselacton captained the King's guard in the west. They fought together; in fact during a fierce battle, my father saved Lord Simon's life. There is little Lord Simon would not do in return. For that reason I believe he will make good on his threats and refuse to release your uncle if I am not found. He may even sentence Falcon to death." She held Curlew's gaze. "You have already lost your parents. I will not have you lose your uncle also."

"Aye, but..." Curlew twined his fingers through her hair. That mere touch made her relive all they had shared last night. She could feel his body moving over hers again, and his lips everywhere. "I need you also. Heron and I do. Sherwood does."

"Let me return to my father just long enough for an exchange to be made. I will come back to you as soon as your uncle is safe."

"If you can. If your father so allows. He will keep much closer watch on you, after this."

"He thinks I was snatched, abducted. I will feed his belief with some tale, say I never saw the faces of my abductors and that I was held elsewhere, far from Oakham. Your folk will be safe. You will be safe." She raised her hand to his cheek.

He caught her hand and pressed his lips to the palm. His breath whispered across her skin as he said, "I am not at all sure I can let you go now."

"Curlew—"

"What if your father insists on wedding you at once to this man you detest?"

"Havers? He will never have me now that I am most assuredly ruined."

"What if he does not believe you ruined? You are meant to be mine, Anwyn—mine, and Sherwood's."

Emotion rose inside her, fierce and tumultuous. She seized hold of him and stared into his eyes. "You listen to me, Curlew Champion. I will return to you at any cost. How can you imagine I can be kept away, when you are here?"

"By all the faith in my heart," he avowed, "I cannot imagine it."

"Then come, my fine lord of Sherwood, and ruin me one more time."

****

"I mean to return at once to Nottingham," Anwyn told the woman who sat cross-legged outside Heron's hut. "Thus will I see your husband fairly returned to you."

Lark got to her feet slowly. Light blazed in her eyes and chased some of the burning agony. Her gaze dropped to Anwyn's hand, linked fast with that of Curlew, who stood beside her, and then returned to her face.

"What is this I hear?" Diera ducked through the doorway of the hut and into the light. "What has happened?"

"My parents are gone," Curlew announced. He looked at his aunt. "They have done what everyone says Grandmother and Grandfather did—become part of Sherwood, together."

Diera gasped, but Lark stood strong, her head well back. "Ah, so it is done, our circle sundered."

"I am sorry, Aunt. You have lost much, your sister and the guardianship both."

Lark smiled thinly. "You know, we none of us wanted to take it up when our turn came. Poor Fal! But I was his strength and he was my wisdom. We became one another's life."

That, Anwyn could understand.

"And Linnet—she was the one who kept us all whole and sane. Now she goes on ahead and the wheel turns. It seems, lass"—she bent her gaze on Anwyn—"you must take your place upon it. And much as I desire the return of my husband, I must ask: how does that fit with taking yourself away to Nottingham?"

"She thinks she can return to us once the exchange is made," Curlew answered for Anwyn, hoarsely.

"Ah. So it seems you do have some courage. It had better be enough. We have had guardians in the past who failed dismally in their duty. But I lie. There has been only one."

Curlew's fingers jerked violently in Anwyn's. She looked at him in question.

Not now. Did she truly hear his voice in her mind? *I will tell you later.*

She clenched his fingers hard and looked Lark full in the face. "I will prove myself and my courage to you, mistress, if you give me the chance."

Lark grimaced. "Have I a choice? Send him back to me, lass, and you will be more than half the way to my favor."

Anwyn nodded. Never in her life had she been required to prove herself to anyone. Her mother had always cherished her. Even Winifred, who had stepped in after her mother's death, had been indulgent. And she had worked hard, since then, to destroy her father's regard. Aye, she had much for which to make recompense.

Curlew looked at Diera, who stood silent, listening. "How does Heron?"

"He does very well." The raspy voice came from behind Diera and made her start. Heron loomed behind her, his hair unbraided and hanging down, bandages swaddling his throat.

"You should not be on your feet!" Diera turned on him, and Anwyn caught a glimpse of her expression as she did. Ah, so the lovely Diera had given her heart to Heron. Anwyn twitched her fingers in Curlew's again. All well and good, so long as Diera did not desire Curlew, for he was hers now and for all time.

But how might that impact this guardianship of three?

Heron looked at Anwyn. "I heard all you said. You leave for Nottingham directly?"

"Aye."

"Come inside first. I think the three of us need to speak together."

"Will that make you sit down?" Curlew asked Heron as they followed him in. The place, dim and quiet, still smelled of herbs.

Heron shrugged. "As you see, I am fast recovering, even though it seems I may never again sing. 'Tis an ugly voice now, is it not?"

Anwyn spoke impulsively, "Naught about you could ever be ugly." She felt an instant surge of emotion from Curlew through their linked fingers, and thought at him, *Do not worry—as I have promised, there is no one for me but you.*

He eased, and Heron tipped his head almost as if he caught the echo of the exchange. "Ah, so that is the way of it. The circle is barely formed, and already the two of you have bonded."

"Well before that," Curlew said.

Heron smiled. "I am glad for you. Comfort him well, lass. He has lost much. And now even you must go from him for a time. But surely you know you cannot, in truth, be parted from him? Never again."

"I am beginning to find my way through these new waters," Anwyn admitted. "It is all strange and, it seems, navigated mainly by faith."

"Very true. And so it seems," Heron added almost wistfully, "it is me for Sherwood, and the hermitage."

"You need not go alone," Curlew told him. "Only think on my parents."

"Aye, but who would go to live in oblivion with me?"

Anwyn nearly spoke. The merest twitch of Curlew's fingers and a slight whisper in her mind kept her from it.

"So, cousin," Heron said in his rough whisper, "your parents have gained eternity in Sherwood. It seems the three of us must take up our duty in earnest. First of all, I wish to thank you both for saving my life. Strong magic, that was. I do not believe I have ever felt any stronger."

"Nor I," Curlew agreed, to Anwyn's surprise.

"I do not know, quite, how we managed that, the two of us and a novice. But it seems, gifted with such power, we must accomplish great things."

Heron reached out and raised both his hands to Anwyn's face. He did not touch her, quite, yet she could feel the magic hum in his hands, see it in his eyes as they caught hold of hers.

"And that means, young Anwyn, you must be sure to come back to us, whatever that requires."

Chapter Twenty-Five

"So you can tell us naught of these vile dogs who stole you away, Mistress Montfort?" Simon de Asselacton asked Anwyn with a frown.

De Asselacton—or the Asslicker, as the folk of Sherwood invariably called him—had shown Anwyn only kindness and forbearance since her return to Nottingham, but he quite clearly did not believe her story, at least not all of it.

"We must identify these men so that those guilty may be brought to justice, and others who are not guilty released." Like Falcon Scarlet, who had been set free that very afternoon. Though Anwyn had not seen him she could imagine Lark's joy, and that of Heron and Curlew, at his return to Sherwood.

And was she now also part of Sherwood, since she had bonded with Curlew, with Heron? Had her heart at last found a home?

She only knew she would do anything for them—for *him*—whatever that meant.

She looked de Asselacton in the eye. "I did not see their faces, my lord. They kept my eyes covered. As I have said, I heard their voices only, and so do not see how I can hope to identify them."

"Tell me again how it was you were captured."

She drew a breath. "I was disobedient, my lord, and did not listen to my father, who bade me remain in our quarters. 'Twas already growing dark when I ventured out. I wanted an adventure and thought to walk to the edge of Sherwood and see if I could catch a glimpse of any outlaws. After all the stories I had heard, well, my lord, it was foolish, as I now know, but my father will tell you sometimes such urges get the better of me."

"Your father has no need to tell me," de Asselacton said. "Where were you when these villains fell upon you?"

"No more than half way to the wood. I heard a noise behind, and then I felt hands seize me, and a sack came down over my head. It smelt of onions. Someone said, 'It is the forester's daughter.' "

Lord Simon glanced at Anwyn's father, who stood beside her, poker straight and silent. De Asselacton's ruddy face looked sour. "The provision of the sack would argue a planned capture. You have not been here long enough, Mason, to earn such enemies."

Anwyn's father remained silent.

"On the other hand," de Asselacton went on, "you push the peasants hard and have made a number of arrests. These men who seized you were peasants, aye, lass?"

Anwyn hesitated. She had no wish to turn suspicion on the innocent. "How to tell? Their voices might have belonged to anyone."

"Describe again the place where you were held."

"'Twas but a hut, old and not well kept, outlying, I think. I do know we turned eastward and headed some distance before we arrived."

"Not into Sherwood, then? Passing strange, that. Mason, we need sufficient information to track down these miscreants. We cannot have blackguards snatching our daughters from beneath the walls—no matter their disobedience," he added with disapproval.

"Aye, my lord. But we will do well not to apprehend the wrong men. The folk are already up in arms over us hauling in the headman of Oakham without what they call just cause."

De Asselacton waved his hand. "He has been released, has he not? And he is but a peasant, after all."

"Highly regarded, though," said Anwyn's father, who was rarely anything but fair.

Lord Simon snorted. "He is probably a wolfshead. I hope I have not made a mistake in letting him go. But I gave my word, and I am a man who keeps his word, as you well know."

Anwyn's father nodded his head. "Indeed, my lord."

De Asselacton fixed Anwyn with another hard stare. "These men who held you, mistress, they did not defile you in any way?"

Again Anwyn hesitated. Her sole defense against Havers lay in claiming to be ruined. Yet how could she send Lord Simon or even her father on a vengeful hunt for men who did not exist? They were bound to seize someone and he—or they—would suffer needlessly. Her thoughts flew madly: how might she best aid Curlew?

She dropped her eyes. "My lord, I would rather not say."

"Aye but, child, you must, if we are to seek for justice."

"Is it not enough if I confide the truth to my father?"

De Asselacton shot another look at Anwyn's father and then relented. "Very well. You will bring word to me, Mason, if measures need to be taken. Meanwhile"—his words grew weightier—"you must curb your lass's tendency to roam. Whatever has happened in the past, we cannot have that here at Nottingham, do you understand? Only look at the trouble it has caused. You will wed her at once to this man of yours, the one you said is willing to have her. Within the next two days." No question but it was an order issued. Anwyn's father bowed his head.

She drew a breath. "But, my lord—"

He fixed her with a glare. "I did not ask you. You may choose marriage to your father's man or the nunnery. Do you understand?"

A chill chased its way down Anwyn's spine. The very thought of a nunnery lent feelings of suffocation, guilt, sorrow, and death. Anything but that.

Almost anything. The memory of Havers' piggy eyes assailed her. How could she endure his touch after lying with Curlew?

Ah, but surely she could dissuade her father when she had him alone. Yet de Asselacton gave him one last glare and said, "I want this settled, Mason, and 'tis my final word upon it."

****

"So tell me, Daughter, were you harmed during your ordeal?"

They were alone in their quarters with night coming on. Anwyn's heart struggled in her breast. She wanted away to Sherwood so badly she ached. She wanted to lie this night long in Curlew's arms.

Everything she did, she reminded herself, she did

for him.

"Nay, Da," she answered, "they were not unkind."

"Then tell me," he sat down beside her, "that I might send you to Roderick with an easy mind, and that you are virgin yet."

In his eyes she saw desperation, shredded patience, and a measure of forbearance. Aye, she had tried him much. He did not know what to expect from her answer, yet he hoped.

She shook her head and his face fell; pain flooded his eyes.

"Who is the man?" He faltered. "There is but one?"

Shame touched her then, that he should think otherwise of her. But aye, she had been running wild, and stories of her behavior had not been gentle.

She said with certainty, "There is but one." One man for her, now and forever.

His face flushed dark. "Are you with child?"

The very idea convulsed her heart.

Before she could answer, her father rushed on, "For Roderick will not have you if you carry another man's brat."

She sat up straighter. "He will not have me anyway, now that I am ruined. He told me as much."

"He and I have a bargain. I have pledged to him that, as the man wed to my daughter, I will elevate him among my foresters as soon as the opportunity presents itself. I have spoken with Lord Simon about it, and he agrees. Measures must be taken to protect Sherwood. We both believe that requires placing it in the hands of a strong overseer. Roderick is not without ambition, Daughter." He paused and wetted his lips. "He has agreed to take you in any condition we found you, upon your return."

The blood drained from Anwyn's face. "No."

"Oh, aye, and I do not mean to let you out of my sight until the marriage takes place. This nonsense we have had from you is surely and truly done."

Anwyn's mind flapped and fluttered against the idea like a bird in a cage. There must be a way out; her father was basically a kind man. Yet she had used up all his kindness and then some. Should she tell him she could not accept Havers because she loved another? But she would sooner die than place Curlew at risk.

"Father, please reconsider."

"Nay, Anwyn. You heard Lord Simon: he wants the matter settled. And 'tis clear you need a stronger hand than mine. I have failed in my duty to your mother. You are not the young woman she hoped you would become."

"Do not say that." A blow, indeed. Tears flooded Anwyn's eyes.

"I pray this match will benefit us all. You will learn to obey your husband and Roderick will earn a fine place once our battle with the rabble infesting Sherwood is done."

"'Tis no battle, Father. I do not doubt folk in Sherwood, as elsewhere, are only trying to survive."

"It has gone on too long. Lord Simon would send word to King Henry that order has been established here, and thus take at least one worry from him, in light of all the unrest westward."

Lord Simon would, rather, curry favor.

"None of that concerns you," her father told her. "You must prepare yourself for your wedding."

"I will not!"

"I have never raised a hand to you, Anwyn. Perhaps that was my great mistake, but your sainted mother would not have it. Now, though, I do not doubt you require firm guidance."

What she required was the sound of Curlew's voice in her ears, the feel of his arms around her, the scent of him as he filled her, the touch of his mind on hers, and the glint of humor in his silver eyes.

She lifted her head. "Would you send me to a man who has promised to beat me? It will not happen, Father. I swear to you, no man will touch me." None but Curlew Champion.

And her father told her grimly, "We shall see about that."

Chapter Twenty-Six

"I received a visit from our grandmother, Wren, while Anwyn and I were in the forest."

Heron's head came up at Curlew's words, and their gazes met. Interest glinted in Heron's eyes and his agile mind leaped ahead with ease.

"Whatever she told you has troubled you. Or are you just missing Anwyn?"

Curlew shook his head. They sat together beside a smoldering fire in Heron's hut. Outside, an autumn rain poured down, its chill matching the bleak cold in Curlew's heart.

Only two things gladdened him Heron's swift and steady recovery from his dire wound and Falcon's return from Nottingham earlier that day. Asslicker had kept his word, at least. Now Curlew had but to get Anwyn back with him where she belonged.

"Both," he admitted.

"She is for you, then," Heron confirmed without bitterness, "and me for the forest, as I said before. I do not mind. She is a lovely, willful thing, but one only has to see how she looks at you to tell what is in her heart. You will have your hands full there, Lew, but I do not doubt 'twill be worth it."

Anwyn's presence in his life was worth anything, Curlew knew that. Yet he could scarcely get his mind around the wonder of it all.

He searched Heron's eyes, rueful and tentative. "You know me, Heron. I think I can safely call myself a humble man. There is naught special about me, save certain pronouncements made before my birth and my place in our triad. You are the one who carries the magic about with you, visible as a cloak. So—why me?"

The amusement in Heron's eyes deepened. He made a graceful gesture with his hands. Gently ironic, he said, "Indeed, there must be something we can none of us see."

"So it would seem, if I can believe what Grandmother Wren implied."

Heron shifted where he sat. The dim light of the room washed over his hair and made a stark line of the wound at his throat, now uncovered to the air. Curlew's heart trembled within him; he had nearly lost Heron. Or had he? Could it be, as Wren had said, that all loss was a lie, an illusion?

"You had better share with me what she told you."

"It sounds mad, and as if I think too much of myself."

"Cousin, I know you. As you just said, you are a humble man. As for madness, well, I think we are all of us a bit mad, in a good way."

"Very well." Curlew drew a breath. "What do you know about those who have lived in the past returning to live again?" At Heron's look of surprise he added hastily, "No, I do not mean resurrection, but rather a spirit finding a home in new flesh. I explain it badly."

Emotions chased one another through Heron's eyes: astonishment, realization, and understanding. "Is that what Grandmother Wren said to you?"

"In part." Curlew's heart quailed within him. "And I have been catching glimpses of a past not my own. Or perhaps my own, after all..."

Heron drew a breath. "Aye well, Lew, you know there is no end in death. We have encountered spirits enough in Sherwood to believe the truth of that. All life is circular and as such has no beginning and no end. The ancients who first came here believed we don many cloaks of flesh over many lifetimes."

"If such a thing might be so—and I am not saying it is—then how could we fail to remember?" Beyond brief flashes—*hot tears raining down onto his face*—and familiar feelings.

Heron smiled wryly. "You speak of madness. Surely it would lie that way, indeed. Only think of the memories of several, or many, lifetimes crowding our minds, the pain of old wounds and losses, the crippling fear. If such a thing be true, our failure to remember must be a mercy."

"That is what Grandmother said, more or less." Curlew frowned. "Yet if two souls who knew one another before, and meant much to each other, should don new flesh and come back into this world from that other to meet again—could they fail to know each other by feel, by longing?"

Interest flickered still more brightly in Heron's eyes, but he did not ask the question Curlew half expected. Instead he offered kindly, "I believe they could not fail to so know each other, Cousin."

Gladness surged in Curlew's heart, along with doubt and another, stronger rush of humility. If what Wren suggested were true, he, Curlew, did not deserve this shocking and miraculous identity.

Moreover, he was not sure he wanted it. Yet he wanted *her*. And he wished a chance to heal her pain even if it meant reliving all the loss and terror over again.

"Lew…" Heron touched his arm lightly. "I know what was said of you before your birth, what the spirits whispered—that you would be the most important person ever born in Sherwood."

"Yet I am scarcely that, Heron. Look at me! Four and twenty, and I have done nothing of note. I have merely lived my life, tried to look after those around me, and searched for the missing third of our triad."

"And spoken always for justice, and been a loving steward of Sherwood. And"—Heron smiled like sunshine in the dim room—"saved my life, you and she together."

Together. So he must believe they were meant to be. "I want her back with me, Heron."

"Aye."

Would she come tomorrow? He wished he could find her with his mind, but he had searched and caught only the barest whispers, which he attributed to imagining. How could he know what was dream and what truth? How tell reality from the product of pure wishing?

"Miracles surround us," Heron told him in his new, husky voice. "Your parents now exist together in Sherwood's sanctity. Mine speak even when apart, between their minds. Should we doubt that those who lived and died for this place should be given the gift of living for it again?"

"You are a wise man, Heron Scarlet."

"Wise enough to wed myself to Sherwood and lie

with the Lady always?"

"It need not be that way. Not since Alric, who shared the power taken up when Robin died, has there been any among the triad who lived the life of the hermit."

"Alric—aye, an intriguing figure, is he not? A deeply holy man."

"Like you."

"Who by all accounts lost out when Lillith chose the warrior-headman Geofrey over him. Sounds familiar, does it not?"

"There is no need for you to be alone."

"Even though Anwyn has chosen you?"

"Nay, but it is all about keeping the balance. For the last three generations it has seemed to poise between the leader, the warrior, and the healer, though they came in many guises. Your parents—warrior and leader—bonded together, but my mother was not left to live alone. Sherwood proved kinder than that."

Heron said ruefully, "Aye, Sherwood handpicked Gareth. And he had only to prove himself under threat of death."

"I am trying to tell you there is one who would take you to her heart even as the Green Man's Lady has done."

Heron quirked an eyebrow. "What is this you say?"

"Well, and I am not at liberty to say, but your quick and clever mind should be able to tumble to it. She is close at hand and she loves you more than her own breath."

As if conjured by magic, a knock sounded on the door. Diera's voice called, and an instant later her dark head poked in.

"I just wanted to say good night, lads," she told them.

Curlew shot Heron a look before he gave Diera a mischievous smile. "You braved this foul rain for that?"

"So I did—I cannot imagine why." Her gaze moved to Heron. "I wished, also, to be sure you have all you need before I go to bed."

Heron's eyes seemed to appraise her. "Come, sit and warm yourself."

"I suppose I might stay a moment or two; Grandmother is asleep and likely to remain so."

She chose a place at Curlew's side, which surprised him until he realized it afforded her a fine view of Heron with the firelight awash over him.

"You know, lass," Heron said to her gently, "you need not keep on fussing over me. I am well enough now. Even the bandages are gone."

She gave him an uncertain look and tears flooded her eyes. A strong woman and one who battled hard, she did not give in to tears easily, Curlew knew.

In a broken voice she said, "I nearly lost you. Had that strike taken you a hair higher—or a hair deeper—you would not be here now."

Heron's expression softened. Compassion came readily to him, always. "I am not so easy to kill as that, Diera. But aye, I am grateful for the tender care you gave me. And," he added, as if teasing, "all the attention since."

Diera's gaze, still locked on his, remained serious. "Can I help but come just to see you? To assure myself you breathe yet?"

"Peace, love. I am not going anywhere, not for a long while. There is too much work to be done."

Fool, Curlew thought. Could he not see? Was Heron so close to Diera he could not interpret what shone even now from her eyes, when he had no difficulty picking up on other signs and portents?

"Aye, well," he said weightily, "the heart cannot help but worry when it cares so deeply."

Heron's eyes flew to his and thence to Diera's face, where they lingered in sudden, rapt attention. *At last*, Curlew gloried inwardly.

Diera did not seem to notice; her gaze was fixed on her hands, which twisted together in her lap as she strove to keep Heron from seeing what she believed he did not welcome.

Foolish children, Curlew thought with deep affection. He loved them both, and in that moment almost thought he could see the ties that linked them all, like threads of glowing light, heart to heart: Diera to Heron, all of them to each other, the faithful to Sherwood itself. He even thought he could catch echoes of beauty, like music, coming from the now-darkened hut where Lark and Falcon lay together, she taking him to her once again following his return.

In that moment Curlew saw it all as a pattern, and each of them distinct pieces making up the whole, the very heart of Sherwood. If only, he thought, he could protect it all forever.

Aye, and he would give his very life to do so, without reservation, even though among the many trails of light he could see one leading away from his own heart, straight to Nottingham.

He came back to himself and realized Heron and Diera spoke together in hushed voices, their heads bent, no longer aware of him. Ah, and he did not belong here;

better to leave them alone.

And if he did, would Diera have her heart's desire at last? Was there also an old magic linking these two, an ancient question long asked and now answered?

He got to his feet and bade them good night; they barely heard.

He stepped out into the pounding rain and lifted his face to the sky.

Come to me please, he begged her in his mind. But the only answer he heard was the voice of the rain.

Chapter Twenty-Seven

"Please, Father, I beg you do not force me to this."

Anwyn extended both hands to her father in supplication. She would get on her knees and weep, if need be. All night long had she lain awake, her thoughts beating against the cage of her mind, seeking a way out. She had even risen in the darkest hours and crept to the door, planning escape, only to find her father sleeping there, his body a barrier stretched across the opening.

Now, with morning come, they had mere moments before they went to meet Havers at the chapel, and she argued the only way she might.

Her father avoided her eyes and his hard expression did not relent.

She seized both his hands. "Da, please!" She used the name she had employed for him since earliest childhood. "Do not be so cruel."

"That is just it, Anwyn: I am at last being kind. Lord Simon has convinced me I did you no service by indulging you so long."

Asslicker, Anwyn thought irreverently.

Her father went on, "Only look to what it has brought us. You ruined! Your mother would never forgive me."

"She would," Anwyn avowed passionately. "Mother understood about love, for she loved you. That I saw my whole life long."

That did make her father look at her. "What part plays love in what you have done, Daughter? Running like a wanton, giving yourself to some man you will not name. Or was your virtue taken?" he appeared almost hopeful at the possibility, and Anwyn's heart sank. Was she truly such a disgrace he would prefer to think her the victim of violence?

"Da!" Desperate, she squeezed his hands. "Do not make me wed Havers. I am in love with someone else."

"With whom?" Her father's eyes narrowed. His quick mind made a leap. "Never say you became enamored of one of your captors?" His hands smoothed her hair. "Daughter, such things happen. Why, even in the Holy Land men have thought to become friends with their jailers."

"Not that, Da. He of whom I spoke is a good man, an honorable man."

"Honorable? And was it he who defiled you? What sort of honor is that? Nay, Anwyn, I have harmed you too much with my overindulgence. I do take most of the blame. But you shall go to Havers now."

"No, please!" She sank to her knees and her fingers twisted in his. "Would you have seen my mother go to another when she loved you?"

He hesitated, and for an instant Anwyn believed she had won. Only let him cry off on the wedding and all would be right. She would find a way to return to Curlew, to Sherwood, where she belonged.

But then regret filled her father's eyes and he shook his head. "We are fortunate, Anwyn, that Roderick is still willing to take you, and you so sorely damaged."

"He wants not me but a place in your favor. He

wishes to elevate himself in your esteem."

"Is that so terrible? Ambition is a fine thing in a man, and what benefits him will benefit you as well. Together, Lord Simon and I have worked out the plans for appointing an overseer for Sherwood, a man with authority in his own right. He will carry Lord Simon's business and demands to the folk in and around Sherwood. I think Havers is the right choice."

"He would be a disastrous choice! His harshness and cruelty would only make more enemies and spread hatred."

"Child, you know little about the workings of the world. Strong men often seem harsh. It is how they enforce their will."

Nay, Anwyn thought, Curlew was both strong and kind. He led with humor, wisdom, and an eye to the good of all. In that instant she longed for him so intensely her heart convulsed in her chest. Surely she had been born for the touch of his hand, the kiss of his lips, and to watch the light move in his eyes. Aye, and she would journey through any pain or darkness to reach him. But how? Could she survive her treatment at the hands of Havers, if she knew she might eventually be away to Curlew and Sherwood?

"Father, please," she breathed once again, and pressed her forehead against his hands.

"Do not weep." Very gently, he raised her up. She could feel his love; her Da did care for her still. And he believed he acted for the best of reasons. But oh, he dealt her a dire blow! "Courage, Daughter. 'Tis time you put your fancies from you and took up the duties of a wife."

****

The rain poured down like hard tears all through the wedding rite. The chapel felt cold and damp, and the priest rushed through his words, no doubt eager to get back to his fire.

Anwyn, not in the least anxious to go home with Roderick Havers, clung to her father when it was done. She could not believe such frail things as muttered vows, spoken unwillingly on her part, could place her in this man's possession. She would never belong to anyone but Curlew, not so long as she lived.

"Da," she whispered in her father's ear at the end, "is there time to change my mind? I would choose the nunnery after all."

He merely shook his head and went out into the rain. Done—it was done. No glad tidings, no celebration. Only home with this man she detested.

According to her Da, they would move to larger quarters soon. For now Havers and his two children lived in nothing more than a room with a sleeping alcove, half a hut partitioned from space occupied by two other foresters.

Anwyn's heart struggled to rise with hope even as they tramped to it through the rain. Outside the castle proper, it did not seem so impossibly far from Sherwood. Yet, she quickly realized, it offered no such thing as privacy. The two men who occupied the other half of it were away on their rounds when she arrived, but Havers' children were there. And he quickly made it clear Anwyn would be expected to care for all.

"Put your things away and begin making the supper. When the lads come back they can join us to eat. Might as well make use of you, eh? And you will keep their room tidy as well as ours. Do as you are told and you need not feel the back of my hand."

Anwyn merely nodded. Nothing but a wattle-work wall divided the two halves of the hut, and she told herself Havers would not think to exercise his marital rights this night, with both his children and those men listening. She could endure his hard words and his cruel stares until tomorrow. Then, while he was away about his duties, she would flee to the forest.

Curlew's face swam in her mind as she struggled to prepare a meal on the poor hearth, with some assistance from Havers' daughter, Agnes. The girl flinched each time Havers spoke, making Anwyn certain she had more than a passing acquaintance with the back of her father's hand.

The meal passed in tense silence. When Havers heard the men next door, he hollered for them to come in. They hovered in the small room, dripping with wet and with mud still upon them.

Agnes leaped to her feet and fetched a rag, with which she began to swab the floor. Anwyn's lip curled—if Havers expected her to scurry round like a trained hound, he had another think coming.

"This is my new wife. She might as well do for you until we move to our new quarters."

Havers did not even pay her the courtesy of telling her their names. Both were rough men, one older and one younger, with leathered skin, like her father's, that bespoke a life spent outdoors.

"Mistress," the younger murmured and avoided her gaze. She saw what might be sympathy in the elder's eyes.

"Well," Havers barked in his hated voice, "are you stupid? Get you up, Wife, and serve them."

Chapter Twenty-Eight

"We took two men found with a deer near Ravenshead," said the elder of the two foresters seated by Havers' fire. "Tried to deny they had felled it, of course, but the arrow through its shoulder matched those in the one's quiver. They will stand trial, one or both of them."

Anwyn's heart, already fully battered by the events of the day, trembled even as she pushed in beside the men to serve bowls of the stew she had made. They discussed their day precisely as if she were invisible.

"And lose their hands, or their lives," the younger threw in.

Havers nodded grimly. "No mercy can be shown. These peasants are like undisciplined children or"—his gaze moved to Anwyn—"a wife who has not felt her husband's anger. They need to learn."

He gestured at her roughly. "Do not just stand there gawping, woman. Refill their mugs of ale."

"The thing is…" The younger man spoke again. "We cannot arrest every peasant we encounter in the forest. And they are all poaching, I am convinced of that."

"To be sure, they are," Havers denounced. "But you see, 'tis difficult for a man with one hand to draw a bow. So you cut off his hand and let his family starve. These serfs resemble rats, in that way. You have to destroy one generation to curb the next." He drank deeply from his mug. "Lord Simon is a careful man, and far too lenient. Were I in a position of authority, it would be hard dealing until these folk, who seem to feel themselves so privileged, stop stealing from their betters."

Anwyn's lip curled again. To Havers, everything was a matter of discipline. And was this the man her father wished to see made overseer of Sherwood?

The conversation and the meal limped on. Anwyn told herself she should be grateful, for at least the presence of these men kept her safe from her husband's attentions.

But they left at last and, almost at once, Havers ordered both children to bed. He bent a look on Anwyn. "I am off to my bed also." He gestured to the alcove. "You will join me as soon as your work is done."

She nodded. She could still hear the voices of the other two men, now on the far side of the dividing wall, which told her they could hear everything she said, as well. Would she let them hear her beg and cry for mercy from this misbegotten troll?

Could she bend her pride enough to ask mercy from him? Could she bear to let him touch her? *No.*

Her eyes stole toward the door even as she kept her hands busy. Outside, the pounding of the rain matched that of her heart. It sounded welcoming, in light of what awaited her in the alcove.

But Havers had barred the door when the other men left. She might have time to dash out, otherwise, but he would surely catch her when she had to pause and lift that bar.

She glanced at the two children, gone to their

pallets against the opposite wall. Agnes's worried gaze caught hers, and she whispered to the child, "Stay in your bed, and do not listen."

The girl ducked her head down beneath her blanket. Anwyn shot still another look of longing at the door. When she turned back, Havers stood at the opening of the alcove, stark naked.

Horror suffused her and stopped the breath in her throat. The fire, which shed the only light in the room, allowed her to see his body: broad and squat, thick with muscle and bristled as a boar. Shadows danced over arms knotted with bulk and sinew, legs like the broken, bandy stumps of trees. Aye, and he stood ready for her, as well, the length of him jutting like an engorged, obscene weapon.

Somehow she dragged her gaze to his face. It wore a look of lordly demand, his little eyes narrowed and mean. "Enough, Wife. Here, to your duty."

Anwyn did not move; she no longer could. As well to toss herself into the jaws of a ravening wolf.

"Come," he insisted, "or will you feel the weight of my hand?"

Somehow Anwyn forced her voice through frozen lips. "You will have to beat me before I consent to let you touch me."

"Aye, well, wench," he advanced on her, "I will take pleasure in that, and what comes after also."

Anwyn's paralysis broke and she fled to the door. But the room, only a few paces across, did not allow distance enough for her to elude him. He caught her, even as her fingers brushed the bar, and spun her about by the shoulder. Before she could blink, he struck her, a smashing blow that took her across the face and knocked her down. Her head hit the door as she fell and she lay stunned for the instant it took him to haul her up and strike her again.

This time her ears rang. He held on to her so she could not tumble down, and bellowed into her face, "Now get you to your bed, and be the whore your father sold to me."

Having never been struck in such a way, Anwyn did not expect her primary response to be one of anger. She felt surprised by it now, but the rage streamed up through her, obscuring fear and even her pain.

"I will not," she spat into his face.

Not a sound came from the other side of the wall, nor from the children's pallets, though she knew they listened. She could expect no help; the children were too frightened and the men considered her Havers' property.

Havers' small, piggy eyes widened in surprise. She doubted many people defied him. "You will," he vowed, "over and over again."

He began to drag her away from the door, but she reached out and seized the bar with desperate hands. With a grunt he slapped her once more, and her fingers bit into the cold iron as if it could grant her freedom. But the only freedom lay in—

Curlew!

She screamed his name in her mind, a cry born of need and longing. *Help me, my love.*

Havers grunted and raised one beefy arm to strike. Anwyn saw the blow coming and cocked her foot to fend him off. A desperate kick, it took him in the stomach and rocked him back so he let go of her.

She lifted the bar from the door. A power not her

own helped her, so it seemed weightless in her hands. She felt strength flood and steady her so she was ready when Havers bellowed and came for her again.

She swung the bar with both hands and met his lunge. *Not the chest, no*, said the voice now inside her, *or he will seize the bar with his hands*.

But Anwyn's first strike, clumsy and badly directed, took Havers in his left shoulder and—by all that was holy—knocked him down.

She swung again even as he fell—once, twice—and battered his naked flesh. Then, the bar still in her hands, she opened the door and fled into the rain.

The door on the other side of the hut opened and a head emerged—the elder of the two foresters, he was. Did he mean to stop her and send her back inside? She glanced over her shoulder. Havers would be coming, unless she had killed him, and she doubted she had. Hurt him, aye, maybe.

She returned her gaze to the forester's face. For an eternal, breathless moment, they stared at one another.

"Run," the man told her then.

She did, into the gathering autumn dark, shocked to see it was not yet really night. Havers had not wished to wait long for his cruel pleasure. But the rain and the early dusk lent their own cover in which she would gladly lose herself.

Where to run? Not home. Her Da might well send her back to Havers. What she wanted was away to Sherwood. As she had ascertained earlier, the foresters' huts lay outside the gates. Yet, disoriented by reaction and the rain, she could not begin to tell her way.

Come along with me, child, said the voice that had already sounded in her head, inside the hut.

She lifted her face like a startled hind. "Who are you? Where?"

Here.

A woman took form beside her, barely visible through the driving rain. Tall she was, with dark hair woven into a braid that flowed down her back. Eyebrows like wings marked a face at once severe and full of beautiful strength.

Anwyn gasped. From whence had she come?

Do not fear, child. Rain streaked the woman's face, though she heeded it not. *Would you not go to my grandson?*

"Your grandson?"

Curlew.

Another spear of surprise pierced Anwyn. This woman did not look old enough to be Curlew's grandmother. But she breathed in ready response, "Aye." Oh, aye, it made the one desire of her heart.

Then I will lead you to him. Fear not, for I assure you I will not get lost in Sherwood.

"I believe you," Anwyn said. And so she did.

Chapter Twenty-Nine

Curlew!

The word—his name—screamed in Curlew's mind and turned him around where he stood. He peered through the rain.

Anwyn's voice. He knew it to the core of his soul, remembered the sweetness of it twining through him when they lay together, claiming him. Had she come at last? His heart leaped impossibly, and he glanced at his aunt and uncle, who sat behind him.

"Did you hear that?"

He would far rather ask Heron, but Heron had gone off to his hut with Diera, ostensibly to speak. Curlew could only hope they were not in fact speaking.

Lark and Falcon exchanged glances, and probably words between their minds. Since Falcon's return they had refused to be parted, and—

Wait. Words between their minds.

He knew what this meant, then, and that Anwyn's call had sounded only for him. Emotions poured through him—gratitude, awe, and glad rejoicing. All his life he had longed for this, the miracle and intimacy of someone's voice in his mind, the deep belonging. And aye, if he could hear her, then truly she belonged to him and he to her forever—no end.

But where was she? How far? And why did he glean fear from her as well as longing? Aye, the longing he shared, by the Green Man's blood he did. Was she somewhere he might find her?

"Curlew, what is it?" Falcon asked, but Curlew barely heard.

Come, meet us. Another voice, one he felt he knew but could not at this moment identify, one of those that so frequently sighed like a wind through Sherwood.

"I must go," he tossed over his shoulder, and moved off even as Lark began to protest.

He stopped only to gather his bow and arrows, without which he seldom went anywhere, and to glance at the door of Heron's hut. Assaulted by the driving rain, it stood firmly shut and revealed no crack of light.

Come.

He abandoned Heron to his fate and followed the call.

Could he lose his way in Sherwood, even in the dark? Surely not now, for he tracked Anwyn's awareness as he might a beacon. Glimmers of light seemed to flash and dance in his mind. The rain crashed down with its own rhythm and music. Secret things moved along with him and memories—not just of him and Anwyn together—stirred in his mind, strange things full of grief and magic.

None of that held him. When he reached her now he meant to never let her go.

Nay, lord, for are the two of you not destined to be together? still another voice asked.

Someone strode beside him, a large man only dimly seen and mostly made of shadow. Like Curlew, he wore a bow and a quiver across his back, along with a great sheepskin cloak.

Curlew did not need to see him. He would know

that rumble anywhere. "Grandfather Sparrow."

Aye, lord, and honored as ever to walk at your side.

"'Tis I who should feel honored, Grandfather, not you. For, there is scarcely a more ordinary man in all England than I."

Sparrow laughed, a deep chuckle that seemed to rustle the trees. *Is that what you think? But are you not lord of all Sherwood?*

"Am I?" Curlew returned.

'Twas said of you, before your birth, that you would be the most important person ever born in Sherwood. Surely, by now, you know why.

Curlew shrugged, still not entirely comfortable with that implication. "It was said. Yet, Grandfather, I have not yet lived up to that prediction."

Well, humility is a fine thing. Sparrow grinned to himself. *And you were ever a humble man, my lord.*

"Why do you keep on calling me that?"

You are about to take the place that was always meant to be yours, in service to Sherwood. Surely that warrants some respect. Or is it truly Sherwood that stands in service to you?

What was the man on about? Curlew could but wonder. Man or spirit—for Curlew could not mistake this presence. Sparrow had been gone since before Curlew's birth. Madness, all of it.

Your grandmother and I have watched you all these years of your growing.

Aye, and seen little enough to inspire them, Curlew would be bound. He had done his duty, tried to prove kind to others, and waited somehow for his life to begin. As it had now, with the arrival of Anwyn.

This way. Sparrow turned him with a touch on the arm. The man felt real. Aye, and so, Heron said, had the Lady when he lay with her.

Awe struck him suddenly at the depth of Sherwood's magic. How he longed to lose himself in it.

Not yet, Sparrow told him. *There is work to be done. But aye, that reward awaits us always at the end.*

"And she? Anwyn? Does she wait also?"

She has been waiting for you a terrible, long time. Women and men, my lord, make two halves of the whole, and no one likes living half a life. I go now to meet my wife even as you go to meet yours. And Heron, bless him, also has business to finish. She will choose him, this time.

"She?"

Diera. She made her decision last time, and chose the leader, the headman. This time, out of love and justice, she has chosen the priest.

"I am not sure I understand."

Nay? Do you believe, my lord, in the eternal nature of life? That the essence of what we are—not the flesh but the spirit—cannot be destroyed?

Curlew wished the man would stop calling him *my lord*, yet he returned patiently, "I must, since I have encountered countless spirits here in Sherwood, and since I find myself conversing now with you."

It is as my wife told you in the forest. It should not be impossible to believe that having put on one suit of clothes for a time a spirit may lay it aside and don another.

"That is not impossible to believe," Curlew could but agree.

Sparrow told him comfortably, *So Diera and*

Heron have donned new clothes to finish old business.

"As have I," Curlew said with both wonder and trepidation. He and Anwyn—whose clothing had they laid down? Dared he believe the truth that whispered ever more strongly to him?

Even though he did not really speak to his grandfather, Sparrow answered. *Have faith in the depth of the magic, my lord. It exists for you.*

Curlew stopped walking and directed a hard look at his companion. Sparrow seemed to waver through the rain, a product of mere belief. Conviction suddenly flooded Curlew; he dared not doubt.

Your lady, my lord. Sparrow inclined his head. *She is there, just ahead. Go to her.*

The rain stilled abruptly. With its passing went the man who had paced by Curlew's side. He stood filled with wonder for one breathless moment while the trees dropped their moisture all around him, like an echo of the rain.

Believe.

The very trees, the air of Sherwood seemed to breathe the word. It pounded up through him from the ground, wrapped him round, and tingled in his awareness.

Ahead of him appeared a vision, aglow in the darkness. From head to toe she shed radiance toward which his heart leaped. He knew her, yet he did not.

Ah, by all the holiness of Sherwood, he knew her.

Her mind reached for him even before her feet carried her forward at a run. He moved toward her also, and years seemed to fly away with every step, so that time tumbled about them like the water dripping from the trees.

Like tears.

She thudded into his arms at last, the way an arrow finds its target. He took hold of her like memory, like relief, and his mind—or was it hers?—cried words of claiming.

My love, at last, at last. I have waited so long. Let us never be parted again.

Chapter Thirty

"My love, why must you go from me?" Marian asked plaintively. She never felt at rest without Robin at her side and especially now, so near her time. She laid her hands on the great swell of her belly as if to caress the babe within. *His* child, lad or lass—blessed child. But she wanted him with her for this birth.

She wanted him with her always.

Robin turned his head and looked at her with a smile in his eyes. By the Lady's light, but she lived for his smiles. They echoed through her being, and allowed her to breathe.

But he straightened and slung his quiver over his shoulder, where he settled it with an unconscious, practiced movement. His brown hair slapped his back, and the morning light flowed over him like a benediction.

"You know I must. We have but one chance to rescue those men before they are hauled away to Nottingham." His expression clouded. "I would leave no one in the Sheriff's hands."

"I do know that." And he, along with his men, had made so many rescues in the past. "Yet, love, I feel a great uneasiness and dread."

He came to her where she stood in the May dawn—Beltane light, that should have brought nothing but joy. He smoothed his hands down her arms with infinite gentleness, and the love inside her stirred, almost like pain.

"'Tis just that you are so near your time, Marian. It makes you anxious, but fear not—Lil will be here with you, and I will not be away long. I will be with you again this afternoon."

"See that you are. I am not prepared to birth this child alone."

"And I am not prepared to miss his or her arrival." He leaned forward and kissed her; the sweetness of it poured through her like light, like need answered.

She curled her fingers around his wrists and spoke into his mind, *You carry me with you always*.

And he responded, as ever, *Always, you carry my heart.*

****

"Geofrey! Lillith! Marian, come!"

The cry pierced the quiet afternoon the way a hail of arrows pierced armor. All day long, ever since Robin's departure, Marian had waited for it as she often waited for a storm to break over Sherwood, with an ache of distress. Now it came—the end of everything.

Suddenly a party of men burst into the village, carrying another between them. A litany broke out in Marian's mind.

No, no, no, no, no, no—

People streamed from everywhere, wailing and exclaiming. Lil was there, her black hair hanging loose down her back, and the headman, Geofrey, with his great air of calm authority.

Marian stumbled to her feet and strove to see through all the backs in her way. She wanted to see. She did not want to see. She counted heads: Will

205

Scarlet she saw—he turned and shot her a look, his face full of fear and agony. The front of his tunic matched his name. And John, the gentle giant, he cradled someone in his arms the way he might a child.

No, no, no, no, no, no—

She moved forward like someone caught in a dream, in a nightmare. They parted to let her through, and she floated up as if made of air.

"He lives." Who spoke the words? Lil, who knelt, her hands already stained red and trembling visibly. "But it is bad."

"Soldiers are after us." The warning tore from Scarlet's throat. "We cannot stay here."

"I do not think we dare move him."

"If we stay here—if they take him—he will die for sure."

The voices came and went in Marian's ears, pounded like her pulse. She stared down at the man sprawled on the ground. His eyes were closed, his face still, his body awash with blood. But she could feel him, feel him still.

Robin!

I am sorry, my love. I did not know. Or he would never have left her. She could not bear for him to leave her.

You must remain with me. Robin, come awake now!

"—must go into Sherwood. The magic there may well save him." Another voice—Alric, their holy man.

Aye, Marian thought, finding hope for the first time. Sherwood would not let Robin go from her, not when he had given so much. Sherwood would hold him, protect him.

"Aye, let us take him to Sherwood," she declared.

They gathered him up without further debate, the six of them together, his bearers crimson with his blood, and carried him to the magic. Marian walked holding his hand, so cold in hers, and the child inside her kicked wildly as if in protest.

"How did this happen?" Geofrey asked as they went.

"'Twas a trap," Scarlet gasped. "The prisoners we sought were not even there. But the clearing was surrounded by soldiers. They aimed straight for him."

John rumbled, "Two of our men, Seth and Michael, gave their lives so we could get Robin away."

"How many wounds?" Marian told herself she did not hear despair in Lil's voice.

"Six." John's voice faltered. "I counted six."

No, no, no, no, no, no—

"He is strong." Alric. "And he belongs to Sherwood. He is Lord of Sherwood."

Sherwood gives. And Sherwood takes.

"Put him down. Lay him down here. We are losing him."

Tenderly, Robin's bearers stretched him on the ground. Marian sank with him, his hand still caught in hers. She could no longer see his clothing for the blood. It burgeoned up from him the way a spring might bring forth water.

John's big hands, already stained red, came out and touched Robin's head.

Robin opened his eyes, deep blue and glowing. Marian knew her world lay there, everything she wanted, everything she was. No hardship could be too great if it brought her to him. He could not leave her.

She could not face such terror.

Robin, I cannot live without you. Do not ask it of me. Anything but that.

You must, love. You are strong.

I am only strong because of you. Tears fell from her eyes, unstoppable. She could feel him still, feel his spirit, yet his hand grew ever colder in hers.

I will always be here in Sherwood.

"Too many wounds," Lil murmured. "Too much blood."

Robin's eyes fluttered closed.

No! Marian screamed at him.

The others worked over him desperately. Lil's eyes met Marian's for a terrible moment; the healer shook her head.

Marian cried aloud, "Do not leave me, Robin—you cannot!"

His eyes opened, their light not yet dimmed. Surely her love, great as it was, could hold him even from death.

"Please." Her hot tears fell down on him one by one like rain. "You must stay with me. You must stay for your child."

So beautiful, you are so beautiful. He spoke only into her mind, his lips waxen and still. *I have loved you from the first moment I saw you. Stay strong. Stay strong for me, Marian.*

She gasped like a drowning woman. *I cannot. My love, my love, my love, you are all my strength. I need you to keep my heart beating.*

I do not go far. Watch for me. Listen for me. I do not leave you.

Inevitable as the setting sun, his eyes closed.

She wailed. Her pain rose up in a cry of maddened and uncomprehending protest.

"But I need you, Robin. I need your warmth. I need your touch. I need your light!"

You have them all.

The words sounded, strong and bright, in Anwyn's mind. She could feel Robin's arms around her, holding her so tight against him. She could feel his spirit wrapped around her, real and vital. Her cheek pressed to his chest, and there she could hear his heart.

His heart.

He stood before her, he lived, he breathed. Again.

Drops of water fell like tears from the trees that surrounded them. But there were no tears now, and no pain—only renewal, only relief, only promise.

Sherwood took. But oh, Sherwood gave.

They drew apart far enough to gaze into one another's eyes. The face Anwyn saw was not Robin's face but Curlew's. She did not mind that, for the same beautiful light shone at her, the same great love.

Joy flowed through her, touched every part of her, eased all the restlessness and answered all the pain.

"'Tis you," she breathed.

"Aye. I told you I would not go far."

"It seemed an insurmountable distance. It seemed an age." Regret arose, sudden and sickening. "But I failed you. I failed you and our daughter."

"Your love never failed."

He kissed her, and the last of the chains binding her heart fell away. She clung to him, knowing what she held in her hands—not just the man she loved, but a second chance. *One thing is certain*, she spoke into his mind, *I will never fail you again.*

Chapter Thirty-One

"No auburn hair," Curlew said lazily. "I do confess I loved your auburn hair."

"Do you complain, my lord?" Anwyn rolled on top of him, flesh against naked flesh, and everything in him came alive with desire. He felt rather than saw her smile, and the teasing note in her voice speared right through him.

"Do you hear any complaints?" he asked, and ran his fingers through her wheaten tresses, relishing the heady sense of possession.

Morning had come again to Sherwood, all last night's rain flown. A sky of clear autumn blue arched above them, and light dappled through the roof of flickering leaves. Curlew barely noticed. They had been so busy rediscovering and reclaiming one another he scarcely knew dawn had arrived.

"Was I more beautiful then?" she asked, and nipped at his lower lip.

"You could not be more beautiful than you are now," he told her honestly.

"That is a proper answer, my lord, and will earn you more kisses." She pressed her mouth to his and poured herself into him. Pure spirit—so she was, and yet he held her in his arms, tasted her, burned for her like fire: true magic.

Still shaken by the revelation that had enfolded

them the instant they touched in the forest yestere'en, he wondered how he could ever have failed to guess. How could he not know her despite the absence of auburn hair and amber eyes?

A sudden thought touched him and he spoke it into her mind, his lips still otherwise engaged. *But are you disappointed in me now? I am so ordinary, far too ordinary to be* him.

Disappointed? She stopped kissing him and her eyes flashed green fire. *Did I seem disappointed last night when I worshipped each and every part of you with my lips?*

By the gods, she had not.

Her eyes danced. *Must I do it all over again?*

I will not say no. Though, faith, I think I should rather take my turn and adore you thus, my lady, this time. His hand stole to her breast. Last night, in the dark, it had been as if he were Robin and held Marian once more, but now, in the light, he could see her, and wanted to discover her all over again.

He touched her cheek and narrowed his eyes; his joy dimmed abruptly. "You say Havers did this to you, gave you these bruises? Your—husband?" He spat the word. "I will kill him for it."

"You will not go near him." Fear flooded her eyes. "I do not wish you to endanger yourself, not for any reason."

"Anwyn, it is the nature of my life to endanger myself."

"Perhaps that has been so, but I forbid it from this moment on. Do you think I have found you only to risk losing you once more?"

Gently he skimmed his fingers over her battered

face and brushed her lips. "I think if we are to learn one lesson, it is that we cannot possibly lose one another."

Wildly, she shook her head. "You cannot tell me that, for you did not live it. You did not have to try and go on alone."

"Back then, your grief would not let you feel me near you still. Surely it would be different next time."

"There will be no next time. Do you hear me, Curlew Champion? I now understand the need that burned inside me, I understand the cause of all my restlessness and for what I sought—you, always you."

Tears filled her eyes. She kissed him through them, and her fear assaulted him, all mingled with her joy. He longed to protect her from such hurt, to take the fear from her, but knew it could not be. For he had taken too much upon himself last time, and it had cost them dear.

Listen to me. He released her lips with regret. *We are being given a second chance. It is the first triad come over again. Then, 'twas me and you—the Lord and his Lady—and the spirit of Sherwood. This time it is you, me, and Heron, who is so closely bonded with the forest he is virtually one with it.* He frowned in thought. *I think Heron was a holy man before. And Diera a healer.*

Lil and Alric. Anwyn supplied their names. *They, too, are finishing and balancing something.* Her eyes held his. *As must I. You say, love, that "we" are being given a second chance to make things right but 'tis I who needs this chance. I must be stronger; I must find the courage I need to not fail.*

And that might well mean she would have to face the same challenges, he thought in trepidation, and this time seek to overcome them. His heart quailed within him. Would he be forced to leave her again, just when he had found her? Aye, he knew, and believed full well, death was naught but a change of form. Yet this time he wanted to have many years with her; he wanted ease and laughter.

"I am a child no longer," she declared aloud. "And with my childhood I put away my great selfishness. I live only for you now, Curlew."

"Do not say that." She had lived for him before, and her spirit had died for him.

"Can I help it?" She caught his face between her hands and moved atop him, parted her thighs and cradled him.

Somehow he resisted the lure of desire. "It must be otherwise, love. Sherwood gives—"

"And takes." She finished it for him. "And I go where sent, but I breathe only for you. One prayer, Curlew—only let me die first, this time."

No. He wrapped her tighter in his arms.

"Ah, you see how it feels?" Her words, loving rather than cruel, vibrated with regret. "See what the mere thought of it does to you?"

He saw. He closed his eyes and held to her, stunned by the sheer risk of loving someone so much.

He said, as if foreknowledge had been given to him, "He will come looking for you—Havers, your husband."

"Perhaps not. He does not truly care about me, save for how I might elevate his position with my father. Da thinks to set him up as a kind of overseer for Sherwood."

Curlew's eyes widened. "What is that you say?"

"Some sort of caretaker, a liaison between the

Crown and the people of the forest. 'Tis a scheme Da and Lord Simon created together."

"Havers would not last a fortnight," Curlew said with feeling.

"Eh?"

"If someone did not put an arrow in his back the first time he set foot here, the forest itself would settle him."

"Truly? How?"

He ran his hands through her hair again, just for the sheer pleasure of it. "Lead him astray, beguile his senses, surround him with spirits, make it so he is never seen again. There are men in plenty who enter Sherwood with evil in their hearts, never to return."

"I see." Her eyes narrowed. "Then it seems we need not worry about him. I will be a widow soon."

"Aye, but much harm may be done before he comes into Sherwood alone. Men may be accused and arrested, more villages burned. So it was in my parents' time. We have had many years of what I see, looking back, as relative peace. Now it all changes."

"Because I have come?" Her lashes lowered over glowing eyes and her voice purred at him, "Would you sooner I had not?"

"Never think it." He drew her still closer. "You were sent to save me. I only hope," he said seriously, "I can be worthy of this great gift."

"Do not doubt that," she told him. "Do not ever doubt again. And smile for me. I have always lived for your smile."

Joy speared through him, defeating all the uncertainty. "Any other orders, my lady?"

"Oh, aye, I have a whole host of them."

She began to move over him, wanton and rejoicing; her body called to his, wooed and raised it. Desire ignited, at least as strong as the love he felt, and flowed through him in an unstoppable wave.

She reared up, her glorious hair her only covering. With pleasure sharp as pain he watched her body flex, all strength and softness, felt her take him inside and rock him until they, the forest, and the morning became ever one.

A woman who knew what she wanted, who had always known; thank the Green God it was still him.

When he filled her, she fused her mouth to his and spoke into his mind, *'Twould be a shame, my lord, not to do justice to this great gift we have been given. Aye, and you have all the strength of the forest itself. Let us see how many times you can love me.*

Chapter Thirty-Two

"Two villages have already burned. And Asslicker has sent out a decree: Montfort's daughter is to be returned or greater pain will follow."

Falcon Scarlet spoke heavily, yet his gaze, on Anwyn's face, remained kind. Never once, since Anwyn and Curlew had come hand in hand out of the forest, had he suggested she should return to Nottingham.

She wondered what Lark thought. If anyone made the suggestion, surely it would be she. Yet Lark's lips remained pressed together in silence, even though her gaze looked mutinous.

Neither Lark nor Falcon knew the truth about her or about Curlew. They had debated long over whether to tell Curlew's aunt and uncle. In the end, Curlew had balked at it.

"How can I stand up before them and declare myself a legend? I have not the self-conceit."

"Yet, love, that is what—who—you are."

"Aye, but such grand ideas have been built of him since his death. I cannot begin to live up to all that."

Heron did know the truth. They had needed to tell Heron, and Anwyn suspected Heron had told Diera, for the two of them were now nearly inseparable. Ancient circles, as she well knew, reached round to meet with themselves again.

Even now, she and Curlew stood before Falcon and Lark with their fingers tangled. She needed that contact whenever possible; even though their minds were always linked, she wanted never to let go of him. Their desire for one another might be prodigious, but the need overshadowed all.

And that terrified her, whenever she let herself think on it.

Now she lifted her eyes to meet Falcon's. "Havers cannot be certain I am in Sherwood."

"Your *husband,* you mean." Lark could not resist getting a barb in.

Curlew leaped immediately to Anwyn's defense. "'Tis not her fault she was forced to wed with him. And you see how he used her."

Aye, they had all seen her bruises when Curlew brought her out of the forest.

Lark shrugged and grimaced.

"What would you do," Curlew challenged her, "if you were treated so?"

Lark answered swiftly, "I would wait until the next time he proved vulnerable and stab him to the heart, make well certain he was dead. I am sure I would not run straight to the person I loved, streaming danger and violence behind me."

Falcon turned to her, touched her cheek and smiled tenderly. "Liar. You would always come straight to me."

They exchanged a look Anwyn now understood in full. Sherwood gave.

Lark visibly softened. "Aye, love. Through fire if need be."

Curlew's fingers clenched Anwyn's. He had

confided to her, whispering the words into her ears, about how often he had yearned for just such a relationship, as for something remembered.

"That is because you did remember, deep inside," she had told him. Now a current flowed ever between them. Her one fear remained that it should once more be severed.

She caught her breath and spoke, not to Lark but to Falcon. "Do you mean to send me back?"

"I have no authority to send you back."

She forced herself to say, "In the eyes of the church and the crown, Havers is my husband."

"In the eyes of Sherwood, however, *he* is." Falcon nodded at Curlew. "Lass, I would not send you if I could."

"Despite the risk in letting me stay?"

Falcon gave her a smile warm as sunshine. "Despite it. Are you not our third guardian and destined to take your place in the next circle?"

"The god only knows why," Lark muttered.

Anwyn did look at Lark then. "And you? Would you send me back?"

Lark made an impatient gesture toward Falcon. "It is as he says. With my sister gone, our circle weakens. You must be ready to stand strong."

"I think," Falcon said slowly, "the two of you should go back into Sherwood. 'Tis not safe for you here. Only let this Havers come looking; he will not find what he seeks."

"But will he not do much damage in the searching?" Anwyn persisted.

"He will not find us so easy to defeat, lass." Falcon asked, "You say you can you use a bow?"

"I can." She lifted her head. "My Da taught me, and well, but 'twas with the shorter Welsh bow."

"Love," Falcon addressed Lark without looking at her, "give her the lend of one of yours. It should be about the right draw for her, and Curlew can guide her in the use of a longbow." He told Anwyn gently, "We all need to be able to fight."

Aye. And Anwyn meant never to be caught helpless again.

****

"I bring ill tidings. Oakham lies burned, and many are dead. My parents have gone."

Heron stood before Curlew and Anwyn and delivered the news starkly, with little emotion audible in his voice but pain rampant in his eyes. He wore a hood well up over his tawny mane and not one but three bows on his shoulder. Diera stood at his side, straight and tall, with a bundle tied to her back and another clutched in her arms.

"Gone?" Curlew repeated, centering on the heart of it. "Not dead?"

Heron shifted his shoulders uneasily. "Who can say? If they are dead, they left no bodies behind. And I can still sense them." He smiled bleakly. "But then, I might well be able to do so even were they dead."

"Aye." Anwyn felt Curlew's thoughts leap and sensed his dismay. "Yet they would not abandon their people, especially in time of such need."

"Their power had nearly waned. 'Tis time for the three of us to accept our places in full—now, while the danger is bright. 'Tis why I am here." He glanced at Diera and corrected himself, "Why we are here."

"Wherever he goes, I now go," Diera stated.

Anwyn reached out and touched the other woman's arm. "Most welcome. Master Heron, how did you find us?"

A glimmer of a smile touched his eyes. "I followed your thoughts. Do not look so distressed, Lady—I can catch but an echo, not enough to tell what love words you may speak to him."

Thank the green god.

"You sparkle," Heron added simply, "the two of you together do. There is power."

Curlew nodded. Anwyn knew how he struggled yet to come to terms with who—and what—he was, could not be sure he had completely accepted the wonder and peril of it. Aye, a humble man to his heart, as Robin had ever been humble—just a serf's son, so he had always said of himself, who could shoot an arrow very well.

But one who had inspired hope and devotion, and love that burned yet. All that lay inside her Curlew. And she would fight to the death to defend him. That meant she must accept her place in full, this time, stand strong, and live up to all it took to be at his side.

She looked Heron in the eye. "What needs to be done? What can I offer?"

"You, Curlew, and I need to strengthen our bonds and enforce the circle as did my parents and Curlew's mother before us. They had an advantage: my mother and his are twin sisters and the three of them knew each other from birth."

"Like you and Curlew," she supplied.

Heron inclined his head.

"I," Anwyn stated, "am the outsider."

"Not a bit of it." Heron glanced at the woman beside him. "I hope you do not mind, but I have confided in Diera about who you are. I can hold no secrets from her, even that."

Shame and regret struck Anwyn deep. She looked to Diera and said, "Then you know how I failed him and our daughter—and Sherwood—last time."

Compassion kindled in Diera's dark eyes and she touched Anwyn's shoulder. "I understand full well what it is to love, and your loss was a heavy one."

"Still"—again Anwyn jerked her head up—"I should have found the strength to carry on. I assure you both I will never be so weak again." She hoped. Could she be sure she could keep from going mad with grief if she lost Curlew? She prayed she need not find out.

"We will be needed back in Oakham," Curlew said.

"Aye, but I thought we should take some time to grow our power first. Three days. Then we will return." Heron added, "By then we must be ready to face anything."

"Tell me what happened in the village," Curlew bade Heron.

Heron's face closed. "That brute, Havers, came with a troop of soldiers, searching, so he said, for his bride, who had either run off or been snatched for ransom, even as she had once before. He bore ugly wounds." Heron's eyes moved to Anwyn. "And held himself as if he hurt, but he was there."

"Was my father not with him?" Anwyn asked, and Heron shook his head.

"He may have been busy searching elsewhere, I cannot tell. Havers spoke to my parents—or, rather, berated them. Mother answered him back. You know, Lew, how she is. She asked what made him think his wife was in Oakham, or in Sherwood. He answered they had searched all Nottingham and, besides, the gates had been closed and guarded when she disappeared. She had not been seen there. Havers became abusive; Ma did not take it well and fired on him.

Anwyn gasped, even as hope stirred in her heart. "A death wound?" With Havers dead, she would be free.

But Heron shook his head. "Ma's shot took him in the shoulder yet hampered him barely at all. And then pitched battle broke out between the soldiers and our folk. Havers called for Ma's arrest and Pa jumped to defend her. Somehow, in all the furor, flame was put to thatch."

He went on, "I, myself, began to fire from cover. 'Twas enough to let my parents and the others scatter and move to safety."

Diera spoke, her voice trembling. "He should not even draw a bow yet, with his wound scarcely healed. And now he will not let me look at it and see the damage."

"No time for that." Heron gestured dismissively. "Most of the villagers gathered what they could ahead of the flames and fled to the forest. I assumed 'twas what Ma and Pa had done. The last I saw of them, she still had her bow in her hands and he attempted to coax her away."

Curlew said, "They may yet be somewhere in Sherwood."

Heron gave a rueful smile. "Oh, I do not doubt they are somewhere in Sherwood! But I doubt they will return."

He reached out his hands, one to Curlew and one to Anwyn. His fingers felt warm when Anwyn accepted them into hers; her other hand lay already fast in Curlew's so they made a circle.

Complete.

The power stirred and rose to travel among the three of them. It glinted with its own radiance and flared like sudden lightning.

Let the old circle form once again. Curlew spoke in both their minds. *Unbreakable, and unbroken.*

Chapter Thirty-Three

"This is my fault, all of it," Anwyn mourned. "The fires at Oakham, your aunt and uncle's disappearance—I have brought trouble down on you once more."

She stirred in the dark, and a tiny shower of sparks erupted around her, bursting like small, reddish stars. So it had been since the three of them forged their bond to completeness at Heron's bidding. Curlew's mind struggled to accept all that had come: too much and far too quickly. Yet the miracle of it began to whisper inside him, even as the presence of the woman in his arms spoke to his heart.

Rightness and staggering completeness: these things he felt for her and for Heron. It was as if the love he had felt his whole life long for Sherwood had been caught in the circle with them, all simmering power.

Yet he felt Anwyn's fear just as clearly, could almost taste it, just as he had felt Heron's weariness and pain when he and Diera arrived. Anwyn sought her way in this new circle, aye, even as Curlew sought his certainty. Still, he knew she feared she would fail him somehow.

"Not your fault," he breathed, and ran his hands through her hair. A new shower of light shed from his skin in turn—deep green this was, like forest shadows.

"But I am Havers' true reason for coming to Sherwood. None of it would have happened, were I not here."

"Were you not here, we would have no circle and no way to defend Sherwood."

He felt the catch in her breath as she contemplated that. They lay naked and twined together with the singing night all around them. He had already loved her once, each movement, each caress summoning memories of what once had been, bright images in his mind: a lively, defiant girl with auburn hair and his aunt Lark's golden eyes, pledges and loving, a marriage in the greenwood, a smile that delighted his heart, and tears, tears, tears.

Why should he be brought to recall this now? Heron had said those who returned were not given to remember, because that way did madness lie. Yet Curlew could barely touch her without the past flooding upon him. Pieces of who she had been, and he also.

It felt like putting on a tunic belonging to someone else, or removing his tunic to find another beneath— that of Robin Hood. Was he worthy of wearing that heavy mantle?

Could he do otherwise?

"I do not wish to cause you any sorrow, any pain," she whispered.

Aye, and he feared hurting her also. He never wanted to make her weep again. Now the hope and belief of so many rested upon him. Somehow, together, they must find a way to overcome the fear.

Slowly, he said, "You know, I heard about him all my life—Robin Hood. He seemed like one of those stars up there in the sky that never burn out, bright and impossibly far away. I am but an ordinary man. How do I reconcile that?"

"Curlew Champion, you are anything but ordinary."

"To you, perhaps. From whence did Robin get his strength? His certainty?"

She moved against him again and wriggled more surely into his arms. "Perhaps he was not as certain as legend has made him. Perhaps he feared and doubted also, but he strode on through the doubt. I believe, my love, your strength comes from those around you—from Heron and your family and the folk you will now lead once again. From Sherwood itself, also, which you carry ever with you."

He had always known he would make any sacrifice for Sherwood, just as he had always believed every leaf and twig here belonged to him, in defiance of the King's laws. Would he give his life over again?

Aye, without hesitation.

Would he give the life of this woman in his arms?

A harder question. He saw, then, the terror she faced. He hoped that this time he would not have to face it in his turn.

She must be able to feel his emotions rise up, even as he felt her fear and doubt. So it was, to be so surely linked in spirit. And that, too, he would lose if he lost her, far worse than losing an arm or a leg.

She murmured, her breath brushing across his lips, "Can you forgive me?"

He cradled her with his hands. "What is to forgive? That you loved too well? Without you, love, none of the rest of it would have followed. Who would have stood up, so fierce, to take the places of Robin and Marian, if not pushed to it by your grief?" *My Mari-anwyn*, he added silently, tenderly, all his remembering in the word.

She trembled at the caress of his voice in her mind. "Back then, Curlew, you inspired love and loyalty, you called people to follow you. They follow you yet. Let me be the first to stand up now and vow to follow you bravely and without wavering, whatever may come."

He saw it then, the truth of why Sherwood had given them to remember—so they would be prepared to take the places for which they had been shaped in the past and were now reborn.

"Aye," he said gravely. "We will wear these cloaks however heavy. But first, Marianwyn, first I will love you and so try to keep the past at bay."

****

"Set the target farther off. I would try and see can I hit it still."

Curlew slanted a look at the woman who stood bathed head to toe in afternoon light, assessed her and almost unconsciously measured the changes. His Marianwyn no longer seemed the wayward lass she had been only three short days ago.

Indeed, he wondered fleetingly if her father would recognize her now. A new determination and certainty possessed her. She had found what she had sought so long.

In him.

Without protest he moved the target, a small scrap of fabric, to a tree farther from where she stood. Since early morning she had worked with Lark's bow, trying to accustom herself to its weight and length. Now Heron and Diera sat together and watched with interest.

"You shoot very well," Diera told her.

Anwyn notched yet another arrow and sighted the

target. "My father taught me, and he is very good, indeed. Plus, my mother's people were all archers." She narrowed green eyes and shot; the arrow sang through the air.

Could she see the faint shimmer of magic that accompanied it? Could Heron? Curlew gave Heron a look of inquiry and saw only amusement in his eyes. "A fine shot, that," Heron said.

Anwyn lifted her chin. "Not good enough. I want it to come to me naturally as breathing."

"When the time comes—if it comes—so it will," Heron assured her.

Anwyn exchanged a look with him, and for the first time Curlew wondered about the connection between them. He, Curlew, had bonded with her, aye, and he had been always bonded with Heron. But he sensed now an alliance between these two.

"Not good enough," she said again. "When we go back I must be ready."

"As must we all," Heron returned, and Curlew felt his frustration. Heron did not like being hampered by his wound. His customary serenity had been ruffled by his enforced immobility. Yet Diera sat beside him, a living assurance he would not overstep himself. Curlew wondered, also, about the relationship the two of them shared. Did it approach what his parents had known?

"You shoot now, Curlew," Anwyn interrupted his thoughts. "Show me how 'tis done."

He took up his bow without conscious thought, notched an arrow and sighted. Since first able to hold the small bow Aunt Lark had fashioned for him, he had done this, almost always without effort.

He heard Lark's voice again, in his ear. *Aye, lad,*

you have a keen eye. Not much I need to teach you, is there? The ability just comes to you.

Aye, the ability had always come to him. But now as he raised the bow and sighted, he felt power come as well, flowing like a river, sparking and leaping the way a fire or a stag would, burgeoning from the very soil of Sherwood to fill and uplift him. Knowing sighted for him and certainty drew the bow. The shot, when it came, arced in a trail of light and clove Anwyn's last arrow clean.

"Ah," Heron breathed.

And Anwyn sighed, "That is what I want. That is how I need to be able to shoot."

****

"I would have us say a prayer together before we return to Oakham," Heron said gravely. Night had settled over Sherwood like a cloak of stars. The air, cold enough to show their breath, danced all around them where they stood beside a small fire. In the morning they would walk out of the forest to face whatever awaited them.

Aye, Curlew thought, best to carry Sherwood with them as surely as they could. For he felt a great wind coming—change, hard and fast. Looking into Heron's eyes now, he saw his cousin felt that as well.

And Anwyn? Curlew turned his gaze on her and caught his breath. She had, indeed, become a woman of will and intent. Each time he loved her she strengthened in his arms. And he had loved her repeatedly.

Just thinking on that had his body quickening with longing. Even when he did not touch her, she whispered inside him.

"Are you willing?" Heron asked.

Curlew nodded.

Anwyn lifted her head in that new way she had and said, "I will do whatever is needed, unsparing."

Heron wordlessly held out a hand to each of them. Anwyn slid her fingers into Curlew's and a shower of sparks erupted all round.

The power rose.

It grew from the knowing in Heron's heart and the determination in Curlew's own; it arose from the element of sacrifice he now felt within Anwyn. All these emotions, he saw, came of love.

The magic of Sherwood consisted of pure love.

Love of place, of past, of identity, and one another, of those who were and would be again.

He knew then, as the power rose to fill him, what it meant to lead, and to battle unstintingly. He understood who would win, in the end.

Those who gave the most love.

For those loved could never be lost; they remained eternally here in this place equally loved. The ties of the guardianship itself were forged of emotion. And he, who had never believed he could lead, now knew how he should—with compassion and kindness, with strength that inspired, and with understanding, all woven out of love.

He could have laughed aloud with it, were he any less awed. For in this instant he saw with new eyes that which had set the very guardianship in motion and lay behind each sacrifice. He saw, again, himself lying in the greenwood, bleeding his life away, and Marian's beautiful face above him, convulsed with fear.

Weeping tears of love.

Gratitude swamped him, because she had come to

him again.

It had all come again.

When he stood filled with so much light he thought he must burst, when it ran in a current from one to the next of them and came round again, when the green light hummed through their blood, Heron lifted his head.

"'Tis well," he said. "Now let us go and claim the future for Sherwood."

Chapter Thirty-Four

"We have taken a prisoner, a right plum one. Now will old Asslicker sit up and take notice!"

The man who spoke, named Marcus, wore a proud look and carried a hard gleam in his eye. A rough fellow and longtime resident of Oakham, his home had recently been burned to the ground. Now he, along with a band of other village men, met Curlew's party on their way back from Sherwood and imparted the news even while his companions, fully six in number, muttered dangerously.

Curlew felt Heron's flash of alarm, even though his cousin's expression did not change. Since they had strengthened their circle, he could sense his fellow guardians' emotions all too easily. Heron burned steadily, but Anwyn balanced like a stone upon a knife's blade.

One of Marcus's fellows, a man called Herald, spoke. "None but Asslicker's new head forester, it is."

Anwyn stiffened. *My father.* Her voice made but a ripple in Curlew's mind, yet sounded clear. So this was how it felt to speak without uttering a word.

He reached out and touched her arm, willing caution. "How did this come to be?" he asked the men.

Yet another, named Alfred, spoke up. Usually a quiet, steady man, he now had a hard set to his jaw, and a hoe resting on his shoulder. "We decided to fight back, that is all, Curlew. Another village burned last night, torched by that devil, Havers, and his men. Two children died. We will stand for no more of it. When Montfort came looking for his daughter with the Sheriff's men at his back, we gave them battle instead of obedience." He jiggled his hoe purposefully.

"Aye." Marcus took it up. "We will no longer roll over for those Norman bastards. Are we not Englishmen true born?"

The longing for justice rang in his voice. Indeed, Curlew thought, and it was an idea his grandmother, Wren, had loosed long ago when she went to Nottingham Castle and demanded of King John the same justice for all his subjects that he granted the elite few. All Englishmen, she had asserted, should claim equal sovereignty. Since that day the notion had never quite gone back into the sack of Norman oppression.

Nor, he acknowledged, should it. It was time, and past time, those born of this soil claimed ownership of their lives in this blessed land.

That did not mean bands of angry men, like these, could be allowed to roam far and wide, claiming their own vengeance.

He stepped forward. "Where is the prisoner now?"

Marcus replied, still aggressively, "A new camp has formed just north from the ruins of Oakham. He is there."

"Injured?" Anwyn asked.

"Injured, aye, but alive." Marcus slid a look over Heron. "Is your father going to return?"

"I do not know. But we—the three of us you see here—have formed a new triad and now hold the magic of Sherwood among us."

"Her?" Still another man spoke. "But she is one of them."

"As was my father," Curlew asserted. He knew Anwyn to be of Welsh and Saxon blood, less Norman than he, but knew also what these men meant. To their knowledge, she had come from Nottingham and brought the enemy in her wake. They must somehow be persuaded to acknowledge that spirit mattered far more than mere flesh. "Would you question the loyalty of Gareth Champion?"

"Peace, Curlew. Gareth was a fine man and a good friend to all of us." Alfred spoke heavily. "But we deal not with the past. For too long have we lived under the heels of those who call themselves our betters. What right have they to burn our homes, to punish us for feeding our families on the bounty of this place where we were born?"

"If they strike at us," Marcus avowed, "we strike back. Six of the Sheriff's men dead, and a prisoner who will surely make Asslicker heed us."

He switched his gaze to Heron. "With your pa gone, are you the new headman?"

Heron shook his head. "I am no leader, but a holy man. Curlew is headman now."

They all turned their gazes to Curlew where he stood, and measured him openly. He met their stares and returned them with the new certainty he had acquired. He would lead, aye, but in a way not seen in four generations.

"Can you accept me? Will you?" he challenged softly.

One by one they nodded.

"There is justice in you, Curlew," Marcus grunted.

His eyes swiveled to Anwyn. "But I still do not understand. How comes she to be one of the chosen three?"

"She belongs to us, to me, and comes granted my wife by Sherwood itself. Will you question Sherwood's choice?"

Before the men could answer, Anwyn came alight in response to those words. Straight and tall she stood with Lark's bow on her shoulder and looked at the men. "I fight with him, and thus with you, to the death if need be. But that man you hold prisoner is my father."

"Best take us to him," Curlew bade.

****

"Oh, Da," Anwyn mourned, and nearly choked on her emotion. Battered and beaten, with bruises on his face and a livid cut across the top of his head, Mason Montfort crouched with his hands bound behind him, tied to a tree amidst the confusion of the new encampment. The whole place wore an air of grim defiance and pain. Everyone within sight watched as Anwyn dropped to her knees at her father's side.

Despite his obvious discomfort, Mason Montfort lifted his eyes to her face in gladness. "Daughter! You are not harmed? How come you here among these outlaws?" Without giving her a chance to reply he looked at Curlew who stood at her back. "You I know—the trickster met in the forest the day we arrived."

Curlew made no answer. Anwyn knew he meant to leave this to her, then. She stole a look at him over her shoulder where he stood, firm and sure, with the brown hair hanging on his shoulders like a mane and his eyes bright as two polished shields. Was she the only one who perceived the faint glow of power around him, felt how something inside him had bloomed and steadied? Her spirit rose inside her at what she saw, for she knew him for who he was—the man who ruled her heart, her mind, and thus her destiny. Thank the good god of this place she could trust him with all she was and rely upon his innate kindness.

She turned back to her father and said, "He is my husband."

"Nay." Distress invaded her Da's eyes, and he shook his head. How many times had she brought such trouble to him? "You are wife to Roderick Havers. In the eyes of the Church—"

Slowly and clearly, Anwyn returned, "I am not." She seized her father's shoulders. "Da, I care little for the Church; by all that is holy and sacred to me, I am wife to Curlew Champion and belong to him body and spirit."

Her father flinched. He directed a scathing look at Curlew, who yet stood silent. "What has he done to you? What, to turn your mind this way? Has he maltreated you, threatened—"

"No, Da, not he. These bruises you see upon me came from Havers, the man you bade me wed. My mind has been always turned in this direction. Do you not remember my restlessness, my refusal to settle? I longed ever for what I could not name. Rejoice for me, Da, for now I can name it."

Her father gazed deep into her eyes and seemed to weigh what he saw there. Refusal warred with acknowledgement in his face.

"So am I to surrender you to this? Living the life of an outlaw in the greenwood, enemy to all I am?"

Anwyn told him, "You can never be enemy to me. Da, I know I have tried you sorely and tested any affection you once held for me." Tears blurred his face before her eyes. "But tell me there is yet some love left between us."

Her father's expression softened slightly. "Of course there is, Daughter. Do you think I do not blame myself for your waywardness? I was not strong enough after your mother died, nor stern enough in her absence. I did not guide you well. Lord Simon convinced me of that and convinced me also 'tis like sending a son away to be fostered at arms—others can often provide the needed discipline. That is why I thought Roderick might succeed where I failed."

"With cruelty? By employing the strap?"

"Only look where my kindness led you!" He shot another resentful look at Curlew.

Softly Anwyn said, "Nay, look where my destiny has led me. Da, I was born to stand at his side. There is no turning from it now."

Grief, objection, and a measure of acceptance filled Montfort's eyes. "And what of Roderick? Whatever you say, he believes himself your husband. He scours the forest for you, and he has the law on his side."

Curlew spoke for the first time. "He shall have to accept that she is lost to him. She has a far greater place to fill here, in Sherwood."

"How can this be?"

"Da, all the things you gave me in my youth were meant to be mine: the love of the land, the ability to read the seasons and the weather, the knowledge of how to shoot a bow." Her voice became husky. "More, the ability to love so deeply it endures anything."

Mason Montfort bowed his head. "You carry a new wisdom, Daughter. If this is truly your choice, I will grant you leave of it. But this places us on opposite sides of a bitter conflict. Those men who seized me speak of ransoming me to Lord Simon in return for Saxon prisoners who have committed crimes against their King. They speak also of demanding rights and a measure of sovereignty for Sherwood."

Gravely, Curlew replied, "'Tis the only way this can end, Master Montfort. The seizures have to stop, and the butchery and the burned villages. Would you not stand against men who burned down your home?"

Montfort looked at him. "There has been much provocation, Master Outlaw—years of it, by Lord Simon's accounting. You and your kind have grown far too bold."

"My kind?" Curlew repeated bitterly. "And what kind is that? A peasant, beneath notice? I think not, for we are of this land, and the land grants its own leave. Who better to hold sovereignty over a place than those born of it? My ancestors' blood has soaked this earth." Aye, Anwyn thought, and his own. "'Tis I will stand in defense of it now."

"Then you will fight and fail," Montfort said almost regretfully.

"But I will fight, nevertheless, for some things are greater than fear."

Montfort's gaze returned to Anwyn's face. "You have chosen a man, I will give you that. And I would do what I could to help you. But lass, for the life of me I cannot see a good end to this."

"Help us find one," she beseeched impulsively. "Let us work together for the sake of all that lies between us, and help me as you have so often in the past."

"I would, but what can I do?" He shook his head. Ruefully, he wiggled his wrists, bound behind him. "Quite truly, Daughter, my hands are tied."

Chapter Thirty-Five

"We are at war now, and no doubt about it," Curlew said heavily. "Two more villages burned and half a score men dead. Things have not been so dire since my grandmother's time."

"Aye?" Anwyn returned. "And what would your grandmother have done in our place?"

Curlew turned his head to look at her. Dawn had again come to Sherwood, bringing radiance that lit both the dying leaves and his lady's hair with fire. A chill morning it was, with the mist not yet burned from the ground, but she wore only that glorious curtain of wheaten silk, and despite their dire circumstances his heart rose. Was there any sorrow from which his Marianwyn could not lift him?

"Grandmother Wren?" He smiled despite himself. "She would have gone storming into Nottingham and demanded justice."

Anwyn tipped her head and a spark of mischief entered her green eyes. Softly, she came to him, naked as she stood, and pressed herself close into his arms. Thank the green god, he thought, they had chosen a place away on their own to spend the night. For his lady, as he well knew, possessed little restraint around him and might well behave so even before prying eyes.

The very thought enflamed him. Only half clad, he felt himself swell against his just-donned leggings. Ah, and had he not loved her most the night long? It seemed he could not get enough. Aye, Sherwood gave.

He growled at her in combined arousal and mock-anger, "This is no time for your nonsense. Have I not just said we are at war?"

"Forgive me, my lord." Her eyes gleamed. "But you know me for a wicked woman. Only give me leave to make it up to you."

She slid down his body slowly, making a tantalizing friction, until she came to rest on her knees, her fingers already at the laces of his leggings.

The breath snagged in his throat, half laugh, half wonder. Nearly a week had they lived together now, and she never ceased to amaze or delight him. Her love was wondrous strong, and he knew—just as he knew all that lay in her heart—she sought endlessly to compensate for all the years they had missed.

How could he ever hope to live without her now?

He caught her face between his palms and tilted it up so her gaze met his, even though he ached to feel her mouth upon him.

Her eyes danced, unrepentant. "I can hear your thoughts, my lord. I know exactly what you want." She added, with a small smile curving her lips, "And 'twill be my deepest pleasure to provide it you."

Marianwyn. Mine. He spoke the words into her mind with gladness and claiming. *Do you know how I love you?*

And she replied, her words enflaming him more surely than her touch, *No more truly than I love you.*

Satisfaction thrummed through him that had little to do with the flesh. All his life had he wished for such a connection and now it came, sweeter than imagined.

241

For she was need and gratification, question and answer wrapped up together. She completed him even as she brought him to the knife's edge of terror, for fear of losing what he had found.

Never leave me, he beseeched.

Light flared in her eyes, magical as Sherwood's heart. *As if I could. 'Tis as you have promised: we will remain together, here, even should one of us—*

She dared not complete that thought, even in her mind.

Swiftly he drew her up from her knees and fast into his arms, where he wrapped her tight. He wished he could pull her inside him, into the place where his need for her lay, keep her there for all time. Aye, Sherwood assured their love would never die. Of their flesh, it gave no such assurances.

She felt what he felt, and as the regret and acknowledgement flickered through him, she trembled.

It shall be me this time, my love.

Eh? He stiffened.

You say we are at war, and I know full well the costs war may bring. If one of us must fall, it will be me. Let it be me!

Nay. Somehow he drew her still nearer. *Who says one of us must fall?*

Her gaze held his. *Have I not come back to make up for my past failures?*

Nay, he said again, *not by dying for me. Marianwyn, if you would make up for aught—and I do not say you must—let it be by standing strong and taking your place in Sherwood's defense. For 'twas not your fault I fell, and you could not have loved me better.*

I could not, she acknowledged. *And I can stand strong in the face of anything*—her eyes filled with tears—*save losing you again. I fear…I fear 'twill crush me, for all my intentions.*

Love. He touched her face gently, caressed her with his fingers, his mind, and his emotions. *Do not think on this thing, and so invite trouble. Such fear feeds on itself. And those fears we admit to our minds too often may come true.*

But it has always been in my mind. Even before I knew you, I desired you, searched for you, feared losing you. Curlew, what can ease this agony I feel inside?

Faith, Marianwyn. Only faith.

She hid her face against him and trembled. *I vow to you, Husband, I will try.*

****

"The attack came at dawn," Heron said bitterly, "while you, like we, were away in the forest." He indicated Diera, who stood pale as death beside him. "Yet another party led by Havers, come after Montfort, no doubt."

Curlew shot a look at Anwyn and asked, "But Montfort was not found?" He could feel Heron's distress and Anwyn's also. So closely were they now linked he very rarely felt alone in his own head.

"Nay, nor where we hold him. But six more are dead, three of them children."

"He slew children?" Curlew heard the shock in his own voice.

Heron met his stare. "He did so deliberately, slaughtered the wee ones, innocents, before their parents' eyes, in an effort to make them speak. But the folk did not know where Montfort is hidden." Heron paused and then pronounced, "The bastard needs to die."

The very fact that Heron, of all men, should call for violence shocked Curlew. But he nodded gravely.

Diera spoke with tears standing in her eyes, "Does he not have children of his own?" She looked to Anwyn.

"He does," Anwyn confirmed, "and treats them to the strap regularly. The man is devoid of mercy."

"Clearly." Heron's eyes glowed with fury. "I have prayed over this, but I tell you fairly, I am not easy in my mind. Danger rushes upon us. I see heartache. And blood."

Diera's hand flew to his and he clutched it tightly. Beside Curlew, Anwyn tensed. Curlew lifted his chin. "We must make resolution, send Montfort back, if need be. We cannot allow Havers to commit such deeds upon our own."

Heavily, Heron said, "I fear even Master Montfort's return will not stem Havers' brutality now. Aye, he travels under the banner of the Sheriff in seeking after Montfort. 'Tis what he says he wants. But you know, as well as I, he desires the return of his wife still more." He nodded at Anwyn. "He will not rest until he has her back in his hands."

Diera suggested softly, "Surely Anwyn's father will be able to curb Havers. He is not an unreasonable man." While caring for Mason Montfort's injuries, Diera had become friendly with him.

Anwyn answered, "My father will speak reason to Lord Simon once back in Nottingham, aye. I trust he will do his best for us. But I am not sure anyone can reason with the beast Havers."

"Yet," Diera still hoped, "Havers must take his orders from de Asselacton."

"Must he?" Anwyn shook her head. "So he may pretend to do. But Havers is sly and cunning. He might well pay lip service to Lord Simon even whilst playing at his own game and seeking revenge."

"One thing I do know." Heron spoke again. "We must make the best possible trade for Anwyn's father. He is one of the few things with which we have to bargain."

Curlew spoke thoughtfully, "Yet we also have right on our side, and courage—and Sherwood. We cannot allow ourselves to weaken. As never before, we must stand strong."

"There is one more possible choice," Anwyn said.

Curlew turned his gaze on her, suddenly alert. He did not like what he heard in her voice or felt streaming from her—a mingling of fear and determination.

She looked at Heron and not at him. "We could simply give Havers what he wants."

"No," Heron said, even as Curlew's heart reared in protest, "not that."

Anwyn tossed her head in the bold, careless way Curlew now knew covered her uncertainty. "'Tis the one sure way to stop the pain and persecution, is it not? To halt his cruelty, the burnings and the murder of babes? I will return alongside my father to Nottingham."

Curlew's heart twisted in his chest. "You will not. You would not, for you promised me we would never be parted—"

Her expression tightened, yet she spoke still to Heron. "Surely you see 'tis the only course."

"And surely you see," Heron returned gently, even though Curlew felt his outrage, "we cannot so sunder the circle. We have only just found you. Would you deprive us again?"

"The circle will hold," Anwyn said unequivocally, "whether I am here or in Nottingham. By any road, 'twill be for but a short time. I will find a way to make Havers rue the day he wed with me, to want shed of me, and then—"

"No." The word thundered from Curlew. He seized Anwyn's wrists and turned her to face him. "It will end no better than last time. What if he seeks to punish you for defiance? What if he insists on his revenge, and your pain? Only think the things he could do to you before you might flee him."

"Curlew is right," Heron said swiftly.

Anwyn did not so much as glance at Heron; her eyes now held Curlew's as if she might never look away.

"Anything is better," she throbbed, "than that he should come after you or harm you in any way. I could not relive that scene. Better another barren death in a convent! Better a thousand nights at his hands—just so you live and breathe the free air of Sherwood."

"Foolish girl! Would you seek to sacrifice yourself—for me?"

"Have not countless others? You know what you are—more than a man made of bone and flesh. You know what you carry inside you: hope, belief in a justice not brought by Norman hand, the chance for a better future and a share in England. What is my small life against all that?"

Curlew's throat worked desperately before he said,

"Everything. Everything, to me."

"And to me," Heron echoed.

She turned at looked at Heron then. "What have you seen at your prayers, holy man? What, that you dare not reveal? I can feel it all inside you. Why will you not say?"

Curlew, too, looked at Heron and saw acknowledgement fill the golden eyes, along with honest fear.

Heron said slowly, "I see danger, aye, a great risk. I cannot say—"

"I can!" Anwyn seethed. "This thing I have always known. I will not let him die in my arms again."

Marianwyn. Curlew breathed it into her mind.

She continued speaking exclusively to Heron. "How do you know I was not made one of your three only so I could play this part? Sherwood gives and Sherwood takes. Let me give, so Sherwood will not take *him*."

A brittle, fragile silence fell. The trees themselves listened, as did the bright morning. Curlew willed Heron to speak, to say something—anything—that would persuade Anwyn she argued for madness.

For, nay, Sherwood would not bring her to him only for the purpose of sacrifice.

And Heron spoke the desired words, "Lady, you act out of fear, but your desire to protect him, to protect us, is misplaced. Our strength lies in three."

And Anwyn repeated, "We are three apart as well as together."

Heron shook his head. "I say we return your father to Nottingham and see can he speak to de Asselacton, and thus curb Havers' ferocity."

Swiftly, Curlew spoke, "I say it also." He ran his fingers down Anwyn's arm to clasp her fingers. "And, my love, it takes but two of us to overrule the third. Now let us hear from you no more talk of sacrifice."

Chapter Thirty-Six

I know I swore I would never deceive you, Anwyn whispered to Curlew in her mind, even while she guarded her thoughts from him and hoped he would not hear. *But this need goes far beyond any promises.*

Another morning and the forest lay silent all around her, heavy with cloud that threatened rain.

Rain like tears.

She pushed that thought away fiercely, afraid to allow it dominance. The party escorting her father back to Nottingham had just departed following a wealth of discussion, and she needed to catch them up before Curlew or Heron tumbled to her intention. At the moment, the two of them conferred together in a huddle with others of their folk who still disagreed about returning Mason Montfort ahead of de Asselacton's release of their own people. She had only moments to act.

She swung her quiver up across her back and followed it with her bow.

"Where are you bound?"

The question caught Anwyn in a grip of iron and spun her around. Diera stood just behind her, straight and tall. Anwyn tried to determine what she saw in Diera's dark eyes. Sympathy? Understanding? Denial? A mist stirred between them and suddenly muddied the distinctions between past and present.

Without conscious thought, Anwyn said, "I know who you were—who you are. You stepped up and took one of the three places after he fell. You know what it is to love, and suffer, and need to protect."

Diera nodded, but Anwyn still could not feel her emotions. And Diera had only to open her lips, or possibly her mind, to alert Heron.

Desperately, Anwyn said, "You were there that day when I lost him, when the blood flowed from him and would not stop for all my prayers. Even the healing power in your hands could not save him."

Diera inclined her head and her dark hair fell forward, half obscuring her face. What did Anwyn see there? And who was this woman before her? A tall, slender maid, keeper of Heron's heart, or the strong yet diminutive healer Diera had once been?

Whoever she was, she said, "This is not then. Why do you fear the past will occur again?"

Wild now with terror and desperation, Anwyn returned, "Do you not see? That is why I was born. It is why all of us have gathered here now, because it must happen over again so I can change the ending, so I can save him this time."

"Or perhaps"—Anwyn heard Lil's wisdom when Diera spoke—"the circle now turns and proves to us nothing can ever be lost, no matter how it may appear to our mortal eyes."

"Then why am I so afraid? Why do I wake with the thought of losing him even though I lie in his arms? You are a woman, and a soul who loves. Surely you understand."

Diera spread graceful hands. "I would not be here, did I not believe in second chances. But, Anwyn, grief comes to those who dwell in fear of it—as does love to those who long for it."

"I have learned," Anwyn said hoarsely, "that grief is the companion of love. I go to do this, Diera, and you cannot hold me. Accompany me if you will. But I pray you do not tell Heron. Are you able to speak to him in your mind?"

Diera shook her head. "That has not yet been afforded us. But Curlew will hear you, or Heron will, through your connection."

"Not if I guard myself from them. Come swiftly, if you are to come, before they see."

Diera stole one look at the men on the far side of the encampment. Then she hiked up her skirts, and together they ran.

No sooner were they away into the trees than the rain came. Weeping, weeping. Bright blue eyes reaching for her through the tears.

Breathlessly, Diera asked, "Just what do you mean to do?"

"Trade myself to Havers for his promise to cease with harrying the folk of Sherwood."

"Do you think you can trust any promise he may give?"

Better, she hoped, than Curlew could rely on her own. She had promised, aye, never to leave him. Surely in the purest sense she did not, even now.

Marianwyn! As if her errant thought summoned it, his voice sounded clear and bright in her mind. She skidded to a halt, and Diera faltered also, staring.

"His thoughts pursue me." Anwyn's heart clenched. "That did not take long."

"Let us turn back."

Anwyn ignored that plea. "Heron instructed the men to take my father by the east road out of Sherwood, did he not?"

"Aye, and Curlew sent archers ahead to guard the way." At Anwyn's look of surprise she said, "You did not know that? Curlew rarely leaves things to chance."

"So, others of our folk are out there?"

"Aye. Let us turn back," Diera urged again.

"Nay, for you heard what Heron said: Havers may well fly the banner of my father's rescue, but what he truly wants is my return. I see no hope but to give it to him."

"You would endure his anger, his vengeance?"

"For Curlew's sake, I would endure most anything."

Diera studied her long. "Then come."

They ran on, Diera now leading the way through the trackless forest on a tangent that Anwyn guessed would intercept the east road. Tension grew inside her as they went, and awareness of a great event approaching. The rain pounded down so loud she could not hear her own footsteps, could barely hear Curlew's voice still calling in her mind.

He came. But he would not catch her in time.

Anything would be better, she told herself again as she ran, than to fail him. Nay, it had not been her fault he fell, last time. But afterwards she had crumbled, shattered, turned from all he loved, and ended her days in the desert of the nunnery, away from the place he rested and away from Sherwood's green light.

Anything would be better than that slow starvation, even pain at Havers' hands.

Marianwyn, return to me.

She closed her thoughts to the desperate voice in her mind. Just ahead through the trees she could see the road, and caught a glimpse of the party bent on leading her father back to Nottingham. She reached out and caught Diera's hand, dragged her to a halt.

Was it better to join her father's party now or follow them to Nottingham? Would the Sherwood group try to send her back to Curlew? They knew how he felt for her—by now most everyone did. But they had little reason to value her of themselves. Still, she would not risk being turned away.

Even as she stood hesitating, the decision was taken from her. She heard a cry ahead, voices raised in challenge and one voice she knew and hated most well.

Havers. Here, now. *No.*

Diera sucked in a great breath and freed herself from Anwyn's grip. "Trouble. We had better turn back."

For an instant Anwyn stood while everything teetered in the balance. Turn back or go forward? Reach for safety or resolution? Dare or fail? The very forest seemed to whirl around her, a wheel on its axis, and Curlew coming, bringing with him a past she needed so desperately to outrun. The future, bright with danger, sweeping in.

One thought only tipped the scale for her: if she did not move forward, how could she protect him? She must protect him.

She darted forward so swiftly she eluded Diera's grasp and headed like an arrow for the clamor of sudden battle, the screams and the peril.

Behind, Diera called even as Curlew cried to her, in her mind.

She burst onto the roadway and into a scene of carnage. The party from Sherwood had halted in the pounding rain to face Havers, who had both foresters and soldiers at his back. Three men already lay dead or wounded to death—two of Havers' and one from Sherwood. Her Da stood with his hands still bound, unable to defend himself. That alone was enough to take Anwyn forward.

Her father saw her at once and called her name, which snagged Havers' attention. The squat forester—her husband—loosed a shot from his bow and turned to face her, maddened as a boar on the attack.

He roared, "So there you are, misbegotten wench!"

Marianwyn! Curlew called at almost the same moment.

What happened next would stand forever in Anwyn's mind. Havers started toward her even as the Sherwood party fell back, still battling the soldiers. Curlew Champion appeared from the forest and leaped into the road.

Faster spun the circle in which Anwyn seemed so surely trapped. It did so jerkily, and in a garish light, every detail standing out too strong. Curlew skidded to a halt in the road. To her horror, she saw he had come away without his bow, no doubt determined to catch up with her and thinking of nothing else.

Even now he parted his lips and called her name. "Anwyn!"

The cry diverted Havers' attention from Anwyn for one terrible moment—one that proved long enough. She saw the heavy hatred fill his mean, little eyes. "Is this your captor then, bitch? Aye, and I can answer the bastard as he deserves!"

Anwyn did not see Havers notch his arrow. It was simply there at the ready when he raised the bow and sighted. Everything within Anwyn roared in protest and she launched herself at him—a few short steps were all it would take to place her body between Curlew and that arrow. But Curlew leaped also and rushed into the shot in an equally thoughtless effort to protect her.

Everything halted. The terrible, merciless circle ground to a stop and all the players stood pinioned. Only the arrow moved, flying, as inevitable as the past, and buried itself deep in Curlew's chest.

Anwyn clutched her own breast precisely as if the wound had taken her, instead. And it had, oh, it had! Then the circle shuddered into motion. The rain pounded down—*like tears, endless*—and Curlew crumpled to the ground, his eyes already closed.

No, no, no, no, no, no—

A few short steps separated her from her heart, which now lay in the road like something slain. She was not permitted to take them. Cruel hands caught her even as she stumbled forward, and a hated voice grated in her ear, "Ah, no! Your lover is he, that outlaw? Dirty slut that you are. But you will not go to him. Nay, Wife—you will come away with me."

Chapter Thirty-Seven

"Does he yet live?" Anwyn asked the question piteously of her father, who tramped at her side, but got no answer. He merely shook his head as he had the all other times she had implored him.

Despite his denial she said, "Surely he lives. 'Twas but a single wound, and he is so strong." He carried the very strength of Sherwood.

But that had not saved him last time. And there had been so much blood. She had seen that even as Havers dragged her away.

Her last glimpse of her love had come when the road turned, and it had the power to chill her to the heart: Curlew sprawled in the road with the others gathered round—both Heron, who must have followed him even as Curlew had followed Anwyn, and Diera kneeling over him. And the rain falling down, weeping.

It had all come round again, her worst terror and her deepest fear.

"It is my fault," she murmured to herself. "I brought this on him even as I strove to prevent it, the very thing I—"

"Be silent!" Havers whirled and ordered her viciously.

She raised burning eyes to him. He had unbound Mason Montfort's hands and tied Anwyn's with the same straps, even over her father's protests.

"We cannot trust her, Master Montfort. Surely you see that. 'Tis worse than we thought. She is in league with those outlaws back there, and has no doubt given herself to that rogue I cut down."

"I do not like this, not any of it," Montfort had declared even as Havers organized his men and moved off, leaving the Sherwood party in confusion behind him, scattered and focused only on their great loss.

And Havers told him, "Let us get out of this accursed forest and safe back to Nottingham, and we shall sort it."

Nottingham, Anwyn thought; no safety lay there nor anywhere else for her now. She did not care what Havers did to her. She would scarcely notice for the weight of her agony.

Did Curlew live? She needed to master her emotions and quiet herself enough to listen for him through the ties that connected them, and those of the triad—him, or Heron. But she could not calm herself. Pain pounded through her like a second heartbeat, grief arose and threatened to unhinge her mind. Words chased one another through her head.

My fault. Brought this upon him. Led him straight into it. Failed him.

Again.

A sob caught in her throat. Had she learned nothing through all the past heartache? Did she not believe their love eternal? Did she not know life rose and fell and rose again, undefeatable as the seasons?

Aye, but still all she could see was him lying there in his blood.

Would she be so weak as to fail him now?

No. Not that.

She eyed Havers' squat back, and the other men who accompanied them. What were her chances of escape, of making it back to that place Curlew lay, of discovering if he yet lived?

Six men—two foresters, neither of them known to her, and the surviving soldiers. Some went before and some came behind. She would not make it twenty strides before they caught her.

She tipped her face up to the sky, to the rain, and sought for strength. Sherwood must lend that to her; she was of the forest now, a part of it, a guardian. Sherwood, she knew, dealt in both magic and stark reality—it gave and it took.

I will give you anything. Only let me reach him.

She thought she saw something from the corner of her eye, a flicker of movement away through the trees that bordered the road. She fought for breath and strove once more to calm her mind. *Help me.*

A stillness came. Through it she reached with her mind, seeking out the pathways that linked her with Curlew—with Robin—battling even as she had failed to do last time to reach him, to find him.

To sense him.

Whispers. Flickering flashes of light. Did he live? If so he could not hear her, and he could not respond. But by the very light of the forest, she felt something.

What was it Curlew had told her? Love made up the strength of Sherwood—the love that bound souls one to another, that which lit the flame of giving, and sacrifice.

Last time fear had made her weak. This time, love would make her strong.

She stopped walking, threw her head back and

screamed aloud. She called to the air, the rain, the deep soil and the eternal fire. "Help me!"

Havers faltered and spun, an ugly look distorting his face. The first arrow came almost simultaneously and thudded into the back of one of the foresters as if in answer to her call.

A hail of others followed. Havers' party sprang into motion. The soldiers drew their swords and raised their shields. The one remaining forester readied his bow. Anwyn's father, having no way to defend himself, dropped to the road and bellowed at Anwyn, "Get down!"

She ignored him and stood where she was, joy pounding up through her. Whatever came now to her aid would not harm her, even though arrows shivered through the air like hard drops of rain. Who had come to her aid? Surely it must be the bowmen Diera said Curlew, in his caution, had sent on ahead.

"Can you see them?" Havers demanded of his men, enraged. And louder, "Show yourselves, cowards!"

His sole response was an arrow that flew with beautiful precision and pierced the top edge of his shield.

"Drive them off!" he hollered then. "Fall in!"

Another arrow streaked in upon him. Anwyn saw it take him in the shoulder just beneath his throat, and her battered heart exulted. But he roared like the boar he resembled, seized the shaft, and pulled the arrow from his flesh.

Anwyn nearly fell down where she stood. Havers stomped forward and caught hold of her even as her knees began to buckle; his merciless grip trapped her as he drew her against him. The iron tip of his knife bit her throat.

"Stop firing," he called into the trees, "or I slay her where she stands."

Go ahead, Anwyn thought fiercely. If Curlew passed into death, she would go even there with him. Inner knowing told her they would then be together in spirit.

But she had a destiny to fulfill. She needed to fight, not crumble and run. She needed to stand strong.

The arrows from the forest desisted. Her father scrambled to his feet.

"Ah," Havers growled in satisfaction, his breath scorching Anwyn's ear, "so they value you, do they? You mean something to them."

"Let me go," she told him, "else you will not leave the forest alive."

"Ah no, wench. You come with me. And you will have your discipline, full earned, in pain."

Her father glared at Havers. "Is this how you think to treat my daughter? It is enough!"

"Peace, Master Montfort. Did you not ask for my help with her? The next time you see your daughter, I assure you she will prove obedient."

Montfort stared, aghast.

Havers called to his men, "You get Master Montfort back to Nottingham safely. These wolfsheads want the woman, and I doubt there are enough of them to follow all of us. We will meet you there." He growled for Anwyn's ears alone, "And we have a score to settle, you and I."

Chapter Thirty-Eight

"You will regret this," Anwyn promised Havers bitterly.

Even as she spoke the words, she strained back for a last glimpse of her father's party. She could still hear them and the sounds of a fight, for no sooner had she and Havers left than the Sheriff's men had once more come under fire from the forest. Did Curlew's bowmen mean to settle with them, then, rather than follow along with her and Havers? Much as she hoped for her father's safety, she longed also for a chance to break free.

But Havers gripped her hard by the neck and dragged her along, heedless of twigs and branches, ever deeper into the trees. Sherwood's fingers raked her face and stung tears from her eyes. She did not care. She willed them to hurt her, if it meant they might harm Havers as well.

Be my defense, she thought with all her will and all her heart, *come to my call, all those who love.* As if in answer, an arrow came from nowhere and seared past Havers' head in a shaft of pure magic. Awareness erupted within Anwyn, perilous and bright. All at once she could feel everything intensely—the distress of her father, now far behind her, Havers' extreme anger, even the force inherent in the falling rain. She could feel the sentience of the trees, and threads of power rising.

That power was for her. She had only to seize and use it.

"Down." Havers shoved her to her knees behind a fallen tree even as more arrows streaked in upon them. The tree, an ancient giant, lay like a corpse covered with green moss. She placed her hands on it and power surged up into her palms, strong enough to widen her eyes.

Havers ducked as an arrow came close enough to kiss his nose. Another streaked from behind and he cast himself onto the ground. The archers were now all around them.

Trapped. Havers was quite surely caught and surrounded. But how could Curlew's archers be here, if they remained behind at the road, fighting the balance of Havers' men?

"Get down, stupid wench," Havers growled, "or do you wish to be killed?" He sneered, "Just like your outlaw lover. 'Tis what he was to you, is it not? You were never captured or held against your will. You went off catting around with him. Admit it."

"I admit it. He is worth a thousand of you."

"A serf? A dirty wolfshead? You fool! I have earned importance and a good place. How could you choose him over me?"

"He, too, has a place. He is Lord of Sherwood."

Havers laughed harshly. "Whatever that may mean, it is his place no longer, for he lies dead. No man could survive such a strike from one of my good arrows."

As if to emphasize his words, an arrow thudded into the tree close beside his head.

"Aye," Anwyn asked softly, angrily, "and just what do you suppose you are likely to survive?"

Before he could answer, she sprang to her feet and lifted her hands. Curlew might well lie dead, she knew not. But she refused to lie down with him, not this time. She would take the power Sherwood offered, revenge him, and fight on. A cowering child, a grieving widow no more, she knew her place in the circle, and meant to accept, uphold, and glory in it.

"Come and get him," she called to the forest.

She knew not precisely whom she summoned. The remnants of Curlew's archers? Others of his folk from Oakham? When they began moving closer, those who had been busily firing upon Havers, she saw the truth.

A crowd of shadowy figures, they blended with the forest itself, slid and shifted with infinite grace and seemed to materialize, all with bows in their hands. The flick of a leaf became a lock of hair here, the glint of a raindrop the gleam in an eye there. The burr on an oak resolved itself into the curve of an ear, a limb an arm, a leg.

The power came with them, even as Anwyn looked into the eyes of the nearest, a woman—those fierce, golden eyes so like Lark's, set in a strong, beautiful face beneath a flowing mane of brown. Anwyn knew her. Had this woman not led her to Curlew the night after her wedding, when she fled Havers? *Grandmother Wren.*

Beside her stood a great, tall man in a sheepskin cloak holding a bow even taller than he. His name appeared in Anwyn's mind: *Sparrow*. On the far side of the circle Anwyn caught sight of his counterpart in size—a veritable giant with a great, brown beard: *John Little*. Beside him stood another man with an untamed, yellow mane and a scarred face: *Martin Scarlet.*

Havers saw them also. "Outlaws! Wolfsheads! Vermin!" he barked. He stumbled to his feet and raised his bow, clearly not sure where to aim first.

"No need to be insulting," said the big man wearing the sheepskin. His voice reverberated oddly, and Anwyn wondered if she heard it only in her mind. But no—Havers heard too, and shifted and faltered.

"Let her go," the scarred man told him.

"Nay. The wench is my wife."

"She belongs not to you but to us," warned another of the men. He had steady hands on his bow, fair hair and dangerous eyes: Will Scarlet. "How dare you come here and think to defeat us? How suppose your small defiance can withstand our power?"

The trees swayed overhead. Havers directed one terrified look up into the branches. Sweat beaded his face and his notched arrow quivered.

The scarred man said, "Your men will never leave the forest, and neither will you."

"'Tis a crime to kill a King's forester," Havers bellowed. "You will all pay with your lives."

The big man with the great beard laughed. "Impossible. We have already given our lives for Sherwood. Go ahead and draw your bow, little man. Shoot."

Havers darted an incredulous look at Anwyn. "What are they on about? What do they mean, they have given their lives?"

The scarred man cast aside his bow and spread his arms wide. "Kill me, if you dare."

Havers swore and then drew his bow in a sharp, vicious movement. His arrow flew true despite his uncertainty, and struck the scarred man in the center of his chest.

And passed clear through him.

Triumph ignited round the circle, touched Anwyn, and streamed through her, bright as fire.

The scarred man showed his teeth in a terrible smile. "Now what say you, vile forester?"

"Impossible! Who are you? What?"

"We are guardians," Curlew's grandmother said, "we who have given our lives, our hope, and our blood in love. Sherwood can never die so long as our love holds strong."

Havers still attempted to sneer, but without success. "You are not real." He waved his hand at the scarred man. "If my arrow passed through you, how can your arrows harm me?"

"Perhaps they cannot." Yet another man stepped forward. Strongly featured and lion-headed, he wore the authority of a village headman: *Geofrey of Oakham*. "Or perhaps they can. Are you willing to risk your life on it?"

They raised their bows once again, every arrow pointed straight at Havers' heart.

He reached out to flick the fletchings of the arrow that had embedded itself in the fallen tree, beside him. His fingers encountered only air.

He grunted. "Nothing there. Illusion, it is all illusion."

Grandmother Wren told him, "You never spoke so true."

"But," the scarred man said, "that tree above you is very real."

He waved a hand. Havers turned dazed eyes to where he pointed, even as the power billowed and rose mightily. It streamed up from the circle, from those who occupied it all together, staggering in its intensity, and struck the ash that stood directly behind Havers.

The tree seemed to fall slowly, as it might if hewed by an axe rather than culled by lightning. Anwyn had time to leap away, yet Havers stood as one enchanted and made no attempt to move aside. She caught one terrible glimpse of his face just before the boll of the trunk struck him full in the back. His arms flew out and he fell amid the crash mighty enough to shake the forest.

She turned her eyes away then, even as the reverberation died. Not so much as one leaf had touched her body. Peace followed the violence of it, and the rain abruptly slackened.

Anwyn met the rueful gaze of Wren, who inclined her head.

"Mother," Wren said, and Anwyn gasped. Aye, this was her daughter—hers and Robin's—the child she had failed so terribly when he died in the greenwood, the living part of him she had abandoned.

"Wren. Can you ever forgive me?" She had not even given the girl her name. Another must have done that, or Sherwood itself. Deeply shamed, she looked around the circle. "Can any of you?"

"My Lady," said the man in the sheepskin. And he bowed to her, went down on his knees in reverence.

One by one the others followed, making a circle all about her, sundered only by the tree beneath which Havers lay. Light shimmered from one to the next of them, and Anwyn felt it flow also to her.

Engulfed by humility and power and devotion, she looked into her daughter's face. "Thank you. Thank you all."

"Well, Lady." Her daughter gave an impish smile. "This takes care of one problem that beset you. Even in the eyes of the Church, I believe you are widowed."

Anwyn shuddered. "I pray rather I am not, for I care little for the dictates of the Church, and this one was never husband to me. I am wed most surely to another. Take me to your father."

Chapter Thirty-Nine

"He lives yet."

Heron met Anwyn at the edge of the encampment and spoke the only words she wanted to hear. Led by Curlew's grandmother—her own daughter—she had come through the sodden forest to this place where the survivors of the skirmish had retreated. Wren, like those others who had helped her, disappeared into Sherwood then; she knew they did not retreat far.

Now she looked into Heron's eyes and gasped, "Where?"

"I will take you to him. But before you see him I must tell you"—Heron's voice faltered abruptly—"it is grave. Diera thinks the arrow pierced his lung. He bleeds from his lips and gasps for air. Oh, and your father is here."

"Da, here? How?"

"He was the lone survivor of the Nottingham party, following that last skirmish. Havers—?"

"Dead," Anwyn said shortly. "Is my Da being held prisoner?"

Heron shook his head. "To speak true, I have not been able to consider what should be done about your father, or aught else. All I can think on is *him*."

Anwyn nodded; she grasped Heron's arm and felt his emotions rise. "I cannot endure it, Heron. I cannot lose him again."

"I know. Come."

Heron led her quickly across the rough encampment. They passed Anwyn's father as they went; he leaped to his feet and called, "Anwyn, lass!"

"I will speak with you anon," she told him.

Heron shot her a look. "How did Havers perish? Did you kill him?"

"Nay, Sherwood finished it," she said briefly.

Heron nodded, though Anwyn barely noticed. For she could see Curlew now, stretched on the ground with a number of people gathered near. Diera bent over him with her black hair hanging down and his blood smeared on her hands.

Anwyn's step faltered. For an instant time itself shuddered and she saw two scenes, one overlaying the other: Robin lying awash with blood and Lil bent over him; Curlew bleeding, bleeding his life away.

Terror, stark, fierce, and crippling, arose and threatened to destroy her hard won courage. All her life had she feared this. And so it had come to her, inevitable as the turning of the seasons. At this moment, she had but one chance, one choice between the weakness of fear and the strength of love.

She saw now that the love never changed, only her response to it: she could admit the light or she could shut it away.

What was it Curlew said? Sherwood was all about light, and all about love.

"Anwyn?" Heron touched her arm and looked at her askance.

She told him, "Come."

She reached the place and fell to her knees at Curlew's side. Diera looked up, her face set and streaked with tears. The others who were gathered, three villagers from Oakham, stepped back. Anwyn barely saw them go.

She looked into Curlew's face—so still!—and her heart convulsed. His eyes were closed; lashes thick and brown shielded all the bright radiance she loved. Blood—his own—spattered his cheeks and chin.

They had hauled open his tunic and the shirt beneath, yet she could not see the wound or any bandaging for the blood. Worst of all, she could hear the wound; it whistled with every painful breath he drew—slow, labored breaths in, and each exhalation marked by a little froth of blood at his lips.

Oh, my love.

The darkness rose and threatened to swamp her again. Seeing him so knocked her back on her heels, back in time.

Do not leave me. Do not dare leave me!

No response. Aye, he was there—the hum that had vibrated between them continuously since first their circle forged now throbbed very low but endured yet.

"It is bad, you can see," Diera's red hands fluttered. "We removed the arrow, but that did not help much. You hear how he breathes, and the blood just comes. I have tried—" Diera's voice broke.

"Only one thing can save him." And that, Anwyn knew with blinding conviction, was not doubt but certainty, the undying certainty of their love.

She reached up and seized Heron's hand. He sank to his knees so they knelt facing each other, Curlew between them. She gazed demandingly into Heron's golden eyes.

"Thank the Green God I have come in time. Take

his hand. You, I, and the circle will save him."

Heron said with regret, "Even that power may not be enough to hold him now."

"'Tis the only thing that can. Always, always he has been my strength. Now I will be his. This time I will not leave go of him."

****

He lay in darkness and peace, floating as if on the swells of a gentle river. The dark, not complete, was marked by little shards of brightness that tailed away to the corners of his vision and gave glimpses of things: the glint of light on green leaves, the white gleam of a hart's hide, the warm beauty of Marian's eyes.

Marian.

He could feel her still, the constancy of her presence, her love like faint music. Regret touched him once more and ruffled the peace.

I did not want to go from you.

Did she hear? Ah, but he could feel her emotions striking at him the way the arrow had, reaching through the intervening formlessness. Almost he thought he could feel the touch of her hand on his.

And the circle.

Matchless magic of Sherwood.

But he did not lie alone, here. Others as formless as he rustled and gathered all around him, those with whom he shared the love of this place, those who cared deeply for it and for him. They shared his peace, and thought flowed effortlessly among them the way light might through Sherwood, and comfort like that he felt in his lady's touch.

His lady.

A great force pulled at him like memory, like

271

desire, like the need to breathe. His darkness, so very harmonious, no longer felt complete. Light flared, seared him, and formed a circle.

It glowed and shimmered with power that possessed sound as well as brightness. It flowed from his hand to hers and thence to that of he who carried inside him the very spirit of Sherwood—nay, not from her hand but from her heart.

It sparked with demand. The sound—that of many blended voices—became one.

I will not let you go. Do you hear? Heed me! I will not let go of you this time.

The dark all around him convulsed in response to her call. His very being quivered to it. The circle of power gripped him still more surely.

Come my lord, my love, my heart. It is not over. There is yet work to be done. Return to me and I promise I will walk not behind you but at your side.

The circle flamed once more, became so intensely bright it hurt the eyes he no longer possessed. Surely it must burn all else away.

Even fear.

Yet he had drifted so far, and the flesh to which he must return lay so damaged. The threads that bound him to it had frayed and very nearly broken. Even for love of her, he did not know if he had the strength.

Then take my strength. Her grip on his hand tightened until it filled him, anchored him. Her very touch became love. *I have enough for both of us.*

Joy stirred inside him, took hold, and then arose like a shout of laughter. He rose with it, spirit spiraling up in answer to her call, irresistible. For, as it had ever been, joy could only flow to joy, plenty to plenty, and love to love.

He broke the surface into life even as the brightness of daylight erupted all around him. Pain came with it, where there had been none, and the staggering need to breathe. But so did the beloved sight of his Marianwyn's face, contorted not by terror but transfigured by certainty. He gazed into her eyes and his world tumbled into place around him. The magic gleamed bright, even as he strained for breath.

One breath taken in shattering pain. Her strength and that of Heron, solid as bedrock, upheld him.

A second breath that tasted less of fire and more of the sweet air of Sherwood. Strength flowed not only through Marianwyn's and Heron's hands but up from the soil at his back, pounding in time with his heartbeat, from the light and the raindrops shimmering on the leaves, from the fire that endured, always.

A third breath came easier; it filled him with magic that sang through him, even as he heard Lil or was it Diera?—say, "Look, only look how his flesh knits! Ah, by the blood of the Green Man—"

"He *is* the Green Man"—Heron's voice—"now and forever more."

Chapter Forty

"A word with you, young man, if I might."

Anwyn jerked her head up at the sound of her father's voice, even though he spoke not to her but to Curlew. Evening had come to Sherwood; a cold breeze fluttered the leaves overhead, and all the fires in camp burned low. Guards stood watch for soldiers from Nottingham, and Anwyn sat at Curlew's side with her hand in his, the same place she had occupied all day long.

But how could she have forgotten about her father? He alone had survived the battle after Curlew fell; he alone could identify Curlew and so betray him to Lord Simon.

All this she thought as she looked up into her Da's worn and kindly face.

Curlew shifted himself on the pallet they had fashioned for him. Well bandaged now, he still had some pain, but nothing like what had come before. She knew because she felt everything he felt—each breath, each twinge. She knew how impatient he was to get up, and that he would far rather face her father on his feet.

She knew, too, how closely Heron watched them from his place at Diera's side, some twenty paces away. She found it so easy now to sense Heron's presence. Their circle had never been stronger.

She wove her fingers tightly between Curlew's and

whispered into his mind, *Peace.*

He eased at that and spoke to her father, "Welcome, Master Montfort, and speak as you will."

Mason Montfort seated himself, and Anwyn searched his eyes. Usually she could easily read her father's feelings, but not this time. Did he come to warn them there must be retribution for this day's events? She would fight, if she must. She smiled to herself grimly; this must be how it felt to be Lark Scarlet, always ready to battle fiercely for those she loved.

Her father said, "I scarcely know where to begin. I have seen things this day I would never have believed possible, had I not beheld them with my own eyes." For the first time he looked at Anwyn. "You have said you claim this man for husband, lass?"

Anwyn drew a breath. Surely she was free to do so, since Havers now lay a pile of shattered bone and flesh beneath a tree in Sherwood. She gathered herself and replied, "Aye."

Her father smiled ruefully. "Yet you took vows before God with another."

"Most surely, Father, I am widowed now."

Montfort nodded. "I have been listening to the talk about camp all this day long, and also sharing words with the young woman, Diera, who helped tend me. It seems all the men who made up the search party from Nottingham are dead—the foresters, and Lord Simon's soldiers, as well. Now you say Havers met his end. How?"

"In the forest, as he deserved."

"Havers," Curlew said shortly, "would have taken what is mine." He struggled to sit up in defiance of his weakness, to face her father on level ground, and

Anwyn felt him draw on her strength. "Sherwood would not permit that, nor suffer him to live."

To Anwyn's surprise, her father nodded again. "There is magic here, I see that. Ah, do not look so surprised. You suppose I could be wed with a Welsh woman and fail to credit the existence of magic? By any road, I know what I saw earlier when my daughter and your holy man raised you up. I saw light. And felt power."

"Da—" Anwyn began.

He stayed her with a raised hand. "Nay, Daughter. This is between the man you have chosen and me." Montfort looked Curlew in the eye. "I am not sure who you are—what you are—besides a wolfshead. I have sworn fealty to Lord Simon and also bear him the duty of friendship. But I have an older duty to my daughter, one born of love."

Steadily, Curlew answered, "That duty I both understand and share. Many are the ties that bind us, Master Montfort. Some cannot be denied."

"Now, I am aware I lie, here, very much in your power. You have naught to do but slit my throat in order to eliminate all possibility of retaliation for this day's events." Montfort crooked an eyebrow. "Or, Curlew Champion, you and I might come to terms."

"I am listening."

Montfort shot another look into Anwyn's face before returning his gaze to Curlew. "Do you recall, Master Champion, the day we first met in Sherwood? You told me you numbered one among Lord Simon's foresters."

"I will never forget."

"And now I learn from Mistress Diera you are a

kind of guardian of this forest, one whose authority she believes reaches beyond Norman laws."

Curlew replied softly, "That I am."

"You could, as I say, slit my throat. But that would gain you little in the long run. You would still be at odds with Lord Simon and whomever he might appoint after me. You would have no return for all the bloodshed and grief spent. And my daughter—my daughter would still live with a man outside the law." His smile, this time, was dour. "Lord Simon has condemned me roundly for my handling of my willful daughter. Indeed, his recommendations precipitated much of what has happened. But, young man, what I have seen this day has set me back on my heels and made me wonder whether love be not the stronger path, after all."

Curlew glanced into Anwyn's face before he said, "Aye, sir, so it must be. But I am not sure I follow your thoughts."

"I wondered, only, if you and I might strike an agreement to benefit all." Now Mason Montfort drew a breath. "Lord Simon and I have determined there is need of a steward for Sherwood. I swore I would give that place to the man who wed my daughter. You, it seems, are he."

For an instant everything stilled, as if even the forest itself awaited Curlew's reply. The leaves overhead ceased to rustle; folks' voices died away, and the flames of their fire flickered low. Anwyn once more felt the wheel of life pause on its great axis before it began to turn again.

"You would grant this place to me?"

"I would, but do not misunderstand: I have not full

authority to do so. With Havers dead and so many others with him, there are many places to fill. Lord Simon will take the opportunity to bring in those to whom he owes favors, and many will be Norman. If you want this place, you will have to earn it."

"How?"

"The most reasonable means would be in competition at the butts. If I propose it, I do not believe Lord Simon will refuse. Can you shoot a bow?"

Curlew began to laugh softly, in wonder. His grip on Anwyn's fingers tightened, and the light inside him intensified. "I can. Indeed, Master Montfort, 'tis the one thing I have ever been able to do well."

"I warn you, 'twill not be easy. If Lord Simon brings in his favorites, they will be eager for the place, and some of the Norman bowmen are very good indeed."

"He is better," Anwyn said.

"You have great faith in the man you have chosen, Daughter."

"I have." Carefully, she asked, "And you will give him leave to compete for this place?" The one for which his heart had reached always, through not one but two lifetimes, and that would at last afford his people a measure of autonomy. "Despite all that has passed between us?"

Her father smiled at her, a real smile this time. "Because of it, Anwyn. You will always be my daughter. But you, lad, can you give up your role of outlaw to deal with Lord Simon and, perhaps, a whole pack of Normans? Can you take on a new identity? For Lord Simon had better not discover who you are. We shall need to say you are newly arrived, perhaps from the north."

"My father came from Leeds, and his sire was Norman."

"Is it so? A useful thing! We shall say, then, you hail from Leeds. If you are willing, that is, to give up all you are."

Curlew smiled wryly and lifted his hands. "And what am I, Master Montfort? Is it not possible to lay aside appearance as easily as a suit of flesh, one life for another? The spirit endures. And I would do far more, for Sherwood." His voice assumed weight, and portent. "For I believe it is time. Look around you, Master. What do you see? Serfs? Saxons? Very few of us can claim that name anymore. We are Saxon, aye, but we also carry Celtic, Briton, and even Norman blood. I think, do you not, 'tis time for us to be one thing— English."

Anwyn's heart rose in gladness, as her father reached out and seized Curlew's hand. The power that hummed between them stirred and reached out also, to embrace them all.

"A worthy goal," said Mason Montfort. "Aye, then, let us begin."

Chapter Forty-One

"It is far too soon," Anwyn fretted. "Your wound has barely closed over. You remember how long it took Heron to heal—how will you ever draw a bow in competition?"

Curlew smiled into her eyes. He could see all she felt there—concern, ownership, and passion. "Do not fear, love. Sherwood sends me to this. I was born for it; those who came before us have battled and bled for it." A measure of authority, a chance to speak fairly for all he loved. "I cannot fail."

She bit her lip and somehow kept from saying what she feared, but he knew. He heard her thoughts so clearly now, both hers and Heron's, when he chose. She knew he should not even be up on his feet after three short days, and she was right—the deep wound so near his heart, mended by magic, might not endure the strain.

But she had returned with word from Nottingham last night, having gone thence with her father in order to convince Simon de Asselacton to call off his search for them and to allay any suspicions he might hold. The competition for the position of steward would take place this very day. If he failed to participate, he lost all hope of winning the appointment. And so he would not count the cost.

Aye, and he had already won one prize, that of

Anwyn returned to him. Their separation had been a fierce drain on his spirit, a thing she no doubt sensed as well. Could he hide from her his weakness?

"I still cannot believe Lord Simon has gathered his champions so quickly," she fretted on. "I confess, I hoped for more time—weeks rather than days. What are the odds of a famed Norman archer being so near, in Grimsby? It seems events still conspire against us."

Curlew reached out and drew her into his arms. Not without mischief, he asked, "And, Lady, did I lack for strength last night, when you required it?" He could still taste her on his lips, and fairly vibrated with the bliss of completeness. "You give me everything I need."

She stared into his eyes, mutinous. She wanted so badly to bar him from this, and knew she could not.

He ducked his head and reached for her lips, a potent temptation. *Kiss me once for luck*, he spoke into her mind, *twice for strength, and thrice just because you love me.*

Gladly she gave the required kisses, but told him, *I only wish I could do this for you. Da says Lord Simon has conjured not just the one, but five competitors—all Norman. You will need to draw that bow many times before it is done.*

He stepped away from her, just far enough to settle his quiver across his back. She adjusted the strap over again, easing it against the bandages beneath his tunic, and with reluctance handed him his bow.

Believe in me, he beseeched. *Can you not believe?*

That calmed her fears just a bit. *I have never stopped believing.*

Heron stepped up, with Diera as ever at his side.

"So, Cousin, you go to do this thing so many years in the making. Curlew Champion, son of a northern Norman squire, is it?"

Curlew smiled. "True enough, the tale. My father was squire before he was knight."

"I need not tell you my hope goes with you. All Sherwood goes with you."

"I have just been busy assuring Anwyn I was born for this."

"So you were." Heron smiled, but Curlew could see the concern in Diera's eyes. She had scrutinized his wound when she changed the dressing this morning. And Heron, as well as Anwyn, must be able to feel the pain that still dogged him.

No matter: if he were, indeed, the most important person ever born in Sherwood, then surely this must be the most important day of his life.

****

It looked like a fair day at Nottingham. Pennants flew in the autumn breeze, and a pavilion had been set up for the comfort of those privileged observers that included Lord Simon and several of his knights. Less exalted folk, many from Sherwood, milled about. Curlew knew Anwyn numbered one among them, for he could feel if not see her. Presenting himself at the field where the butts had been set, he struggled to ignore the many distractions and measure his competition.

No trouble identifying them. They stood already out where the targets were set in a row, some conversing and some fiddling with their bows, all Norman. Most, he imagined, would be well known to Lord Simon, and some favorites brought in with haste, even as Mason Montfort had previously been brought.

Aye, and he saw then just how clever Anwyn's father had been, granting him an identity virtually unknown and unquestionably Norman. And had not Sherwood assured he did carry a measure of Norman blood?

As if conjured, he saw Montfort approach across the green sward.

"Good day to you, Master Champion. I am that glad you have come." Without giving Curlew time to reply, he lowered his voice. "Are you fit? I did not mean for this to take place so soon, but after losing most of his foresters as well as a slew of soldiers, Lord Simon has a fire under him. What of your wound? I have been worrying over it."

"You and Anwyn, both. She is here somewhere, and fretting enough for all of us."

Montfort nodded and turned to survey the gathered archers. "'Twill not be easy, lad. They are all very good. The man with the yellow hair and the greedy eyes is Lord Simon's cousin, Le Blanc, in England on a visit from Normandy. The fellow beside him is head forester at Telligate. I have seen them all shoot. If they measure up to their abilities, you will need to prove faultless."

Curlew nodded. He doubted not his aim; if anything proved wanting, it would be his strength.

"Then come along."

Curlew followed Montfort across the damp green grass, his hide boots seeming to float somewhere above it. They paused directly in front of the pavilion, and Montfort called, "My lord, the last of our competitors has arrived. This is Master Champion of Leeds."

"Ah, the man of whom you spoke." Lord Simon's

dark eyes appraised Curlew closely. "You shoot with a longbow, my good man?"

"Aye, my lord," said Curlew in a clear voice. "My father's bowmaster was Saxon."

"Interesting. Then let us begin."

The other competitors eyed Curlew also as he moved to his place at the end of the line. The men took up their bows and composed themselves; he slid his off his shoulder and shook the hair back from his face, assessing the targets and the light as he did so: sun nearly at its height but situated enough to the south at this season to cause some glare. The distance would, aye, be challenging, but nothing he could not manage.

His bow, the best Sherwood had to offer, was cut from yew grown at the heart of the forest, with its living essence in the wood. Polished by the touch of his hands, it now came to him easily, without conscious thought, a part of him. But he knew it had a mighty draw, suited for shooting great distances from under cover, ordinarily no trouble for him.

Lord Simon rose to his feet and spoke. "This is a competition for the place of Steward of Sherwood Forest. The man who wins it will assume great responsibility. He will manage the resources therein, interact with the folk who dwell nearest that great expanse, and act as liaison between them and Master Montfort, here, and thus me."

About fricking time, said a voice beside Curlew. He turned his head and saw a man standing there, one with a mane of fair hair, bright blue eyes, and a deeply scarred face. Martin Scarlet. *I have waited long for some measure of authority in Sherwood. My lord, do not miss your mark.*

Have I ever? Curlew returned.

Martin turned those dangerous eyes on him. *Nay, but you and I know just how deep that wound of yours goes.*

Aye, Curlew agreed, *and we both know also how to endure pain.*

Martin grinned at him with warlike assent.

Steady on, my lord, said another voice, this one at Curlew's other elbow, and deeper. The man there wore a sheepskin cloak and had eyes as dark as Sherwood's mysterious heart—Sparrow Little. He offered the great bow in his hands. *Would you not rather shoot with this?*

Curlew shook his head. *I could not hope to draw that,* he told Sparrow.

You do not need to, said his grandmother—his daughter—Wren, at his back. *You need only be who and what you are.* A shower of gold magic erupted all around them. *The Lord of Sherwood.*

Chapter Forty-Two

"Competition will continue among these candidates for the place of steward," Mason Montfort intoned, "until all but one has been eliminated. Begin!"

Curlew drew a hard breath. Last to join the line, he would also be last to shoot, a difficult enough position. He knew himself surrounded by a trio of past guardians, and he could feel Anwyn's presence somewhere in the crowd, along with others from Sherwood who stood out in his consciousness like shards of light. And he could feel power simmering, balanced among Wren, Sparrow, and Martin.

The rest, he knew, teetered not on his skill but, as Martin said, on his endurance.

He looked at the targets—six of them—each with five concentric rings and a center of black, small yet relatively easy to hit at this distance. But the distance, he well knew, would increase with every round and extend clear across the sward.

"Each competitor," Montfort concluded, "must hit in the black, or he is eliminated."

Martin snorted rudely. *They call that a competition?*

Hush, Wren scolded. *They begin.*

So they did. Montfort nodded to the man from Normandy, first in line. "Monsieur Le Blanc."

Le Blanc raised his bow and sighted in one elegant

movement. He shot quickly, and his arrow clove the black at the center of the target.

Amid applause, the next man, called Doucette, followed. A breeze came up as he released his shot; his arrow landed barely within the black, but was allowed.

Nerves, that, Sparrow muttered.

The next three, Masters Etienne, de Langarde, and de Rouen, followed suit. Curlew raised his yew bow and sighted.

Curlew—Curl-yew, his mother's voice, full of love, tumbled into his ear. *You are in that bow, lad, as you are in everything.*

He drew and pain—far worse than he expected—blossomed in his chest and bit hard. Had his wound torn open? Surely not so soon.

But his arrow found its mark true. Hastily, the targets were moved back some fifty paces. Still an easy shot for him.

The second round passed without any elimination, and the targets hurtled back again. Curlew, fearing his wound had indeed opened, thought only of keeping it from distracting him. Two of the competitors were very highly skilled—the fellow from Normandy and the man beside Curlew, called de Rouen. He, the eldest among them, had a hard eye and wore a cruel sneer.

No fit master for Sherwood, as Sparrow opined.

There is but one master for Sherwood, Wren pronounced. *We have all worked tirelessly for this moment. My lord Curlew, shoot!*

Shoot he did, when his turn came—aim still true, but now he could feel blood well up against his bandages and begin to trickle down his chest. No matter: Doucette, the man prey to his nerves, was eliminated.

One down.

Pain speared deeper when he drew and released his next shot. His arrow hit, but barely within the mark; Montfort gave him a concerned look and de Rouen, beside him, made a rude sound.

Curlew barely noticed. The pain now possessed his chest and reached for his lung; he could hear the wheeze in his own breath. Pray no one else could.

When he shot next, his fifth round, the pain nearly blinded him. But his arrow still found its mark, which was more than could be said for Etienne's.

Two down.

The targets were now distant, indeed. The wind, cold as the kiss of winter, gusted over the field and snapped the pennants on the pavilion. Curlew's eyes could no longer perceive the black at the center of his target. He would need to rely on another ability and sense for it.

Anwyn's voice bloomed in his mind. *How bad is it, love? I feel your pain.*

Peace, he told her even as his strength wavered.

Lean on me, take my strength, she bade. From nowhere, a rush of warmth came to buoy him up. He steadied where he stood.

"Shoot!" Montfort cried.

The Norman, curse him, made his mark. De Langarde's shot was spoiled as a barely-visible blur of magic shook his arm.

Three down.

Curlew could now feel blood soaking the sark beneath his leather tunic. The breath rasped in his lungs and de Rouen, only an arm's reach away, looked at him askance. "This becomes perhaps too difficult for you, Master Longbow?"

Curlew shook his head and drew still more heavily on Anwyn's strength. Where was she? Truly, it did not matter, for she was always inside him.

As was Sherwood.

De Rouen missed his next shot. He protested it even while Curlew stood swaying slightly on his feet. De Rouen, Montfort, and the men toting the butts all inspected the target before the man agreed to retire.

Four down, and the targets—only two of them now—moved back again and blurred before Curlew's eyes.

It is about faith, Martin Scarlet said. *You do not need to see the target.*

Aye, for he must become the arrow even as he was the yew tree, and the fire in the heart of the stag who fell, and the water that beat in the blood, the breeze that caressed all, and the mighty, enduring rock of this place called England. He was the arrow, the bow, and the target as well.

Le Blanc, his only remaining competitor, shot at a target now so distant no one save the men who toted the butts could see the mark. They hollered—the arrow had hit.

Curlew raised his bow, blind now to everything save the pain. The bright, cold afternoon wavered around him and a mist floated before his eyes. Anwyn's strength, inside him, pounded like his heartbeat and magic whispered, it whispered—

Green leaves, golden light, the presence of the god and men who worshipped, all one.

He released his shot in a shower of pure magic. It

glowed around him, obscuring everything else, even the pain, and he flew. He was the arrow, and the wind rushed past him, ruffled his fletchings even as certainty burned in his heart like the light of Sherwood that could never die.

And reaching the target he became that also, and thudded into its heart.

The circle that was the wheel of existence shuddered on its axis, flamed with brightness, and turned ever more swiftly. Curlew found himself back on his feet with the two men from the butts running toward him, and Anwyn at his side. How did she come to be at his side? Aye, but so she had always been.

And Montfort, also there, shook his hand.

"Have I won? Did Le Blanc not make his mark?" he asked Anwyn's father.

Satisfaction filled Montfort's eyes. "He touched the black, but your arrow is dead center. They are displaying the targets now. Congratulations, Master Champion, you have earned your place."

Earned it, aye. Suddenly, despite his pain, Curlew wanted to shout with joy. He had not earned this prize alone—rather had it been won through the sacrifice of many, through loss and blood and agony.

Sherwood gives, he whispered to all of them, *and Sherwood does not always take.*

"Master Champion?" de Asselacton stood suddenly before him, acceptance in his face. "I hear your father hailed from the north—Leeds, is it?—of a good Norman family."

"Aye, my lord, so he did."

"He would be proud of you, I do not doubt. That was some of the finest marksmanship I have ever seen.

I trust you will prove just as skilled and steadfast a steward to Sherwood, look after our interests there, and see to the welfare of all."

Curlew felt the weight that had rested always on his back lighten until it made no burden at all. "Upon that, my lord, you can rely."

****

"'Twill be a sacrifice, you know," Anwyn murmured. "We will no longer be able to live in Sherwood. Da says we are to have a house of our own near Oakham, just as soon as it may be built."

"I deem that no sacrifice," Curlew replied.

They found themselves alone at last at the end of this day that had brought him so much, and outside the walls of Nottingham. There they had paused at Anwyn's insistence so she might change his bandaging before heading back to the forest. Only a few more nights would be spent there, yet he felt no lack, for Sherwood dwelt always inside him.

Anwyn refastened his tunic and looked into his face. He got to his feet, and her hands slid tenderly up his chest to lodge in his hair. "It is as I feared, my husband; you have injured yourself much."

"And gained much. Sherwood now rests in my hands—something of which my grandmother Wren, those who fought at her side, and all those since could but dream."

Gladness flared in Anwyn's eyes. "'Twas a shot in a thousand—nay, in ten thousand, my lord. And I felt the magic of it. You were not alone."

He shook his head. "I flew in that arrow and all of them with me."

"Do you think you will heal quickly enough to take

up this wondrous position?"

He smiled gently. She had nearly wept when she saw the mess beneath his tunic. "'Tis naught Sherwood cannot heal."

"Then, my lord, are you able to kiss me?"

"My lady, I am."

He bent his head and her sweetness rushed at him like magic, like light, curled through him and flowed in a stream of warmth to his ravaged flesh. Ah, and it would not take Sherwood, for her love made him whole.

He drank from her until the breath came more easily in his lungs, until the pain faded and joy filled him, making him heady with it. Only then did she release his lips and give him her matchless smile.

"It is well, my lord. I need you whole and hale, not only as steward of Sherwood, but for the coming of our child."

"Child?" Sudden gladness arose and shouted inside him, along with a sense of rightness, strong and deep. Another chance this was, another turn of the wheel, and an arrow shot into the future.

He cradled her between his hands, the most precious light of his world. "There is no mistake? You are certain?"

"Oh, aye, I am very certain." His Marianwyn tossed her head. "Just as I am sure to my heart this child will be a girl—another blessed daughter of Sherwood."

A word about the author...

Born and raised in western New York, Laura Strickland has been an avid reader and writer since childhood. Embracing her mother's heritage, she has pursued a lifelong interest in Celtic lore, legend, and music, all reflected in her writing.

She has made pilgrimages to both Newfoundland and Scotland in the company of her daughter, but is usually happiest at home, not far from Lake Ontario, with her husband and her "fur" child, a rescue dog. She practices gratitude every day.